D0231159

Lie With Me

Also by Sabine Durrant

For adults

Having It and Eating It
The Great Indoors
Under Your Skin
Remember Me This Way

For teenagers

Cross Your Heart, Connie Pickles
Ooh La La! Connie Pickles

SABINE DURRANT

Lie With Me

MULHOLLAND
BOOKS

HODDER

WITHDRAWN FROM
DÚN LAOGHAIRE-RATHDOWN COUNTY
LIBRARY STOCK

First published in Great Britain in 2016 by Mulholland Books
An imprint of Hodder & Stoughton
An Hachette UK company

1

Copyright © TPC & G Ltd 2016

The right of Sabine Durrant to be identified as the Author of the Work has been
asserted by her in accordance with the Copyright, Designs and Patents Act 1988.

All rights reserved. No part of this publication may be reproduced, stored
in a retrieval system, or transmitted, in any form or by any means without
the prior written permission of the publisher, nor be otherwise circulated
in any form of binding or cover other than that in which it is published and
without a similar condition being imposed on the subsequent purchaser.

All characters in this publication are fictitious and any resemblance
to real persons, living or dead, is purely coincidental.

A CIP catalogue record for this title is available from the British Library

Hardback ISBN 978 1 473 60833 7
Trade Paperback ISBN 978 1 473 60834 4
eBook ISBN 978 1 473 60830 6

Typeset in Plantin Light by Hewer Text UK Ltd, Edinburgh
Printed and bound by Clays Ltd, St Ives plc

Hodder & Stoughton policy is to use papers that are natural, renewable
and recyclable products and made from wood grown in sustainable
forests. The logging and manufacturing processes are expected to
conform to the environmental regulations of the country of origin.

Hodder & Stoughton Ltd
Carmelite House
50 Victoria Embankment
London EC4Y 0DZ

www.hodder.co.uk

BAINTE DEN STOC

WITHDRAWN FROM
DÚN LAOGHAIRE-RATHDOWN COUNTY
LIBRARY STOCK

For Francesca

August 2015

It struck me in the night that it might have started *earlier*. I sat up in horror and, in the darkness, used my fingernail to scratch the word 'BOOKSHOP' on the inside of my forearm. It has gone now: the skin is inflamed due to an infected insect bite, which I must have further scratched at in my sleep. Still, the act of writing did the trick, as it tends to. This morning I can remember well enough.

Hudson & Co: the secondhand bookshop in Charing Cross Road. I have been assuming it began there – that none of it would have happened if my eye hadn't been caught by that silly little shop assistant's red hair. But am I wrong? Were the forces already in motion, in the weeks and months before that? Does the trail of poison lead back, long before the bloody girl's disappearance, to university? Or before then, even – to school, to childhood, to that moment in 1973 when I struggled, puce-faced, into this unforgiving world?

I suppose what I am saying is, how much do we collude in our own destruction? How much of this nightmare is *on me*? You can hate and rail. You can kick out in protest. You can do foolish and desperate things but maybe sometimes you just have to hold up a hand and take the blame.

BEFORE

Chapter One

It was a wet day, one of those grey, drizzly London afternoons when the sky and the pavement and the rain-streaked buildings converge. It's a long time since I've seen weather like that.

I'd just had lunch with my oldest friend Michael Steele at Porter's in the Charing Cross underpass, a wine bar we had frequented since, at the age of sixteen, we had first discovered the discretion of both its location and its landlord. These days, of course, we would both have much rather met somewhere less dank and dark (that chic little bistro on St Martin's Lane specialising in wines from the Loire, *par example*), but nostalgia can be a tyranny. Neither of us would have dreamt of suggesting it.

Usually, on parting from Michael, I would strut off with a sense of groin-thrusting superiority. His own life restricted by the demands of a wife, twin boys and a solicitor's practice in Bromley, he listened to my tales of misadventure – the drunken nights in Soho, the young girlfriends – with envy in his eyes. 'How old's this one?' he'd say, cutting into a Scotch egg. 'Twenty-four? Saints alive.' He was not a reader and a combination of loyalty and ignorance meant he also still thought of me as The Great Literary Success. It wouldn't have occurred to him that a minor bestseller written twenty years ago might not be sufficient to maintain a reputation indefinitely. To him I was the star of 'Literary London' (his phrase) and when he picked up the bill, which he could be depended upon to do, there was a sense less of charity than of him paying court. If an element of mutual bluff was required to sustain the status quo, it was a small price to pay. Plenty of friendships, I am sure, are based on lies.

That day, however, as I returned to street level, I felt deflated. Truth was, though I had kept it to myself, life had recently taken a downward swerve. My latest novel had just been rejected, and Polly, the twenty-four-year-old in question, had left me for some bum-fluffed political blogger or other. Worst of all, I had discovered, only that morning, that I was to be evicted from the rent-free flat in Bloomsbury I had, for the last six years, called home. In short, I was forty-two, broke and facing the indignity of having to move in with my mother in East Sheen.

As I have mentioned, it was also raining.

I trudged along William IV Street towards Trafalgar Square, dodging umbrellas. At the post office, a group of foreign students, wearing backpacks and neon trainers, blocked the pavement and I was pushed out into the gutter. One shoe sank into a puddle; a passing taxi soaked the leg of my corduroys. Swearing, I hopped across the road, wending my way between waiting cars, and turned up St Martin's Lane, cut through Cecil Court, and into Charing Cross Road. The world juddered – traffic and building works and the clanging of scaffolding, the infernal disruption of Crossrail. Rain continued to slump from the sky but I had made it doggedly beyond the Tube station before an approaching line of tourists pulling luggage thrust me again out of my path and against a shop window.

I braced myself against the glass until they had trundled past, and then I lit a cigarette. I was outside Hudson & Co, a secondhand bookshop specialising in photography and film. There was a small fiction section in the back where, if I remembered rightly, I had once pilfered an early copy of *Lucky Jim*. (Not a first edition, but a 1961 orange Penguin with a Nicolas Bentley drawing on the cover: nice.)

I peered in. It was a dusty shop, with an air of having seen better days – most of the upper shelves were bleakly empty.

And then I saw the girl.

She was staring through the window, sucking a piece of long, red hair, her features weighted with a boredom so sensual I could feel it tingle along my fingertips.

I pinched the lit tip off my cigarette, put the remainder in my jacket pocket and pushed open the door.

I am not bad looking (better then, before everything happened), with the kind of face – crinkled blue eyes, strong cheekbones, full lips – I've been told women love. I took trouble over my appearance, though the desired result was to make it look as if I didn't. Sometimes, when I shaved, I noticed the length of my fingers against the chiselled symmetry of my jaw, the regularity of the bristles, the slight hook in the patrician nose. An interest in the life of the mind, I believed, was no reason to ignore the body. My chest is broad; I fight hard even now to keep it firm – those exercises I picked up at Power Pulse, the Bloomsbury gym, over the course of the free 'taster' month continue to prove useful. I knew how to *work* my look, too: the sheepish, self-deprecating smile, the careful use of eye contact, the casual deep-in-thought mussing of my messy blond hair.

The girl barely looked up when I entered. She was wearing a long geometric top over leggings and chunky biker boots; three small studs in the inside cartilage of one ear, heavy make-up. A small bird-shaped tattoo on the side of her neck.

I dipped my head, giving my hair a quick shake. 'Cor blimey,' I said in mock-Cockney. 'Rainin' cats and dogs out there.'

7

She rocked gently backwards on the heels of her boots, resting her bottom on a metal stool, and cast a glance in my direction. She dropped the spindle of ruby hair she'd been chewing.

I said, more loudly: 'Of course Ruskin said there was no such thing as bad weather. Only different kinds of good weather.'

The sulky mouth moved very slightly, as if vaguely in the direction of a smile.

I lifted the damp collar of my coat. 'But tell that to my tailor!'

The smile faded, came to nothing. *Tailor?* How was she to know the coat, bought for a snip at Oxfam in Camden Town, was ironic?

I took a step closer. On the table in front of her sat a Starbucks cup, the name 'Josie' scrawled in black felt tip.

'Josie, is it?' I said.

She said, flatly: 'No. That was what I told the barista. I tell them a different name every time. Can I help you? Are you looking for anything in particular?' She looked me up and down, taking in the absorbent tweed, the cords, the leaking brogues, the pathetic middle-aged man that wore them. A mobile phone on the counter trembled and, though she didn't pick it up, she flicked her eyes towards it, nudging it with her spare hand to read the screen above the cup – a gesture of dismissal.

Stung, I slunk away, and headed to the back of the shop where I crouched, pretending to browse a low shelf (two for £5). Perhaps she was a little too fresh out of school, not quite my audience. Even so. How dare she? Fuck.

At this angle, I smelt damp paper and sweat; other people's stains, other people's fingers. A sharp coldness in here too. Scanning the line of yellowing paperbacks, phrases from my publisher's last email insinuated themselves into my head: 'Too experimental . . . Not in tune with the current market . . . How about writing a novel in which something actually *happens*?' I stood. Bugger it. I'd leave with as much dignity as I could muster and head off to the London Library, or – quick look at my watch – the Groucho. It was almost 3 p.m. Someone might be there to stand me a drink.

I have tried hard to remember if the door jangled; whether it was the kind of door that did. The shop had seemed empty when I entered, but the layout allowed anyone to hide, or lurk – as indeed I was now. Was he already in the shop? Or not? Do I remember the scent of West Indian Limes? It seems important. But perhaps it isn't. Perhaps it is just my mind trying to find an explanation for something that may, of course, have been random.

'Paul! Paul Morris!'

He was standing on the other side of the bookcase, only his head visible. I took a brief physical inventory: close-set eyes, receding hairline that gave his face an incongruously twee heart shape, puny chin. It was the large gap between the two front teeth that sparked the memory. Anthony Hopkins, a contemporary from Cambridge – historian, if I remembered correctly. I'd bumped into him several years ago on holiday in Greece. I had a rather unpleasant feeling that I had not come out of the encounter well.

'Anthony?' I said. 'Anthony Hopkins!'

Irritation crossed his brows. 'Andrew.'

'Andrew, of course. Andrew Hopkins. Sorry.' I tapped my head. 'How nice to see you.' I was racking my memory for details. I'd been out on a trip round the island with Saffron, a party girl I'd been seeing, and a few of her friends. I'd lost them when we docked. Alcohol had been consumed. *Had Andrew lent me money?* He was now standing before me, in a pin-stripe suit, hand out. We shook. 'It's been a . . . while,' I said.

He laughed. 'Not since Pyros.' A raincoat, pearled with drops, was slung over his arm. The shop assistant was looking over, listening to our conversation. 'How are you? Still scribbling away? Seen your byline in the *Evening Standard* – book reviews, is it? We did love that novel you wrote – my sister was so excited when you sold it.'

'Ah, thank you.' I bowed. His sister – of course. I'd hung out with her a bit at Cambridge. '*Annotations on a Life*, you mean.' I spoke as loudly as I could so the little scrubber would realise the opportunity she had passed up. 'Yes, a lot of people were kind enough to say they liked it. It touched a nerve, I think. In fact, the review in the *New York Times* said—'

He interrupted me. 'Any exciting follow up?'

The girl was switching on a blow-heater. As she bent forward, her silk top gaped. I stepped to one side to get a better view, caught the soft curve of her breasts, a pink bra.

'This and that,' I said. I wasn't going to mention the damp squib of a sequel, the disappointing sales of the two books have had that followed.

'Ah well, you creative types. Always up to something interesting. Not like us dull old dogs in the law.'

The girl had returned to her stool. The current from the blow-heater was causing her silky top to wrinkle and ruche. He was still prattling away. He was at Linklaters, he said, in litigation, but had made partner. 'Even longer hours. On call twenty-four seven.' He made a flopping gesture with his shoulders – glee masquerading as resignation. But what can you do? Kids at private school, blah blah, two cars, a mortgage that was 'killing' him. A couple of times, I said, 'Gosh, right, OK.' He just kept on. He was showing me how successful he was, bragging about his wife, while pretending to do the opposite. Tina had left the City, 'burnt out, poor girl', and opened a little business in Dulwich Village. A specialist yarn shop of all things. Surprisingly successful. 'Who knew there was so much money to be made in wool?' He gave a self-conscious hiccupy laugh.

I felt bored, but also irritated. 'Not me,' I said gamely.

Absent-mindedly, he picked up a book from the shelf – *Hitchcock* by François Truffaut. 'You married these days?' he said, tapping it against his palm.

I shook my head. *These days?* His sister came into my mind again – a gap between her teeth, too. Short pixie hair, younger than him. I'd have asked after her if I'd remembered her name. Lottie, was it? Lettie? *Clingy*, definitely. Had we actually gone to bed?

I felt hot suddenly, and claustrophobic, filled with an intense desire to get out.

Hopkins said something I didn't completely hear, though I caught the phrase 'kitchen supper'. He slapped the Hitchcock playfully against my upper arm, as if something in the last twenty years, or perhaps only in the last two minutes, had earned him the right to this blokeish intimacy. He had taken his phone out. I realised, with a sinking horror, he was waiting for my number.

I looked to the door where the rain was still falling. The red-haired temptress was reading a book now. I twisted my head to read the author. Nabokov. Pretentious twaddle. I had a strong desire to pull it from her grasp, grab a handful of hair, press my thumb into the tattoo on her neck. Teach her a lesson.

Turning back to Hopkins, I smiled and gave him what he wanted. He assured me he would call and I made a mental note not to answer when he did.

Chapter Two

It was two weeks later, a Tuesday afternoon in late February, when he made contact again. I was still – just – living in Bloomsbury. This was the deal: Alex Young, the owner, a violinist with the New York Philharmonic, let me have the place in exchange for feeding the cat. I only had to clear out when he and his boyfriend were in town. Lamb's Conduit Street, with its organic coffee shops and chic 'old-fashioned' gentlemen's outfitters, was my spiritual home. The flat on the top floor of a tall Georgian building, filled with nothing of mine and everything of his (paintings and white bed linen, mid-century furniture, an Italian coffee machine), presented to the world the kind of man I wanted to be. But the arrangement was coming to an end, and I was trying not to think about it.

When my phone buzzed, I was sitting in a worn velvet armchair with the *London Review of Books*, savouring a moment of winter sunshine. It was shining low through the long window, the shadow of the square casements casting a hopscotch pattern on the Turkish rug. On the table next to me was a cup of coffee and a cheese sandwich; I was eking out the last of the bread. Persephone, of whom I had become fond, was curled like a sliver of mink on my knee.

I didn't recognise the number, but my guard was down. In the pub the previous night, I'd met a young graduate called Katie, who was trying to break into journalism. I'd written my contact details on her palm, told her to get in touch if she wanted some advice. As I picked up, I was already imagining the meeting ('my place probably easiest'), her breathless deference, the bottle of wine, the gratitude, the tumble into bed.

'Paul Morris,' I said, with the clipped professionalism of a busy man.

'Ah! I've caught you.'

Not Katie. A male voice – one I didn't immediately recognise. Some jobsworth from one of the literary organs that occasionally employed me? Dominic Bellow, a fellow Soho barfly, who edited *Stanza* magazine, had recently lobbed me the new Will Self to review, and my copy was late. (That's the problem with under-employment: even the things one has to do tend not to get done.)

'Yes,' I said doubtfully. Too late to pretend it was a wrong number. I'd announced my name.

'Hello. I'm ringing to entice you down to the wilds of Dulwich.' *Dulwich?* 'Tina's longing to meet you.' *Tina?* 'Mind you, I'd better be careful. I know what you're like around women. I've never forgiven you for Florrie.' He laughed loudly.

Florrie. Of course. Not Lottie. Florrie Hopkins, the sister of Anthony Hopkins. Andrew. Whatever his name was. I remembered, in the bookshop, the way he had said 'litigation', his mouth stretched out to the side, the click of his teeth.

'Great,' I said, thinking, *Shit.* 'Lovely.'

'How about this weekend? Saturday? A grateful client has just sent me a rather nice case of wine – thought it was a shame not to share it with friends. Châteauneuf-du-Pape. 2009. Tina was going to do her signature slow-cooked lamb. Moroccan.'

I'm not proud of myself. When you are on your own living hand to mouth, you make judgements: the cost and inconvenience of trekking to the wastes of south-east London versus the possible rewards of doing so. A good meal, a decent glass of French wine, they added up. Connections, too, are something to be alert to. I was about to be homeless and you never know who might prove useful. Also: exactly how rich *was* he? I thought about the cut of his suit, the way it had fitted so snugly over his shoulders, the softness of his palm as he'd shaken my hand. I was curious to see his house.

The cheese sandwich of curling Mother's Pride stared balefully. 'Saturday,' I said. 'Hang on. Yes. I'm away in New York next week but Saturday's OK. Saturday I can do.'

'Fantastic.' He gave me the details and we disconnected.

I sat in the chair for a while longer, stroking the cat.

His address led me to a wide tree-lined street in the further reaches of Dulwich, a good ten-minute hike from the nearest station: Herne Hill, on the same line out of Victoria as Michael's gaff in Beckenham where I often went for Sunday lunch. This was a very different kind of *banlieue*; less pinched and harried. It was where my tosser of an agent lived, and it figured. Here the roads were wide and self-confident. Even the trees seemed pleased with themselves.

Andrew's house was a large, detached, late-Victorian villa, with a gabled roof and an arc of drive in which three cars were parked at awkward angles. Most of the front was covered in creeper, an abandoned bird's nest in the crook of a drainpipe. The slatted blinds were open in the front bay and, between the wood, lights glowed, shapes drifted, a fire flickered.

I stood back, behind the hedge, and tried to light a cigarette. It was windy, coming in gusts, and it took several matches. Under my arm was a bottle of wine I'd bought at the shop by the station. A Chilean Sauvignon Blanc: £4.99. The blue tissue paper, wet from condensation, was beginning to disintegrate.

A large car drove slowly past, indulging its suspension over the speed bumps. Three teenagers ambled along on the opposite pavement, lugging musical instruments. They paused under a street lamp and stared at me; one of them whispered and the others laughed. This was the kind of place where a single man without a family, or a dog, or a Volvo 4x4, *or a bloody cello*, stood out. I turned my face away, back to the privet. Tangled in some twigs at eye level was a stray piece of silver tinsel. Cigarette dangling from my mouth, I pulled and brought out a Christmas bauble – red, decorated with a snowflake in white frosting. I slipped it into my coat pocket. Then I took one last deep suck, threw the cigarette to the ground and stamped it out.

It's odd to think that, at this point, I could still have walked away, turned on my heel and headed back to the train station with my Christmas bauble, a fag butt the only evidence that I had ever been there.

I thought I had the wrong house at first. The door was answered by a woman with hazel eyes, a wide, open face and thick, curly hair which she had tried to tame with a green silk scarf: surely too bohemian to be Andrew's wife. I held my arms out at each side, brandishing the wine in one hand: here I am.

The woman appraised me for a moment and then said: 'You must be Paul Morris. We've been waiting for you. Come in, come in. I'm Tina.'

I put out my spare hand and she shook it, drawing me into the hall, where a large glass chandelier shot the light into pieces; small lozenge-shaped fragments across the floor and walls. Dark bannisters curved up a sweeping staircase. I removed my tweed coat and she opened a large French armoire and hung it up. I felt exposed, my chest tightening, as she opened the door to a drawing room where a group of strangers standing by a piano turned to stare. A fire flickering in sequence. An overly sweet smell of burning candle. Elaborately framed photographs on every surface of children in swimwear and salopettes.

A memory stirred, sediment at the bottom of a well. A tea-date with a boy from school. The suit my mother had put me in; the glance the boy's mother had exchanged with her son. I swallowed hard.

Andrew came towards me. 'My dear fellow,' he said. 'So glad you could fit us in before New York.'

'New York?' I said. 'Oh yes, a work trip. Lightning. I'll be back before I know it.'

I held out the wine and Andrew took it, his eyes on mine, cradling my £4.99 Isla Negra with its neck in his palm, and the base in the inside of his elbow, like a sommelier. Tiny shaving pimples dotted his neck. 'Come and meet everyone!'

I was wearing my best suit, no tie, and a white shirt with the top three buttons undone. I was overdressed. Every person there was in jeans, with polo shirts for the men and flowery tunic tops for the women. I took a deep breath, adjusted my cuffs and stretched my mouth into a smile, the kind of smile I knew women loved.

'This is Paul, the old university friend I was telling you about.' Andrew led me to the piano and ran through a list of names: Rupert and Tom, Susie and Izzy – a blur of chins and sharp noses and thin legs, cashmere, dangly earrings. 'Oh, and Boo,' he said, delivering the name of a short, chubby woman he had almost forgotten.

A cold flute of champagne was pressed into my hand and I found myself the centre of attention. I felt my anxiety ease – I often blossom in such circumstances – and before long, I was leaning against the piano, hamming up the arduous adventure of my journey. The Tube, the train, the bloody walk. I turned to berate Andrew. 'No one else was on foot. It was like being in LA. I had to flag down a car to ask directions. Twice.' Andrew laughed loudly. 'Paul's a novelist,' he said.

'You're a novelist?' Susie said.

'Yes.'

'You were – what? Twenty-two when you wrote *Annotations*?' Andrew said.

I smiled modestly. 'Twenty-one. My last year in Cambridge. I was twenty-two when it was published. It was number nine on the *Sunday Times* bestseller list.'

How clean and innocent the words. I was aware of them landing on fresh turf and taking root – seedlings of hope, new shoots.

'How exciting. Have you written anything since?' asked Susie.

I felt my smile harden. 'Bits and bobs . . . a couple of shorter novels you might not have heard of.'

'Is it true everyone has one novel in them?' a voice said, behind me.

It's an annoying cliché. I turned my head to see who had uttered it. In the doorway stood a slim, slight woman, with shoulder-length blond hair, wearing an apron splattered with flour.

She stepped forward and put out her hand. Silver bracelets jangled. She had a small pointy chin and her mouth was lopsided, painted in a pale pink lipstick that didn't suit her. There was something child-like about her, despite her obvious age. Nothing special, but more attractive at least than any of the other specimens on offer. 'I'm Alice,' she said. 'We've met.'

She did look vaguely familiar, but I couldn't place her. 'Have we?'

She put her head to one side, her hand still out. 'Alice Mackenzie?'

Andrew pushed himself off from the piano. 'Paul – you remember Alice? I'm sure you've met before, not least that night in Greece.' He laughed.

A chasm yawned beneath me. I didn't like thinking about Greece. I decided to ignore her outstretched hand and bent to kiss her cheek. 'Of course,' I said.

She didn't move – her face still crooked towards mine. 'You've been smoking. I can smell it.'

I put my hands up in a gesture of surrender.

She leant even closer, bringing her hands up to the collar of my shirt, touching the fabric, and breathed in deeply, wafting the air near my mouth towards her nose. 'Don't apologise. It's delicious. Right. Back to the kitchen. I'm needed.'

She disappeared again through the door. Andrew watched her go.

'Alice is amazing.' Boo had moved closer. 'A real force of nature.'

'Oh, really?' She had seemed quite ordinary to me.

'Yes. She is quite incredible.' She raised her voice: 'Alice was how old, Andrew? When she lost her husband?'

Andrew spun round. He closed his eyes. 'Um. Ten years now since Harry died, so yes, early thirties. Their kids were still little.'

'Unlucky,' I said. 'Cancer?'

'Adrenal,' Boo said. 'It's terribly rare. He had stomach pains, which they thought was appendicitis. By that stage it had already spread and he was dead within three months. But she was so strong; she kept it together for the children.' Her tone was both reverential and self-satisfied, as if by reporting the saintliness of this Alice she was conferring some of it upon herself.

'Alice is a wonderful mother,' Andrew said. 'And an extraordinary lawyer. She's not a money-grabbing corporate shark like me.' He paused, allowing room for silent demurral. 'Alice works for Talbot & Co – you know, the famous legal aid company in Stockwell. She mainly represents asylum seekers.'

'And battered wives,' Boo said.

'She is closely involved in Women Against Sexual Violence, Women for Women's Rights, Women for Refugee Women . . . the list goes on.'

'She launched the Finding Jasmine campaign,' Boo said, as if I knew what the fuck she was talking about.

'You have met before,' Andrew said. 'That night on Pyros – we were all having dinner together down in the harbour when we saw you. Do you remember?'

I dug my hand into the back of a chair and leant back. 'I probably wasn't at my best that night,' I said carefully.

'You were a bit the worse for wear, old chap. A little out of control.'

I scratched my head, aiming for comedy. 'Sunstroke.'

Andrew made a clicking noise with his tongue. 'Retsina.'

I glanced at Boo. 'Haven't drunk retsina since. Aversion therapy.'

Two deep dimples dented Boo's cheeks. I'd dismissed her as too fat and posh for my tastes, but now I looked at her properly I saw she was quite pretty: white-skinned and blue-eyed. The way she was standing was sexy, too: shoulders back to show off her ample cleavage, her short plump legs tapered in their optimistic skinny jeans, her toes turned out, like a ballet dancer.

I smiled at her, avoiding Andrew's eyes.

'It was a long time ago,' he said.

'Dinner is served!' Tina was standing at the door, brandishing a wooden spoon. Tendrils of wiry auburn hair had flown loose from the bandana, and her cheeks were flushed.

I was the first to leave the room, and I followed her along a corridor into an enormous white and cream kitchen. An island, containing a sink, where Alice was washing lettuce, divided the space. Stainless steel pans dangled from a metal contraption hung from the ceiling and at the far end huge glass doors led on to the garden. A small section of patio was lit by the glow of the kitchen; the rest disappeared in layers into the darkness.

The others were coming in behind us. A male voice said: 'It's the parking I'm worried about.' The table, shiny mahogany, was elaborately laid. Andrew started lighting candles, using a long elegant contraption, black with 'Diptyque' written along the side. Click. Click. Tina, with a scrappy piece of paper in her hand, was telling people where to sit – embarrassed, pretending to find her writing hard to read.

I stood by my allotted seat, my back to the kitchen, facing three large paintings which covered the wall. They were hideous: semi-abstract seascapes in bright clashing colours – turquoise and orange, a liberal use of white. Not my thing at all. I prefer a nude.

'They're mine,' Tina said, over my shoulder. 'So don't be rude.'

'I wasn't going to be. They are so . . . vibrant. I love how you've caught the light.'

'They're Greece actually. Pyros where . . . where you've been. The view from Circe's House. We go every year – thanks to Alice.'

We both looked round. Alice, who was still fiddling about at the sink, looked up at her name and smiled at us vaguely.

Tina turned back. 'It's coming to an end, though, sadly.'

'What is?' Andrew had taken his seat at the head of the table.

'Pyros.'

'Terrible shame.' He raised his voice. 'Poor Alice. End of an era, isn't it?'

'What, Greece?' she said, bringing a steaming bowl of tagine to the table. 'Yes. My lease has come to an end and the fucking freeholder wrote to me in January to say he's selling the land to developers. The tossers who built the Delfinos resort. Still, at least we have a stay of execution in the house if not the land – you're coming to Circe's this summer, Tina and Andrew, aren't you? One last hoorah.'

'Of course.' Andrew got up again to make space for Tina to squeeze past his chair. 'The kids would kill us if we didn't. We'd literally be dead.'

'Literally?' I said.

'Good.' Alice sat down opposite him at the far end. She made a small dramatic gesture with her napkin, flapping it on to her lap. 'Eat up, everyone.'

I looked at her for a moment, and then at Andrew, and at Tina, who was sitting somewhere in the middle of the table. Anyone would think Alice was the hostess here. Was it, in fact, *her* signature Moroccan lamb, not Tina's at all? I helped myself to a spoonful and then realised I should probably have served my neighbours – Susie, on one side, Izzy on the other. 'Sorry,' I said, offering it. 'I've got no manners. You can tell I went to boarding school – the panic at mealtimes, every boy for himself.'

'Boarding school? Which one?' the balder of the two men asked.

I told him where I had spent my formative years, and I could see he was surprised. The school has an academic reputation and I dropped a hint about my scholarship, too, mentioning I had been in the scholars' house. Tina picked up on this. 'Clever old you,' she said. 'Not just a pretty face.'

'Oh, did you know Sebastian Potter?' Izzy said. 'He must be about your age.'

'No,' I said too quickly, and then: 'I recognise the name. I think he might have been a couple of years above me.'

'Oh, OK,' she said. 'Big school.' She shrugged, her top slipping forward over the bones in her neck, the feathers in one of her earrings tangling in her hair. (Of course I knew Sebastian Potter. He was one of the bastards who made my life a misery.)

I turned my attention to the food. It was delicious, actually – the sauce tasted of orange flower water and saffron; the meat was wonderfully tender. Whether it was Tina who made it, or Alice, frankly for this alone it was worth the trip. Andrew had poured the wine, too, from a glass decanter – presumably the 2009 Châteauneuf as promised. It slipped down smoothly: no complaints there.

Around me the conversation wound on drably, past Tina's wool shop, Ripping Yarns, to plans for the velodrome, to the school where people at the table appeared to have children. A new head of sixth form had just been appointed but the old head was missed; one of the science teachers wasn't up to scratch; Boo's daughter hadn't got on to the Duke of Edinburgh scheme. It was over-subscribed and names had, of all things, been pulled from a hat. So unfair. Boo's husband, who was away for work, was going to go straight in the moment he was back.

'Do you have kids?' Susie asked me.

'No.'

'This must be so dull for you then.'

'Not at all,' I said.

'We should watch what we say,' Alice added. 'He's probably making mental notes for his next novel.'

It was another predictable comment. I'd lost count of the number of times people had said it. Alice was still wearing the apron, dotted now with gravy as well as flour. She'd applied a fresh layer of that hideous lipstick; it was smudged on the edge of her glass.

I felt a sudden desperate need for a cigarette. My legs jangled. I made my excuses, pushed my chair back, and walked over to the expanse of glass, where I fumbled until I found a mechanism that would slide it open. I slipped through a crack, quietly sealing the door again behind me.

The garden was in shadow – a long, wide lawn, edged with shrubs. At the end, skeleton trees against the sky and an expanse of dark nothing: a playing field. A brown smell of earth and damp.

The house, lit up behind me, was exposed – the candles on the table, the glint of cutlery: every detail visible to anyone who might be lurking down there. A shout of laughter, a scrape of chair. Boo's voice shrieking, 'No!'

I moved out of sight. An ironwork bench lurked on the grass, hidden from the kitchen by shrubs. I perched on the edge of it, trying not to get my trousers damp. A climbing frame and a trampoline with tall black sides, hulked like convict ships on the Kent marshes. The moon came out, dappling the grass, and disappeared again. An aeroplane crossed overhead – an angry snarl on the wind.

I lit my fag easily enough this time. It was cold. I should have gone to get my coat. I wondered how quickly I could go home. The evening had been fine – I'd managed – but, now I had eaten, there was nothing here for me. No women. No work. No whiff of a house-sit. I inhaled deeply, drawing the nicotine into my blood.

A sudden loud burst of conversation, a shot of warmth – immediately sliced off. I turned. Alice was standing on the terrace. I kept still in case she decided to go back in, but she took a couple of steps across the lawn and saw me.

'Hi,' she said.

She made a quick gesture to rearrange a bit of her hair at the back – that thing women do, with such a touching air of secrecy, half-tweak, half-smooth, as if they believe there is only one position in which their hair is acceptable. I find it oddly moving.

She took a step closer. 'I thought I might bum a cigarette off you – if that's OK?'

I felt the usual flicker. Why don't non-smokers buy their own? Or *not* smoke? 'Of course,' I said gallantly, reaching into my jacket pocket.

She perched next to me, elbows on her knees, and I handed her a cigarette. I made a wry reference to the femininity of my brand – ultra ultra low-tar Silk Cut – and she laughed, though I was only trying to distract her from my lighter. It was the long, thin stick Andrew had left on the table. I slipped it back into my pocket and continued to fondle it. It was matt black, soft to the touch.

She inhaled deeply. 'Lovely,' she said. 'I don't *actually* smoke. Your typical social smoker. But it's getting harder and harder to maintain the habit these days.' She set off on a riff – how e-cigarettes were ruining all her fun, how the opportunities for 'the mild stoned fugginess' she enjoyed were drying up.

I said: 'I suppose you can't ask someone sucking on an electric vaporiser to "give us a vape"? Not unless you want a mouth full of caramel-flavoured spittle.'

'Exactly.' She laughed. Her eyes, almond-shaped, were a cat-like green under arched eyebrows.

'How did you first meet Andrew?' she asked. 'I forgot to ask.'

'I was at Trinity with him.'

'Ah. Cambridge. Of course.' She smiled. 'Did you know him well then?'

'Not particularly.' I sat back on the bench – damp or no damp – and tilted my head to the sky. 'I knew his sister a bit.'

'Florrie. Yes of course.'

'You know her?'

'We were best friends at school. I met Andrew through her. I used to visit her in Cambridge. In fact, I'm not sure you and I didn't meet there, too.' She smiled. 'I have a lot to thank her for. Andrew and I are *great mates.*'

Great mates. She gave a high artificial laugh. She was one of those women who gush and flirt, but it's all fake. They hold back everything that matters. You never find out what's really there. *If* anything's really there. Terrible in bed, too.

She studied her cigarette closely, then looked up, and said coyly: 'You don't remember meeting me before, do you? In Cambridge, or in Greece?'

'You do look familiar.' I dropped my cigarette and screwed it into the grass with my heel. I decided to cut to the chase. 'But listen, Alice. I'm really sorry. All evening I've been a bit embarrassed about this. I don't know why Andrew invited me. That Greek thing, I was a mess then. It was what – eight years ago?'

'Ten.'

'It's not a period in my life I'm proud of. We'd been on one of those booze cruises. I lost my friends; the boat left the port without me. And then I bumped into Andrew and luckily he helped me out. But I'll be straight with you – the details are, to this day, rather hazy.'

'Do you want me to tell you what I remember?'

25

'If you must.'

She laughed. 'You burst into the taverna where we were having dinner. You were wearing a purple T-shirt that said "Zeus Nightclub" on it. You were shouting and being rude. You started singing.'

'Was I?' I winced. I was encouraged by the fact she seemed to find it funny. 'Zeus, yes. I remember that T-shirt. And ... singing ... singing was never my strong point.'

'Andrew sorted you a taxi. Poured you into it: I think that's how he put it.'

'Andrew is a gentleman.'

A shout of noise from the kitchen. Alice took a last look at her stub of cigarette and flicked it into the flower bed. She was wearing a little purple cardigan, the sort of thing an old lady might wear, and she pulled it together at the neck. Her face grew suddenly serious. 'Every detail of that night is etched on my memory. I remember everything. It was such a terrible time.'

'I heard. Your husband ...'

'I don't mean Harry.' She shook her head, let out a small, bitter laugh. 'He died the year before. No. I mean that night, the night Jasmine went missing.'

If I searched hard enough, somewhere in the murky depths of my mind I could find what she was talking about, but it was just scraps, oddments, broken trails.

'Remind me,' I said.

Alice frowned. 'Jasmine. Jasmine Hurley. You were there. Poor Yvonne, her mother. God.' She let go of the cardigan and her hands waved in the air, fingers tense. 'It was in the papers. You must have heard about it the next day, read about it. Where were you staying? Elconda? Even the Pyros police, who were hopeless from the beginning, would have taken their enquiries at least down there ... Surely you remember.'

I bowed my head, embarrassed, as ever, to be found emotionally wanting. She had prodded my memory, though the details were still vague – a teenager who ran off, a single mother, a dodgy boyfriend? 'Yes, yes, of course,' I said. 'I do. I'm sorry.'

She rested the fingers of one hand on the bridge of her nose. I patted her shoulder, putting as much anguish and concern into my face as I could muster. I was keen to get back inside now. It wasn't just the cold. I was feeling inadequate, and also nettled – the two emotions merging and doing each other no favours.

Through the cross-hatch of shrubbery, lights flickered from the kitchen. Andrew was walking around the table, the decanter in his hand glinting. Tina had crossed to the other side of the room, and was bending to lift a bowl – trifle? – out of the fridge. Boo had her arms in the air: she was trying to take off her cardigan and she'd got her top tangled with it. I caught a flash of skin and bra strap.

A high-pitched chirrup brought my attention back to Alice. She wiped her eyes and wriggled her mobile phone out of the front pocket of her jeans.

'Phoebe – my eldest – wanting to be picked up from a party,' she said, studying it. 'Well, she'll have to get the night bus. I've had far too much to drink.'

She tapped a quick text, saying as she did so: 'Honestly, she's nearly eighteen and about to leave home. You'd think she'd have learnt a bit of independence.' She slipped the phone back into her pocket, angling her hip forward to make it easier. 'Though God knows what I'm going to do when she's gone. I can't walk past her room without imagining it empty.'

She shivered, hunching her shoulders together and rubbing her lower arm. 'I suppose we'd better go back in.'

'Let's see your phone again,' I said.

She kept my gaze. 'Why?'

'Go on.'

A small smile. 'No.'

'It's got rabbit ears, hasn't it?'

I made a quick movement – as if to put my hand into her pocket. She jerked away, giggling, then with a childish petulance, pulled it out and threw it at me. 'Go on then. Feast your eyes. Laugh all you like.'

I turned it over in my lap where it had landed and said flatly: 'Your iPhone cover is in the shape of a blue rabbit.'

'My son, Frank, gave it to me. It was a present!'

'Do you take it to work, you big-shot lawyer you, to your very important meetings?'

She was grinning. I noticed then why her mouth was lopsided. A tiny puckered arrow pointed up at one corner, a small scar.

The feeling came from nowhere. She hadn't flirted. She was not my type – about twenty years too old for one thing. So I don't know what it was – Boo's bra maybe, or the thought of Alice's hip warm beneath her jeans pocket. Or something quicksilver about her movements. Or maybe, even then, I had subliminally registered the prospect of an empty room in a comfortable house. But when I saw that scar I had a sudden desire to lick it.

Chapter Three

I rang Andrew for Alice's number the following morning. If he was surprised, he hid it well. He said, 'Of course, hang on,' and then blustered for a few seconds, muttering, 'Sorry . . . stupid me . . . wait a sec . . .' He was, he said, a 'technical idiot' – couldn't work out how to access his contacts list while remaining on the phone. 'Tina!' he shouted. Then, finally, 'Right, here we are. Alice Mackenzie. Work, home, or mobile – or maybe all three?'

'Mobile,' I said. I was rolling the Christmas bauble from his hedge between my fingers, feeling the glitter turn to grit.

'OK.' He paused. 'You going to ring her now, or after your work trip?'

'What work trip?'

'New York.'

'Oh yes.'

He paused again, and then said: 'Look, I know I'm being an arse. But I can't help being protective. Ali's had such a tough time – Harry's death was so awful for her. She's kept it all so brilliantly together and her kids are fantastic, but she's still vulnerable. She is special to me, to Tina, to both of us. I don't want her to be hurt, or to be messed about, or . . . There – I've said enough. Lecture over.'

Would a better man have said, 'Fair cop. My intentions are purely dishonourable. Your words have made me see sense, and I will respectfully back off.' Frankly? Would *anyone* have

29

listened to his self-serving, conceited little speech and said that?

I wanted to say, 'I'll do whatever I like, you interfering little twerp,' but instead I made all the right noises. So credible was my claim to decency, I half believed in it myself.

The number was duly delivered, recited slowly, each digit apparently wrenched from Andrew against his better judgement.

I arranged to meet Alice in ten days' time, on a Tuesday night: an odd choice, but her diary was packed with university visits and appeal deadlines and parents' evenings, 'unbelievably complicated'. It was too long a wait. As the days went by, I began to go off the idea. By the time the night in question arrived, I had forgotten what I had seen in her in the first place.

Still, a date's a date and I am nothing if not gallant. Andrew Edmunds, a small intimate restaurant in Soho, was my go-to venue in those days. It was perfect for such occasions: candle-lit, quirkily arty. I liked to think it said something about *me* that I was so at home there. Plus, I got a discount: thirty per cent off in exchange for having tutored the manager's daughter. GCSE English Literature: *Othello*. (She got an A.)

I was early, and disconcerted to find Alice already there, drinking a glass of wine and sifting through some papers. When she saw me, she stuffed them into a voluminous leather bag, along with a thick alligator-skin A3 desk diary, and quickly got to her feet, putting out a hand for me to shake. She was wearing a navy-blue skirt with a buttoned-up white shirt, and flat knee-length black boots. Her hair was pulled back, and she was wearing no make-up but for a slash of the unflattering pink lipstick.

She apologised for looking 'office-y'. She had been in court all afternoon: a Congolese teenager, a model A-level pupil at school in Barnet, who was due to be deported when she reached adulthood in a month's time. Yes, I was right, it was emotionally draining. Her own daughter was almost exactly the same age, which added an extra layer.

'Phoebe?' I said. 'The one who is moving out?'

'Yes. She has a place at Leeds in September to read English. If she gets the grades.'

'Oh. Not until September.'

'It'll come soon enough. I can't bear it. She'll leave such a hole.'

'You could get a lodger?'

'She wants to be a journalist actually. Andrew said you wrote for newspapers sometimes?'

'I do. And if she'd like any advice, I'm happy to help. Anything to help her on her way.'

'That would be kind. Thank you.'

We ordered food – wild sea trout and the guinea fowl special. I learnt more about her children. Phoebe, the eldest, followed by two boys (Louis, sixteen and Frank, fourteen). She mentioned her dead husband several times. 'Frank is straightforward,' she told me, 'just like Harry, up for anything.' Louis was a darker character, going through a difficult stage, 'but then of course he misses his father more.' She sighed when she said this and, with the middle finger of her left hand, lightly padded the pouchy skin under her left eye. Her eye was dry, so the gesture seemed staged or, at least, well practised; an instinctive check, perhaps, from a time when there would have been tears there. I felt as I had in Andrew's garden, that even when she was apparently opening her heart, she was keeping a great deal back.

My chair was near the entrance to the kitchen and the waiter jogged it every time he passed – through the doors, out again. I began to find it hard to concentrate. I felt agitated, knees twitchy, not at my best. As soon as the plates were cleared, I decided to call it a day by asking her back for coffee, and was astonished when she accepted. It was raining and the pavements were slick with it – or perhaps I'm making that up: all my memories seem to involve rain. She whistled for a taxi, a proper scalp-shrinking two-finger whistle, which abruptly turned me on, and when we pulled up in my street ten minutes later, insisted on paying. She professed herself 'charmed' while we were still climbing the stairs, her shoulder bag bashing against the bannisters, and she stood in the doorway of the flat, raving in self-conscious delight at my taste and cleverness. 'Oh yes. Oh yes. This is *lovely*.'

I lit a cigarette and busied myself in the kitchen over the coffee machine, listening to her move about the sitting room, knowing, with each particular creak in the floorboards, where she was standing: by this picture, or that bookcase.

'I love the "twiggy bird"!' she cried. She was in front of the black and white print above the fireplace.

'A dry-point etching,' I returned. 'It's a Kate Boxer.'

'You play?' she called a little later. She was poking in Alex's pile of sheet music to the side of the sofa.

'Terribly rusty,' I called back. 'Not since I was a child.'

I had a quick tot of whisky from my emergency supplies, and then a couple more. Persephone wound herself around my legs and I gave her a saucer of milk. I wasn't quite sure what my next move should be. Was this a seduction? I didn't know how it worked with the older woman. Would she expect something rather more gracious and prolonged? In which case, why was I bothering? It didn't cross my mind to tell the truth: that the life the flat purported to reflect wasn't mine – not because I was embarrassed, though I might well have been, a forty-two-year-old man with nothing to his name but a few bin bags in his mother's attic. No, I didn't see the point. So what if I was due to be evicted in a week? I didn't expect ever to see her again.

When I brought the coffee through, she was sitting on the sofa, studying that framed Trinity College photograph. It was Alex's of course, but as he and I had met there, it might just as well have been mine. 'I took it off the wall in the loo. I hope you don't mind. I'm looking for you.' Her finger traced along a row of young, plump, pompous faces. 'Ah!' She smiled. 'Longer hair . . . Where's Andrew?'

I leant across to peer. Etiolated face, peaked nose, sanctimonious expression. 'In the middle at the front.'

'Oh yes. Also longer hair.'

'*More* hair.'

'Don't be naughty.' She laughed, and then looked again at the photograph. 'I can't see Florrie. Is she here?'

'No. She came later. In my third year.'

She put the picture on the sofa to one side of her, and then looked at me. 'Were *you* happy?'

I paused for a moment, wondering what she meant, and then said: 'Yes, very.'

'I remember, when I visited, thinking the place was very grand, and the people there were either very grand or very small. At Bristol, where I was, you could be anything. But there, you were one or the other.'

I experienced a small internal tremor. 'Perhaps that's true.'

She took a sip of her cappuccino. A lock of her hair fell forward. I could see the strands of grey in with the blonde.

'What about you?' I said. 'Were you happy as a child?'

It was one of my usual chat-up lines. Alice responded to type: a self-deprecating shrug, and then a sort of glow – perfectly content to talk about herself for hours. She had grown up in north London, the only child of a lawyer and a university lecturer. Private school, then Bristol, where she had met Harry. A golden life, a lucky life, she said.

'It's hard, isn't it, living with privilege?' She gestured to the flat, the artwork, the items of mid-century furniture, the shelves of books. 'Do you ever feel guilty at how easy it all is, how much people like us have been given on a plate by our parents?'

I felt another tight spasm in my chest, a need to unburden, as if I might tell her how it *wasn't*, what a struggle it had been not to lead the life of my parents, how I had always hated the smallness of their ambition, their willingness to settle with meekness and mediocrity. I wondered at the extent of *her* privilege. How rich was this lady bountiful? How much had Harry left her? How big was *her* house? I managed to nod sagely. 'Yes. I suppose one has to be mindful of that and . . . well, do one's best to give something back.'

She rested her hand on my arm. 'I knew you'd understand. It's why I do what I do. Andrew berates me for not joining a firm like his, for not doing commercial law, but it wouldn't make me happy. I've always fought for the underdog, for people who don't have a voice of their own.'

She shook her head and took another sip from her coffee. 'You write books,' she said. 'That's a generous act in some ways. You have to open up.'

'Yes. You really do.'

'Are you working on anything at the moment?'

I offered her a cigarette, but she shook her head. I lit one for myself. 'Yes, actually. A novel about London, about immigration, about the dispossessed. State of the nation, kind of thing.'

All lies.

'Do you have a publisher? I don't know how it works.'

'Sort of.' I leant back, and changed the subject. 'Andrew said you do a lot of work for charity?'

'I'm on various boards. Finding Jasmine is my main commitment. It's what I feel most passionately about. Andrew helps me. In many ways, it sums up what I was just saying. You know, Jasmine wasn't a sweet little middle-class blonde toddler like Madeleine McCann. She was fourteen. But that's still a *child*. She deserved just as much police, and media attention, and yet no one seemed particularly interested.'

'Well done, you, to have done one thing to rectify that,' I said, trying to sound interested myself.

She picked up the lighter from the table where I had placed it and turned it over in her hands. The words 'Diptyque' flashed silver against black in the light from the lamp. 'I know you're a terrible womaniser,' she said. 'I'm not quite sure what I'm doing here.'

I was taken aback. 'I'm not,' I said.

'Not what?'

'A terrible womaniser.'

'Andrew says you're a bad man.'

'Really? Gosh. Well, I don't know what he means by that . . .'

'He says you treat women badly. You don't respect them.'

'Really? He says that?'

She was looking at me very carefully now.

'Maybe,' I said, doing my best to muster a sleepy smile, 'I just haven't met the right woman.'

Her coffee cup was on her knee and she put her finger into it to scoop out the last of the foam, and dabbed it on her tongue – a flick of white on pink. Her eyes were right in mine as she did so. Was she flirting? It seemed unlikely, and yet bizarrely flattering if so. (Despite everything she said, she still wanted me.) 'I must go,' she said, not moving.

What did I have to lose? I shifted my leg very slightly, steering myself gently towards her, shoulders already manoeuvring into position. She limboed out from under me, stood up and shrugged on her coat, doing up the buttons, enfolding her body in the straps of her bag: putting herself away.

At the front door of the building, I kissed her clumsily. I had had a bit too much to drink. My mouth impacted with a corner of her lips and rested there wetly. She pressed her hands flat against my chest. I could feel the warmth of her palms through my shirt. Was it attraction or rebuttal? An inch in either direction, a finger slipped between the buttons, and her motive would have been clear. But I wasn't sure. I sensed a rigidity in her elbows, a tension in her forearms, and I was almost relieved when she pulled away.

She rang the next day, much to my astonishment. In fact, I stood up when I heard her voice, already scanning the flat for a dropped lipstick or forgotten scarf, some reason for her to have called. She was walking. I could tell by the shortness of her breath. She said something about 'putting a date in the diary' and I imagined her leaning against a wall and hoisting that big appointments book out of her bag.

It turned out it was tea she was suggesting. That Saturday, if I were free. Phoebe would love to 'pick my brains' about journalism if I was really sure; perhaps I could put some work experience her way.

I should have said no. The evening had not been a success. But I was vain and flattered, and was idly interested in the thought of Phoebe, and so I said yes.

Chapter Four

She lived in Clapham in a tall, narrow Georgian house on a fairly busy road. Next door was a dump: the front door painted in rasta stripes, a shopping trolley half buried, upside down, in overgrown vegetation. Rap thumped from an upstairs window. Alice's house in contrast possessed an air of shabby gentility: peeling grey railings topped with acorn finials; cast-iron pots trailing the brown remnants of last summer's geraniums; an empty 'Riverford' box waiting for its weekly replacement of organic veg.

The girl who answered the door had a small oval face between hanks of long blonde hair. She was wearing tiny denim shorts over black tights, the top half of her body swathed in an enormous hand-knitted cardigan. When she saw me, she turned away to shout 'Mum!' up the stairs, and then, to me, 'Yeah, do you wanna come in?'

She walked ahead, and I followed her along the hall, down a narrow flight of stairs, into a basement kitchen: Aga, pine table, pots with herbs, a smell of baking and daffodils, with a strong undertone of garlic. A tabby cat clattered out of a cat-flap, but a brown Labrador, sitting in a corduroy dog bed in the corner, stretched out its front legs and then slowly lumbered over, tail wagging, to thrust its nose into my crotch.

I edged away, and found a chair at the table. The house was quiet, except for the distant sound of television and the muffled pummel of next door's bass. Phoebe stood by the

Aga, twisting her nose ring. She was not that much younger than Polly, my recent squeeze, but I sensed her contempt for me, or perhaps specifically for the leather jacket I had chosen to wear. Or perhaps for the shoes. (New white Converse – I wasn't sure about them.) Not that I particularly cared. Her looks did nothing for me either. She was pretty enough but her hair was badly bleached and her eyebrows were plucked into high thin arches. Half-waif, half-whore. Not my type. I mean – one or the other, surely.

I made a stab at conversation. 'So – Phoebe, is it? I hear you're planning to study English at Leeds. Is the course any good?'

She tipped her head and said, with unnatural politeness: 'I hope so. I've been told it is.' She closed her mouth at the end of each sentence as if she were sipping at the words, speaking slowly to an elderly relative. 'I haven't yet had a chance to visit.'

The dog was still nudging away at my groin, which I discouraged with movements of my knee. 'Oh well, you've got plenty of time.'

'You were at Cambridge, Mum said. With Uncle Andrew. They were talking about it last night.'

Uncle Andrew? *Last* night. I felt uneasy. 'Where *is* your mother?'

She went to the foot of the steps and shouted: 'Mum. MUM. He's here.'

A fraction of silence and then a distant shout and a series of soft thumps. 'He's here? Oh, why didn't you say? Louis – that's enough TV!' Her feet hammered the last flight of stairs and she burst into the room. She was wearing tight running trousers, a silver-grey zip-up tracksuit top, and caramel Uggs. Earrings like tiny, tiered chandeliers dangled from her lobes.

'Paul! Thank you for coming.' She swept over, all movement and light, her hair loose. She pushed the dog out of the way. 'Off, Dennis. Leave the man alone.' She kissed me on both cheeks. 'Phoebe, have you thanked him for coming?'

'Yup,' Phoebe said.

'Right, well, I'll make some tea. You two get chatting.'

Phoebe and I looked at each other. I suspect we both felt we had done our chatting. I had a sinking sense of dread that I was about to be revealed as a fraud. I tried to cover the embarrassment, pompously drilling Phoebe about her expectations of journalism and delivering a small, rather more heartfelt lecture on the shrinking of newspapers and the competitive nature of the job market.

Alice, drying her hands on a tea towel, said: 'Phoebe would love some work experience after her A levels. Wouldn't you, Phoebs?'

'Yes, I would,' Phoebe said with the same sibilant over-pronunciation as earlier. 'If you could help?'

'What sort of thing?'

'I thought I might get a job at a magazine – maybe something at the *New Statesman,* cos I'm into politics, or maybe *Vogue*? Mum said you might have some contacts I could use. Everyone says it's all about who you know.'

'I'll have a think,' I said calmly.

She drew her cardigan tightly around her. 'Or maybe telly? Do you know anyone there?'

I stared at her. 'Not really.'

Her phone made the noise of a hunting horn and, looking at it, she said: 'Mum, can I go to Dolly's now?'

Alice said: 'Yes, OK, but I want you back tonight.'

Phoebe stood up. 'Bye,' she said to me over her shoulder. 'Thanks.'

A hole at the back of her tights revealed a patch of blue-white skin like a bruise.

'It was nothing,' I said.

Alice straightened a large picture on the wall, a framed collage of photographs, black and white, full colour, sepia; big smiles, funny costumes, exotic holidays: family life at its most boastful. In the centre was a photograph of a man on a beach, with a baby on his knee, curved brown arms and summer stubble, eyes wrinkled against the sun – Harry. He looked handsome and manly. Here he was in the middle of his world: skiing holidays and skippered yachts, champagne, blonde heads and Rolex watches. Men like him had made me angry all my life, everything they had, everything I didn't. I felt a sharp jolt of envy and resentment, immediately followed by a more comfortable, of thought. Harry was dead and I was sitting in his kitchen.

Alice had moved away from the picture and was tidying up rather aimlessly, as if she had a purpose other than me for being there. A series of clatters and a male shout from upstairs. 'MUM. Going out!'

She rolled her eyes.

'Which one's that?' I said.

'Louis. Frank's at a friend's.' She stood at the bottom of the stairs. 'Take a coat; it's raining!'

Heavy footsteps and the slam of the front door.

'I never made the tea.' She consulted her watch. 'Oh fuck it. Glass of wine?'

'Well, I wouldn't say no,' I said.

She opened a cupboard and brought out a bottle of Merlot, which she opened with a Screwpull, clutching it for traction between her thighs – rather sexily actually.

'Do smoke.'

She handed me a chipped saucer and threw open the window above the sink. It was raining modestly. Declining to have one herself, she sat back, subtly shielding her nose and mouth with her hand. After a bit she began to shuffle a pile of papers in front of her, absent-mindedly chewing one lip.

When I asked what they were, she told me they were flyers for the dinner-ball benefit in aid of Finding Jasmine. She said, her voice high and tense, that this year was the ten-year anniversary and they needed to raise more money for 'the next phase'. Yvonne, Jasmine's mother, was coming down from Sheffield and she wanted everything to be perfect.

She passed me one of the flyers. On the front was a photograph of the young Jasmine, wearing a flowery bandana and holding a ginger kitten to her cheek, and next to it a computer reconstruction of how the missing girl might look now. I studied the picture as she was talking: a pretty twenty-three-year-old with a high forehead, narrow face, blue eyes, large mouth. It was probably inappropriate, but my instinctive response was to wonder whether the people who construct these composites err, out of tact, on the side of pulchritude.

I didn't say that of course. I nodded slowly, hoping to convey a heart full of empathy and commiseration. 'Poor girl,' I said. Alice slumped back in her chair and took a first big gulp from her glass and then delicately wiped the wine from the corner of her lips.

I swirled my glass, watching the wine swing and crumple like crimson velvet. 'Do you really think she's alive?'

She looked me straight in the eye. 'I think she is alive.'

I gathered up what I could remember, sweeping the details together. 'But the mother's boyfriend . . . wasn't there something . . . Didn't the police . . .?'

'No. The police were wrong about that. And he's been cleared. It's absurd that anyone – you! – should still think that. They wasted so much time. It's true Karl and Jasmine had a volatile relationship. She was jealous of him taking away her mother's attention. And he's that kind of bloke, bit of a talker, still a bit of a child himself – not old enough to be the adult in the situation. He and Jasmine had rowed that night, it's true.

But if you had seen his grief . . . and the way he has supported Yvonne over the last ten years. No. He didn't kill her.' She shook her head, small angry shakes. 'No.'

'Where's Jasmine's dad in all this?'

'He left Yvonne when she was pregnant.'

'And were there ever any other suspects?'

'Not really.' She shook her head again. Her earrings rattled. 'A few eyewitness accounts of strange men hanging around, but nothing concrete. Migrant workers from Albania, but . . .'

She took a swig and put the glass back down on the table. The wine shuddered. Her mouth pursed, tight, angry. 'There was never a body. On an island like that – that's important. They searched the coastline, the hillsides thoroughly. No ferries left that night and by the next day the police were at the port watching. Everyone was out, looking. The sea isn't tidal. So no. Instinctively I just know.'

'She ran away?'

'Perhaps. Or she was taken. Illegal adoption rings are rife in that part of the world. And then Pyros is so close to Albania, you only have to get across the channel . . .'

'But would a teenage girl be a likely candidate? She was fourteen, did you say? Wouldn't that be too old?'

'Yes. I suppose. Though the other possibility is prostitution. One of the things she argued with Yvonne and Karl about was that she was going out all the time – she'd met a boy in the village. He never came forward. For a long time we investigated the possibility that she had been taken to Athens. It's an unbearable thought. I don't know, but I will find out. I won't rest until I do. I know that's a cliché . . . but . . . if you've ever known a mother lose a child . . . the not knowing. It's unbearable, the pain. It never goes away.'

'And what about the idea that she might have left of her own accord?'

'There's a small hippy community on the west coast of the island – a hangover from the seventies. Germans, Scandinavians, a few Brits. They don't live in caves any more but they're still a strong presence – occasionally you see them in the tourist towns. I've always thought they were involved. That she might be living with them. She was, from everything Yvonne has told me, quite a simple girl, but a bit odd maybe. There's a theory – quite a plausible one – that she did run away and has been living with them, and has either lost her memory, or been brainwashed, that perhaps she wanted to come home and was prevented, that drugs might have been involved.'

'But haven't the police looked?'

'Yes, but . . . Too late, you know?'

I didn't really know, and I didn't really care. I was bored of the subject. The dead girl – because of course she was dead – wasn't bringing out the best in Alice. I wanted more of the sexily efficient businesswoman from dinner with her deportations and hearings. Or the grubby domestic goddess from Andrew's house. I remembered the laugh I had wrung out of her in the garden – a girlish tinkle with a filthy undertow; the way she had licked the cappuccino foam from her finger. I knew as well as anyone how life gives us certain roles to play. But I had had enough of her goodness, of feeling in the wrong, of this misery memoir. The Merlot was a good one – fruity and soft, warm blood in the mouth. I'd have another glass and, unless things changed, be on my way.

'Anyway,' she said. 'Let's lighten the mood. You haven't come all this way to talk about that.' She gave a lopsided grin.

I stayed all evening.

Alice found another bottle of wine and, moving with speed around the kitchen, opening cupboard doors and hurling ingredients, produced a bowl of pasta with homemade pesto, and a salad of tomato and cucumber and feta: a Greek salad, in fact, 'though nowhere near as delicious as the ones you actually get in Greece'.

She made a staggering amount of mess – cucumber peelings left flopping over the dirty Magimix; a glug of olive oil spilt on the top of the Aga, the white plastic packet that the feta came in dropped on the floor and forgotten. Oblivious to the chaos she was creating, she talked in a stream about leaving Pyros. The kids had loved it there when they were younger, but now they had social lives in London that needed to be constantly stoked, they were less interested in coming. Perhaps it was good this summer would be their last. 'Everything comes to an end,' she said. She was chopping tomatoes and she stopped in mid-cut. She gazed out of the window, which was still half open, on to the wet garden. 'No matter how hard you try to stop it.'

She picked up the knife again, and said, as an afterthought, 'If you haven't got any plans this summer, you should come.'

Once it was cooked, she suggested we took our plates upstairs and ate in front of the fire. The sitting room was soft and cosy, with mismatched sofas and mohair throws, thick velvet curtains, and threadbare Turkish rugs. Bookcases lined the alcoves. A corduroy beanbag was positioned in front of the television; headphones and PlayStation handsets were scattered on the floor. The fire was real and, once she had revived the embers with another log, comfortingly warm. The tabby cat was curled against a tapestry cushion and was happy now to be stroked. Alice drew the curtains and I saw her face, for a second, reflected in the glass, a ripple of fractured lights, and I remembered the passage in *To the Lighthouse* when Mrs Ramsay, serving stew, feels a sense of coherence, of stability. In my case, of course, it may have been the hope of sex.

Alice sat on the floor, with her plate on the coffee table, and I sat on the sofa, elbows awkward, leaning down. When I finished my food and had mopped up the last gritty green juices with a piece of bread, I stood and wandered over to study the bookshelves more closely. Alice was telling me about a Muslim woman from Bexleyheath who, after years of abuse, had stabbed her husband to death with the kitchen scissors. To be honest, the subject was making me feel a bit jangly.

The lower rows contained bestsellers, thrillers, an extensive run of Hornblowers. But on the top shelf was a clutch of old green and orange Penguin editions (Simenon and Ngaio Marsh; George Orwell; *The Great Gatsby*), and some hardbacks in colourful dust jackets. My eye snagged on a distinctive black spine with a slash of yellow, and I reached up to pull the book out: *The Rachel Papers* by Martin Amis. I flicked it open. 1973. A first edition.

'God!' I yelped.

Alice had been watching me closely. 'Harry loved Martin Amis,' she said, her eyes on mine. 'Public schoolboys often do, I've noticed. Sex and money and a rich dollop of self-loathing.'

'I'll ignore that,' I said, bringing the book back to the sofa and sitting down. The cat slunk off the cushion and joined me, nudging to get on to my knee. I held the book above its body and turned the pages with reverence.

'Gussie,' Alice said. 'The cat, I mean.'

I felt I could hardly breathe, in case I damaged the pages. 'It's signed,' I said.

Alice sighed. 'He probably bid for it off eBay. He was susceptible to extravagant impulses, was Harry.'

A note in her voice made me put the book down, carefully to one side of me, and look at her. Her eyes had a glassy aspect. 'Have it,' she said. 'Go on. It's yours.'

I pretended not to hear. 'Do you miss him?' I said.

She nodded. 'I've forgotten what it felt like to be held . . .'

A stutter in the atmosphere between us, a faltering. The room darkened. A noise against the window, a splatter of rain, as if someone had thrown a handful of small stones at the glass.

Alice shook her head and laughed. 'I'm not a nun. By *him*, I mean. I've forgotten what it felt like to be held by *him*.'

She kept her eyes on the carpet. After a few minutes, I tipped the cat gently off my knee, and made the worst mistake of my life: I unzipped the silver-grey running top to her navel, pushed aside the rather nasty nylon material to expose her surprisingly bra-less breasts, and pulled her towards me.

Chapter Five

The following week I moved back in with my mother. I can't help thinking things might have been different if I hadn't.

The railway cottage in East Sheen, where I had grown up, had changed very little over the years – the same thread-bare carpet, the same lingering smell of cabbage, the same trains rattling out the back. My father had gone, of course – a heart attack delivering pastoral care at Wandsworth Prison, where he was chaplain – and my mother had made certain improvements to my tiny single room: a pine shelf, with puny brackets, 'for your books', a new lamp from BHS ('Ta-da') and above the single bed, a framed copy of the review that appeared in the *Times Literary Supplement* of *Annotations*, the paper yellowing with age behind the glass. It had always been stifling at home – the weight of my parents' expectations, their oppressive pleasure in my success, my own gaping sense of failure. But now the atmosphere was heightened – my mother warily cheerful in the face of my encroaching sense of suffocation. As she warmed us 'a couple of nice lamb chops' while maintaining a constant stream of chatter – she had taken the faulty kettle back to Dickins & Jones and had been served by a lovely girl ('black but couldn't have been nicer'); nice Jenny, from church, had offered to host next month's WI, 'which is a relief because of my knee' – it was immediately apparent desperate measures were called for.

'All those bags of stuff you've got in the attic,' she fussed over dessert, a Tesco apple crumble with Bird's custard. 'I thought I might bring them down.'

'Leave them there. It's fine.'

'Or maybe, as you're so busy, I might sort through them.'

'No,' I said abruptly. 'Don't touch anything of mine.'

That night, as I sat with her in the front room, watching a ghastly soap opera she described as 'one of my programmes' – I ran through my list of contacts. In the past, I'd always found something to save me – a colleague or cohort needing a house-sit, a girlfriend wanting more of me, the generosity of other peoples' parents I had carefully charmed. In extremis, Michael had bailed me out, but now the twins had taken occupancy of his spare room. For the first time in fifteen years, I felt trapped, forced to face my own demons.

Until this moment I had given no further thought to Alice. One night had been enough to satisfy whatever had drawn me to her in the first place. But as the soap opera finished and my mother changed the channel for a detective show set in the 1950s, I began to think about her. The sex had been enjoyable enough. The house was warm and comfortable. I'd got a free book. (I had sold it to one of the posher dealers in the Charing Cross Road for £500. It would have been more but there was a mug ring on the back cover.) And there was always the daughter's imminently empty bedroom to consider.

In the ad break I slipped out to the kitchen on the pretence of making tea. She answered, sounding pleased, and we arranged to meet the following week – supper at a fashionable bistro in Clapham.

That first proper date was not cheap (she insisted on the "taster menu"), but I treated it as an investment. I courted her. I courted her hard. I figured out what formula would work best and applied it, decided what buttons to push and pushed them. The way she had confronted me with my bad-boy image at Andrew Edmunds had been as sexually charged as foreplay – she was clearly aroused, like many women, by a bastard. But she had made it obvious, too, that she liked an underdog, and put her faith in the goodness of the human spirit. Over that first dinner, I eked out a sob story about a woman who had broken my heart at college ('No, not Florrie'), and my subsequent fear of being hurt, my issues (of course) with commitment. We said goodbye chastely in the street afterwards, but the next morning, I sent flowers, with a care-fully composed message ('Thank you for being different'), followed up by texts, increasingly flirtatious in tone. (It was so lovely to spend time with you . . . Can't stop thinking about you . . . Mrs Mackenzie: do you realise the effect you have had on me? . . . Come to bed with me, please.)

It took me two weeks and two more dates to win her over properly, to bring that final plea to fruition. Over that period I convinced her that she had affected me creatively as well as emotionally. I confessed my writing had been blocked until meeting her and that for the first time in years I felt in touch with real emotions. I was working hard in the London Library every day, finishing the manuscript for which breath in publishing circles was now bated. I pumped out the clichés, and watched as she absorbed them all, marking how she took responsibility for this reincarnation of my abilities and energy.

A certain amount of ducking and diving was needed to maintain my credibility. She had no idea I had left Lamb's Conduit Street. Or that a small creditor problem – certain bar bills it had become urgent to avoid – kept me out of Soho. I had lost my free pass to the London Library, too, now Alex had returned and requisitioned it. Instead, I spent my days browsing the books sections of south London's charity shops, or drinking tea in Bun in the Oven, a cheap cafe at the end of Sheen Lane. To cover my tracks, I made sure Alice and I met exclusively in Clapham – a tactic I presented as thoughtfulness. It gave her time to nip home to freshen up, or check on 'GCSE coursework' (I even had the lingo down pat). I let her know 'kitchen suppers' were fine by me too. 'You are understanding,' she said, throwing together pasta puttanesca or chicken cacciatore (she was a wonderful cook). 'I don't like to leave the kids too many nights in a row.' In reality, although I soon palled of teenage sulkiness across the table, I was delighted to avoid spending money. Dating a woman of her standing was not cheap. There was one tricky moment, for example, when I realised she was assuming I would accompany her to the Finding Jasmine benefit: at £90 a head! I found myself inventing a godchild's birthday to get out of it.

My target may initially have been that spare room – by September I planned to be close enough to Alice (maybe as a sort of friend with benefits) to take it over organically, for it to be the natural next step. But as the early weeks of our relationship went by, the idea of something more permanent began to take form. I imagined myself perhaps not her husband but master of the house – of her feather-down king-sized duvet, her claw-foot bath, her stocked fridge, her cat. I mused idly on the subject of Harry's life insurance. Her kids were a pain – a sweaty, hulking fug of grunts and hormones. But the thought was not unpleasant. I wasn't in love with her. I looked at her objectively, and noticed her age: the tight lines across her brows, the cross-hatching to the side of her eyes. It was a complicated desire, maybe a mental captivation rather than a physical one, to do with her energy, her confidence, her ability to sort the most complicated of plans or problems. When she took a call from a colleague at her law firm, or from one of her many pressure groups (Women Against This, Lawyers For

That), I would feel aroused just listening to her. The sheer competence of the woman took my breath away.

And there was something else, too, enflaming me, something more sensitive, to do with a certain unattainability, a nagging sense even during intercourse that she was holding back. She seemed keen enough – she asked earnestly after my 'oeuvre' and laughed at my jokes, took off her clothes at my request, revealing a pale, limpid body, with stretch marks prettily etched across her stomach and a full crop of pubic hair. What she didn't do, despite all my efforts, was reach orgasm – a penetrating blow to my *amour propre*. Once I had returned to bed, having disposed of the condom, she made satisfied noises and nuzzled her face into my neck, sighing as if she were replete. One night I decided to confront it head-on (so to speak). I propped myself on my elbows and gazed down into her half-closed crescent eyes. 'Your turn,' I said, about to go down. 'No excuses.'

But she wriggled out from under me, swivelling sideways, tugging at the duvet, until she was sitting, hunched, on the side of the bed. She pulled a worn towelling dressing gown over her shoulders. 'I don't any more,' she said flatly. 'It's not that I don't enjoy it – I do, I love it all – but I don't come.'

'Perhaps it would be . . . easier . . . more satisfying for you if you were on the pill?'

She shook her head. 'It's guilt, I think.'

'Harry,' I said. I closed my eyes. 'Of course. Poor Alice.'

I peppered her neck with kisses until she squirmed away, laughing. Her bedroom – a sluttish room, scattered with discarded clothes and jewellery, fairy lights and dusty candles – had an ensuite bathroom, which she wandered into. I could hear her peeing. I threw myself back into the pillows, arms crossed above my head, chest expanding, and made light of it. 'All the more for me,' I think I said. But I thought about Harry: a big, solid, dead man in the well of her bed. And I felt a hard, gritty resolution form, a vow that one day soon not only would I have her, I'd have her completely.

The house in Pyros hadn't been mentioned since the night we first slept together, but I hadn't forgotten her vague invitation. It was a slow thought at the back of my mind that I would spend the summer with her there and that, on our return to Clapham, she would ask me to move in. Greece was a major part of my campaign.

It was an encounter with Andrew that first made me falter.

Alice, I was always aware, saw a lot of Andrew. They met up both professionally and socially. (It was Andrew who had gone with her in the end to the Finding Jasmine benefit.) I didn't encounter him again for a while, but I was unpleasantly aware of his presence nevertheless. One Saturday, I found a silk-lined scarf on the back of a chair, which Alice said belonged to him. On another occasion, he had left an envelope on the kitchen table with forms for her to sign. I wondered a couple of times if I smelt his aftershave – Trumper's West Indian Limes.

I didn't like it. He was a threat, one I would, sooner or later, have to do something about.

It was early April when I saw him again. Alice and I had spent the afternoon in bed, with a bottle of wine and the *Guardian* crossword. Maskarade, a relatively new setter, had set the puzzle around *Under Milk Wood*, in celebration of the play's anniversary. Alice, in playful mood, professed herself enchanted by my knowledge of the text and characters: Lily Smalls, Captain Cat, Nogood Boyo, etc. I began to show off – 'Lie down, lie easy. Let me shipwreck in your thighs,' I quoted, but she wasn't taking me as seriously as I thought. 'You're my nogood boyo,' she kept saying. 'Aren't you?' She was tipsy enough to find it hysterical. 'My nogood boyo.'

I took it in good part at first. I kissed her. But as she went on, the joke ('my nonononogood boyo') seemed to be at my expense and I began to feel hot and scratchy. I got out of bed, with a huffy shuffle of the duvet, and pulled on my boxers before remembering I had nowhere much else to go. Doubly nettled, I rummaged for my cigarettes in the pocket of my discarded jeans and walked to the window. I hoiked open the sash.

'Come back and shipwreck in my thighs,' Alice cooed. She knew I was cross, but was making a play of not noticing.

I sat on the ledge and lit up, using the curtain to protect my semi-nudity from the street below. I stared down. Fat wodges of white blossom clustered on the cherry tree. A thin sun reflected on the houses opposite, yellowing the brickwork, glancing off the glass. The shopping trolley had gone from the next-door garden. I remember wondering if the council had collected it, or whether it was still there, buried and disintegrated. I imagined triangular heaps of rust under the brambles, ants crawling. I wondered whether anything could ever be said completely to disappear. I took a few deep puffs, and watched the ash at the end of my Silk Cut lengthen into a precarious tube, before flicking it out.

The silver-white dust floated on the air in tiny fragile lozenges. I noticed voices from below, the gate opening and people accumulating in the front garden. I jumped off the sill and peered down. They were hidden by the porch. Deep in the house, the doorbell rang.

'Visitors,' I said.

'Oh yes,' Alice replied, pulling on the green sweater dress she had been wearing before I took it off. She thrust her bare feet into a pair of suede ankle books, and briskly threw her head forward and then back: a quick way she had of sorting out her hair. 'Andrew, Tina and the gang – they've come for an early supper. Thought we'd have an Indian takeaway'

She stood at the door and smiled at me, her head tipped to one side. She seemed sober now. 'You coming?'

When I didn't answer, she left the room. I stayed where I was for a moment, feeling disconcerted, outwitted. I hadn't met any of her other friends. We'd spent all our time alone. Why hadn't she told me they were due?

I could hear her voice, mingling with Andrew's. Tina's laugh, the sitting- room door opening and closing, footsteps descending to the kitchen.

I got up and pulled on my trousers. My shirt was crumpled under the bed. The door to her wardrobe was open. Some of Harry's clothes still hung there. I'd been through them before, and pocketed a couple of ties I liked the look of. Now I ran through the hangers until I found a shirt I liked: pale pink with a subtle textured pattern. The label read Charles Tyrwhitt. It was a little wide in the collar, but would do. I buttoned it up slowly.

Tina saw me first. She was leaning against the Aga facing the door and I saw her eyes widen with surprise and also pleasure – I think about that moment quite a lot these days. She looked at Andrew and her expression tightened into something more cautious. 'Paul!' she said.

Andrew was sitting at the table with his back to me. His head whipped round. In that split second I saw him take in the shirt and my bare feet. I saw him acknowledge that I had been in Alice's bed, that there was something I could do with her (not a finance meeting, not a quick lunch) that he couldn't.

He made to stand up and tangled his feet in the feet of the chair. He swore and, rubbing his calf, hopped towards me, a small piece of theatre that gave him a moment to collect himself. 'Old man!' he said with exaggerated bonhomie. 'Where've you come from?'

'I was upstairs.'

'Nice to see you.'

I shook his hand, smiling into his face. 'It's been a while,' I said.

'Gosh, yes. But then here you are! Alice. You dark horse. How life moves on.'

Alice was getting a six-pack of Coke out of the fridge. 'Oh grow up, Andrew,' she said, shutting the door with her elbow. She sounded annoyed. 'We're all adults here.'

She noticed the shirt. 'Oh,' she said, flushing.

'Do you mind? Mine was crumpled.'

She shook her head, and turned away.

In the garden, a tall, thin teenage boy with a stick in his hand was trying to whip the head off a tulip. A girl of about seventeen, with very short hair, boyishly cut, in baggy jeans and sneakers, was sitting on a swing, a rotten old thing that dangled from the arm of an apple tree, scuffing the grass with her shoes to spin herself round.

Tina, who was wearing a rather peculiar outfit, a big black linen dress like a depressed artist's smock, saw me looking. 'Our kids,' she said, adjusting her hair, which was pulled back in a tortoiseshell clip. 'Daisy and Archie.'

Alice said to me: 'Paul – you couldn't go and round up my lot, could you?'

I liked that – being given something to do. It showed Andrew I belonged.

I ran upstairs, shouted at the boys to get out of their bedrooms and then took the last flight of steps up to Phoebe's attic room. The door was ajar, and I was about to push it open when I saw her through a crack in the frame, and I paused, angling my head to see in. She was lying on the bed on her stomach looking at her laptop, bare feet in the air, her arse tight and round, her T-shirt twisted to reveal a strip of white skin across her lower back.

I thought I had been quiet, but after a moment she said,

'Coming,' to let me know she *knew* I'd been spying, that she wasn't to be underestimated.

I'd have to watch her.

Back in the kitchen, Alice had found a menu in a drawer and Andrew was writing down what people wanted. Dennis was nosing around and Andrew pushed his head away a couple of times, with an expression of distaste: not a dog-lover, then. (I made a fuss of him to show I was.) Alice seemed tense. She kept laughing and moving things: a pepper-pot, a newspaper. At one point she grabbed a child – Frank – and held on to him, one arm across his chest, almost for protection. Intriguing. I wondered if I was unnerving her, the adjustment of integrating her new flame with her old friends. Yes, possibly I was right. She kept giving me jobs to do: collecting cutlery, finding bottles of Beck's, rummaging in the fridge for lime pickle and mango chutney and Hot Pepper Jelly (the woman had it all). I felt Andrew's eyes on me the whole time.

'How's the oeuvre?' he said.

It was the phrase Alice often used.

'Coming along,' I said.

'Don't be modest.' Alice broke off from laying the table to wrap her arms around me – rather as she had hugged Frank earlier. I smelt beer on her breath. 'He's been writing in the London Library every day and it's really coming together. His agent has a lot of interest already.'

I smiled. Tina said how clever I was. Alice released me and Andrew started talking about a committee meeting that was imminent – a special fund for 'review and investigation'.

I looked out of the window. The teenage girls, Phoebe and Daisy, were sitting on garden chairs, just outside the kitchen door. The way Andrew's daughter was sitting, her legs crossed, her elbow resting on her knee, suggested a French insouciance. She had an edgy, petulant air that reminded me of someone, but I couldn't think who. The loose wool jumper she was wearing had fallen off her shoulder, revealing a turquoise bra strap and a pale triangle of skin – a particularly sexy combination.

The food arrived and we sat down at the table. I was next to Louis, who in my opinion was Alice's least attractive child – a large boy with a face full of acne. He was causing her a lot of trouble. The headmaster from his school had been on the phone a couple of times. Bullying issues. I wasn't going to waste my time with him so I talked across the table to Tina, asking after the wool shop. 'Oh, you know,' she said. 'Whole new shipment of alpaca delivered on Friday!' She glanced at Andrew. 'Big important stuff!'

It upsets me when women do that – put themselves down. Men like Andrew encourage it. I remembered his patronising laugh when he brought up 'her little business' in the bookshop.

'I'm so impressed by anyone who sets up on their own like that,' I said. 'I hope you're proud of her, Andrew?'

'Of course,' he said.

He began to dominate the meal. His father had dementia and had recently been admitted to a residential home. His mother, who had suffered health problems of her own, was not coping. It was terribly unfair. There had been a lot of tragedy in her life. Alice took Andrew's hand and kept hold of it. 'I know,' she said. 'I know.'

'Horrid,' I agreed.

Daisy was dipping her finger in the little plastic pot of mint raita, then dabbing the speckled yoghurt on to her tongue.

I realised then who she reminded me of.

'Gosh, you look like Florrie,' I said. She could have been Andrew's sister right there in front of me.

She looked up, still licking her finger again. 'People say that, yes.'

Everyone else had gone quiet. Had I been indelicate, interrupting Andrew?

'Sorry,' I said, and made a gesture for him to continue.

Alice looked at me and then back to him. 'Perhaps your mother'd like to come out this summer?' she said. 'Yvonne and Karl are insisting on staying at the hotel, so we've got room. Would that do her good?'

Her tone was cool – it was obviously not a proper offer – but it did its job, from my point of view, by turning the conversation to Greece.

'Do Yvonne and Karl come every year?' I asked.

'No. They came once or twice at the beginning. But this year it's the tenth anniversary of Jasmine's disappearance so they're making a special trip.'

'As a sort of pilgrimage?'

'Kind of.'

She was looking at me, and I smiled back expectantly. 'How nice,' I said. I'd finished my plate of lamb saag and had polished off a couple of Beck's. I leant back in my chair. This is my moment, I thought. She will invite me again – publicly. It was the logical conclusion to the evening. Maybe she had even asked the others over this evening for that reason. Whether I accepted, of course, was still up to me. But the offer, and all that it promised, was about to be laid open for my consideration.

'This year,' Phoebe said, 'I'm getting a proper tan.'

'If it's our last time ever we must hire kayaks!' Frank said.

'Too right!' Tina laughed.

'Unless we have another invasion of the jellyfish,' Phoebe added.

'Oh gawd,' Andrew yelped. 'I'm not peeing on anyone's sting no matter how much they beg me.'

'I can't wait for that delicious baklava they served last year at Giorgio's,' Tina said.

'Nico's,' Alice said.

'Was it?'

'No, Giorgio's,' Andrew said. 'You were too pissed to notice.'
They all laughed.

'This year,' someone said, 'we must swim out to Serena's
rock.' Whether this was the rock's real name, or a reference to
a funny story involving a person called Serena, I didn't know
because nobody filled me in. I sat there, like a lemon from the
tree in the Pyros house garden, like a 'saganaki prawn' (Tina:
'I can't wait – washed down with a carafe of that delicious
local rosé').

'It all sounds wonderful,' I said, in the next lull.

Andrew looked at me, a smirk on his face. Alice laid her
arm along the back of his chair.

'Coffee?' she said, after a few minutes.

'How about you boys go to the park for a kickabout?' Tina
said then.

The boys pushed their chairs back and stood up.

Phoebe said loudly, her tone unreadable: 'Paul – what about
you? You fancy a kickabout?'

I was taken aback. What was she suggesting? That I was on
a level with the teenage louts rather than the adults?

Alice said, 'I'm not sure Paul is a kickabout kind of a man.'

Louis said: 'He's more of a layabout kind of a man.'

I noticed Andrew laugh. I had the ingenuity to leap up and
lunge at Louis. 'Ha ha, very funny,' I said, getting his
Neanderthal head in a head-lock, and jabbing at him, as if we
were the greatest of friends, as if it were a tease between
chums. He pulled away and, as he climbed the stairs, I saw
him rub his lower arm. Dickhead.

I waited a few moments until I heard the front door close,
and then I went upstairs to use the bathroom.

There was a bottle of wine on the table in the hall, which I felt like smashing, there, on the chequerboard Victorian tiles. Instead, I picked up a small package that sat next to it – a gift wrapped in tissue paper. It felt like a bar of soap. My tweed coat was hanging, among a lot of other coats, on a row of over-laden hooks and I slipped it into the inside pocket. I doubted Alice had even registered its arrival. I'd give it to my mother.

I turned. Tina was standing at the top of the basement stairs. Had she seen me? No, she was smiling, but as if she didn't want to be, and she was making a nervous action with her hands, splicing her fingers together and then pulling them apart, sharp cutting movements.

She said: 'Are you serious about Alice? I'm sorry I have to ask.'

I let a beat pass. 'Of course.'

'It's just you won't hurt her, will you?'

I managed to restrain myself. 'Of course not.'

She took a step forward and grabbed my sleeve. 'I know you're not the sort of man who usually . . . well, perhaps not what she needs. But . . . we . . . whatever happens, however it pans out, just don't do any damage, will you?'

I made a small bow. My teeth were gritted, but I hid them with a smile. 'My intentions, I assure you, madam, are entirely honourable.'

She looked at me for a long moment and then, as if she were satisfied with what she saw, said: 'Sorry. I shouldn't have said anything. Andrew worries, that's all. She deserves to be happy.'

'And so do you,' I said pointedly.

I smiled as pleasantly as I could and walked past her to the bathroom, hoping I'd unsettled her.

How dare she, or Andrew, make judgements about what kind of a man I was, or wasn't? It was none of their business what I did. I had no intention of hurting Alice, and even if I had, she'd be fine. She was the one with the house, the friends, the money. I was the one who had *nothing*. I sulked for the rest of the evening, and, in the flurry of my own self-righteous indignation, managed to bury the thought that Tina might be right.

Chapter Six

Greece, after that, was all I could think about. It nagged away at me like a toothache.

I lay in my single bed at my mother's house and churned with resentment.

I listened to the kid playing in the next door garden, the thock-thock of wet Swingball on plastic bat, the yapping of a Yorkshire terrier two doors down, my mother's radio, Simon Mayo, up loud, and thought about ten years before. A package deal with a girl called Saffron. A cheap flat on the main drag, a hotspot of nightclubs (Let Zeus blow your mind) and pool-bars and Irish pubs; lights flashing neon outside the window, a smell of fried fish and diesel, mopeds screaming.

We bought tickets for a boat trip and I remembered the rough grip on your forearm as the captain helped you in, the tip and swell of the deck, the push of people, knees and foreheads, and sunburnt cleavage. The cold green bottle jolting against my lips, and the music, 'Zorba the Greek', loud and jangly and scratchy, that we took out of town with us, and onto the sea, the rising bouzouki, and the water, away from the scum of touristville, an extraordinary aquamarine blue: patches of clarity, between the dark rocks, moments when you could see down twenty feet to white sand, small fish flashing. And teenage girls in bikinis, and the nail-varnish-remover tang of retsina at the back of my throat.

The bad afternoon, the one I had tried to forget, came in fragments – drink and an argument, Saffron's hand in the air, a bottle at my head, the naked limbs of another woman.

I opened my eyes and the room closed in on me: a box of Mansize Kleenex my mother had left helpfully on the bedside table, the three framed photographs of 'Old Sheen', nailed slightly too high on the wall, the small useless wrought-iron fireplace, painted gloss white, the spider plant in its grate.

Why shouldn't I be part of Alice's plans? Why shouldn't I go to Pyros? I was her boyfriend now. Wasn't it my due?

At Michael's for Sunday lunch, I could talk of nothing else.

'I can't believe you want to go,' Michael said. He had cooked roast chicken with all the trimmings in his Sunday uniform of sweat pants and slippers and was now picking at the bits in the pan. 'You don't like holidays, and you don't like leaving London.'

'I could do with a break. It's been a tough winter. And now living with my mum. A small sojourn would suit me down to the ground.'

Ann, a solid, plain woman who was deputy head in a secondary school, said: 'It's a family holiday. By definition kids will be involved.' She gestured to the garden where hers were fighting for possession of a plastic tractor. 'Family life: isn't it your idea of hell?'

'They're not small kids,' I said. 'They're teenagers. Three boys, two girls – both seventeen.'

Michael stopped picking at the Pyrex and gave me a look.

'They'll be wearing bikinis,' I added.

He grinned, and then looked at his wife, sheepish. She showed her irritation by getting to her feet, doing up the top button of her jeans which she had undone while we were eating. 'Your pride's dented,' she said, filling the dishwasher. 'You only want to be invited so you can turn it down.'

'It's the affront of having been invited once. She hasn't repeated the invitation since we slept together. I don't understand it. I thought sex was something I was quite good at.'

Michael gave me an indulgent look. 'Come to Wales with us,' he said. 'The twins would love to share a tent with Uncle Paul.' It was a fiction we all indulged that I was a favourite with their boys. 'I know camping's not quite your thing, but in my experience Greek accommodation can be pretty basic too. I'm talking about loos.'

'Knowing Alice,' I said, 'it'll be luxurious.'

'So, Paul Morris,' Michael said. 'What first attracted you to multi-millionaire Alice – what's her surname?'

For a moment I couldn't remember, then it came to me. 'Mackenzie.'

I saw him and Ann exchange a glance – almost pitying.

'Maybe she doesn't realise you *want* to come,' Ann said. 'I love you, Paul. You know I do.' (I didn't actually. She had always seemed uniquely impervious to my charms.) 'But you aren't exactly a big one for commitment.'

'She's too old for you!' Michael said, standing up and wrapping his arms around his wife. He buried his chin in her hair. 'Forget it! Find another young floozy to entertain us with.'

I shut up after that, piqued at being misunderstood, at being patronised. Maybe I had long played up the part of the roué, but I still felt cross, indignant, as if they weren't taking me seriously, and left their house early.

In case Ann was right, I made it my mission to make it clear I wanted to come. I dropped endless hints. We had drinks one wet night at a trendy bar in Brixton. Swags of blossom lay sodden on the pavement. A tarpaulin over the entrance sagged and dripped. 'British weather,' I said, as we shrugged off our coats. 'Don't you just hate it? If we could depend on a month of sun – two weeks, even – we'd be a happier nation.'

'Vitamin D,' Alice said.

I put on a self-pitying voice. 'You're lucky. You've got Greece. I don't know how I'll bear it.'

No dice. 'Poor you,' she said.

I met her for a coffee in Covent Garden the following Saturday. She had been shopping for Phoebe's birthday present and began pulling out items for my inspection – itsy bitsy pieces of fabric – a frilly top and a short denim skirt, a pair of gold-studded corduroy shorts, a tiny orange vest, and then, *pièce de résistance*: a bikini! The bikini was green, with yellow palm trees and pink umbrellas slashed across the pattern; 1950s in style, with a halter-neck and well-upholstered cups. Not sexy enough for my taste.

'Very nice,' I said, sounding out my appreciation. 'For you?'

She slapped my hand. 'Don't be ridiculous.'

'For Phoebe to take to Pyros?'

'Yup. Holiday gear masquerading as birthday presents. I'm shameless.'

I stared into her eyes. 'So who is going this year?'

'Yvonne and Karl will be staying in a hotel, so in the house it's just us lot.'

'Just you lot,' I repeated.

'We'll have so much clearing up to do.' The waitress, a sweet little thing in a black miniskirt, shimmied over and Alice paid the bill. 'Do you want to come back to Clapham for lunch?' she said. She narrowed her eyes suggestively.

'I'm on a roll, work-wise,' I said coldly, and shoved off pretty sharpish. I regretted it later. I bought a sandwich in Subway at Victoria instead. Pathetic.

I had ground to make up after that. It does no good to be petulant. I needed to increase the attack, and lighten it at the same time. An idea came to me a couple of days later. My mother had brought my bin bags down out of the attic and left them on the bedroom floor. I rummaged through until, tangled up in a stolen hotel towel, I found the purple T-shirt I had brought back from Elconda. 'Let Zeus blow your mind' it read in jagged black lettering.

I wore it under my jumper the next time I was at Alice's house. We were upstairs in her bedroom, and I did a slow striptease, disco-dancing while I undressed, until I was just in the Zeus T-shirt and my boxers. 'Let *me* blow your mind,' I said, pressing her up against the dressing table.

'Stop it, stop it!' she said. 'I hate that T-shirt. It reminds me of that night. You were so drunk, you were so . . . *awful.*'

I continued to gyrate. 'God, you'd look damn good in a bikini,' I told her, my hands running up and down her body. 'That's all I'm after.'

'Oh Paul, behave,' she said.

It wasn't until the first week of June that I had a breakthrough. Michael had passed on a couple of free theatre tickets he couldn't use. The play, a political satire set in the former Yugoslavia, was at the National on the Southbank and I arranged to meet Alice there straight from work.

She was edgy and distracted. One of her clients was up for deportation, and she was on her phone when I arrived. It wasn't until the interval that she got the call she'd been waiting for. We were sitting at the bottom of a small flight of steps between levels. I was scooping at a honeycomb ice cream, using the tiny plastic shovel provided, waiting for her to finish. I kept having to jerk my shoulder out of the way to let people pass.

She hung up and sighed heavily. 'No joy,' she said.

'Poor old Alice,' I said. 'You really need a rest.'

'I'm not the one who needs pity.'

'Not long until your holiday now.' I was hot in my jacket. I remember thinking I should have left it on the seat. 'Maybe you'll be able to forget about it for a bit.'

'I won't be able to forget about anything,' she said. She'd been flicking through the programme, and she pointed at a photograph of the lead actor. 'I *knew* I recognised him. He's in *Casualty*.'

'A drama I have never watched, and never intend to.'

'Too lowbrow for you of course.' Her voice was dark and heavy. 'Paul Morris stooping to *Casualty*: as if!' She cast the programme to one side. 'Sorry. I'm tired. No. I'll have too much to do. U-Haul are coming in September for the furniture, but there are clothes in wardrobes, food in cupboards to be cleared – for ten years we've just chucked stuff in.' She sighed. 'I could just leave everything for them to deal with – they're bulldozing the land; they could just bulldoze the house with it. But . . . well, terribly British of me to think I need to tidy. Oh God, and there's Hermes to sort too.'

'Hermes?'

'An old pick-up truck that came with the place. Hermes, the God of speed – ironic obviously. It hasn't worked for years. I could sell it if I could get it going.'

The bell went for the second act. It was all or nothing. I felt vertiginous. 'What you need,' I said, 'is a professional mechanic.'

'I do. If I can find one on Pyros – I suppose they must exist.'

'Or a sexy handsome man who might just have got his hands dirty in his university holidays by helping out at McCoy & McCoy Motors Ltd, Mortlake's premier car service facility. MOTs and general maintenance.'

'Really?'

'No repair too big or too small.'

She let out a gurgle of laughter; more genuine than anything I had heard for a while. 'You're joking. Tell me you're joking.'

I stood up. 'Often, while U' – I drew the letter in the air with my finger – 'wait.'

'Are U' – she made the same gesture – 'offering to mend my truck?'

I shrugged and reached back to put my hands in my back pockets. 'Perhaps you've got me wrong. Perhaps I'm not so highbrow after all.'

She stood up. She was standing on the step above me and our eyes were level. She said, 'I know we've all been talking about what fun it'll be, but it won't, not really. I'll be feeling sad at leaving. Plus, as it's the ten-year anniversary since Jasmine went missing . . . Yvonne and Karl . . . It won't all be roses. You might not have that good a time.'

The second bell rang. I put my hand under her elbow and steered her back towards the auditorium. I couldn't stop smiling.

When we reached the end of our row, she turned again to look at me. An elderly man and two younger women scrabbled to their feet, pushing their bags and coats out of the way, to make room for us to pass. Alice still had her back to them. She didn't move.

'I'm in,' I said.

She considered me for what felt like a long moment and then she bent forwards. 'Good,' she whispered. 'I'm glad.'

She kissed me lightly on the lips. And then she turned and edged, with small, dainty steps, along the row ahead of me.

I followed, shuffling sideways. I tripped over a coat, smiled at one of the women, wobbled, made a face, apologised. I must have looked as if I were too big for the space, like a clumsy oaf. But I felt as if I could soar. I had *won*.

September 2015

I didn't sleep much last night. The itching has become almost unbearable. My whole forearm is red and inflamed, but the area halfway along, the site of the original bite, is pallid and hard, the entry wound long absorbed by the flesh around it. I've lost all sensation there – it's as if a peach stone has grown under the skin. Everywhere else, I've scratched so hard I have blood under my nails. The cycle – the stinging pain, then the itchiness, then the stinging pain – is driving me half insane.

I was allowed to see the prison doctor one morning, a middle-aged man with large hands and heavy lines etched into his face. He didn't speak much English and my Greek is no better, but there was a tangible sympathy coming off the man that almost made me weep. He gave me a cream for the infection – antibiotic, I suppose – and an ointment for the psoriasis on my face and hands. He showed me what to do, miming a dab with the thick tip of his enormous finger, and a more general window-cleaning-style rub. But where those medications are now, I don't know.

Things go missing all the time here. I pulled my bed apart looking for the cream, upended the thin, solitary drawer on to the mattress. As I fruitlessly sifted through its meagre contents, I was remembering packing for the holiday, how carefully I had chosen each item – a white shirt, chinos, a pair of Vans I found on sale. I had planned to take the purple T-shirt with me, the one from Zeus nightclub. Worn at the right time, it would have, I thought, an amusing, ironic effect on the company. But I couldn't find it.

I've been thinking – not about the bachelor flat in Bloomsbury, nor the family house in Clapham. It's my mother's house in East Sheen that keeps coming into my head: the little single room with the window onto the garden, the gloss fireplace, the spider plant in its small caged grate.

I think about that room empty.

THEN

Chapter Seven

The heat woke me, the sun burning my eyelids, probing through my clothes, down to the skin. Sweat had collected in the small of my back. My holdall was propped under my head and I could feel the jag of the zip, stabbing into my scalp, and a rigid object – my washbag – against my neck.

Unbending my legs, I swivelled round stiffly and sat up, adjusting my eyes. It was early but the light, glaring through the plane trees, was already intense, the sky an indigo blue. The air was sultry with the smell of fresh bread, and eucalyptus, aniseed, and something less pleasant – urine. In the distance, the rattle of shop shutters being lifted, the snarl of a motorbike. An elderly woman on the other side of the street was staring at me.

The bus was still parked up in the lay-by. Last night it had appeared dashing, with its blue and white paintwork, triumphant like a flag. Now, sober and in the brightness, I could see the rust above its wheel arches, the filth splattered across the windows. All the seats, including the driver's, were still empty.

I rubbed my face, trying to loosen the ridges caused by the imprint of the bag across my cheeks.

My head throbbed. My mouth, scratchy with nicotine and aniseed, tasted bitter. Was it too early, I wondered, for another drink?

*　　*　　*

It had been a ludicrous journey, an act of thrilling absurdity. Alice had told me to 'look on FlyBest', and to book on to the Thomas Cook flight that left early Sunday morning. There was a BA leaving at a more sensible hour but it was much more expensive and the red-eye meant that, even with a two hour time difference, 'we'll be in the pool by teatime'.

'You should be able to get a ticket for about five hundred quid,' she said. 'They'll have gone up a bit since I booked mine. But at least we'll arrive together. Andrew's booked a mini-van to get us up to the house. I'm sure we can squeeze you in.'

We were in bed, after the theatre, and she was lying under my arm, her mouth soft against my shoulder, her fingers stroking my chest. I murmured, 'That's what I'll do,' glad she couldn't see the shock in my face. It hadn't occurred to me the flight would be so expensive. I had planned to ask Michael to tide me over, but even I would be embarrassed to touch him for that much.

The next day I looked on FlyBest. The Thomas Cook flight was running at £682 – the BA £1,200. By scrolling down a few pages, I found a cheaper alternative. Under 'Duration', in place of 'Non-stop 05hrs10', it read, '2 stop(s) 17hrs40'. The flight left Heathrow seven hours *before* the Thomas Cook, at 10 p.m. on Saturday, and arrived five hours *after* it, at 5.40 p.m. on the Sunday – and ten minutes after the BA landed from London. I booked it.

'The BA?' Alice said, when I told her, slightly put out.

'I've got a meeting in the morning with an American publisher. It's the only time she can see me. I could say no but . . .'

'No of course you shouldn't.' She paused to think. 'There's not much point you hiring your own car. If you don't come with us, you'll have to get a taxi up to Pyros. It's a good two hours and it'll set you back at least 200 euros.'

I'd already Googled. I'd be in time to catch the last public bus from the airport. 'To hell with the expense,' I said. 'I'll be in the pool by teatime.'

At first it had gone according to plan. I left London on a cold wet August evening and caught the 10 p.m. flight to Munich, arriving at 12.50 a.m. local time. I spent the night on a bucket chair in Departures, and took the red-eye to Athens, where I was due to make a connection in the early afternoon. Here was where it began to go wrong. The Aegean Airlines plane, scheduled to take only fifty-five minutes, was grounded due to a technical fault and I finally arrived at Ionnasis Vikelas International Airport, Pyros at 10.15 p.m., almost five hours later than I'd intended, having missed the last bus.

I leant against the wall by the shuttered Avis desk to ring Alice. I felt a small thrill as I did so; the rush of the lie. I apologised profusely for not having spoken to her sooner – I'd been trying and trying: did she not have a signal? 'Most of the time,' she said coldly. I battled on. Basically, there was a slight change of plan. I was ringing from my publishers' office. The American editor I'd stayed behind in London to see had kept me waiting until the afternoon. I'd had no choice but to tear up my BA ticket and instead would 'catch the early flight out' the following day. 'It was worth it; I'll tell you all when I see you.'

Alice's voice softened when she realised I wasn't bailing. She was sad, but she understood. 'Everyone sends their love,' she said.

I hung up, and with an electric charge in my legs, a euphoric surge of unexpected freedom, walked jauntily along the airport access road towards the outskirts of Pyros town. The sky was a dark neon blue, the trees and buildings clear against it. The air, even this close to the runway, was warm with oregano and mint. Lights and noise, the spit and smell of roasting meat led me down a web of roads to what appeared to be Pyros central. I walked past a strip of tourist tavernas, in which shrieking women with sunburnt shoulders applauded a troupe of finger-clicking 'traditional dancers', and found a small, dark, nameless bar, populated by what I imagined to be genuine Greeks. I remember very little after that except that I drank a lot of ouzo and charmed some rather lovely young girls and that, at some point in the early hours, one of the genuine Greeks, imaginary or otherwise, escorted me to the stationary blue and white bus and the urine-streaked neighbouring bench on which I now perched.

I got on early, as soon as the bus driver appeared, and secured a seat near the front. The heat rose as the bus filled – an elderly woman with bow legs and bad teeth; a loved-up Australian couple; an intense-looking youth in decoratively zipped jeans. A greasy-haired man across the aisle was wearing a black suit and open leather sandals; his toenails were thick and dirty, curled like the end of traditional Greek shoes. I'd repeat that observation to Alice, I decided: she'd enjoy it. I was looking forward to seeing her, all the more after my secret escapade. Surprisingly, I was missing her.

The bus left at 10 a.m. with a great deal of clamour and rattling. It took a while to leave the town. We groaned and swayed, obstructed by traffic and tourists; the driver accelerated and braked, gesticulated and hooted. More people climbed on; at one point the driver disembarked to shout at another driver. But eventually the straggle of American-style fast food outlets ('McChicken'; 'Kojax Burger') and supermarkets ('OK'; 'Super Buy') gave way to marble emporiums and DIY warehouses, the engine eased, and we began to make some headway.

I wasn't entirely sure how long the journey would take – two hours in a taxi might be double that in a bus. I was bored of the Dickens I had brought for the journey (*Barnaby Rudge*), and didn't feel up to *In Cold Blood*, the Truman Capote I planned to read by the pool. In my bag was a guide-book to Pyros, which Michael had given me as a leaving present, and I reached up and fetched it from the overhead shelf.

The last time I came to Pyros I knew so little about the island it might just as well have been somewhere in the Atlantic. Opening the book, I was surprised to learn it was not to the south of the mainland, where I thought all the islands huddled, but to the west. A map on the inside cover showed a long mass of land, shaped like an elongated gourd, and a list of 'Quick Facts' informed me it was, at 800 km², the largest of the Ionian islands, more heavily populated than Kefalonia, or Corfu, its near neighbour. Tourism was heavily concentrated in the south, while the mountainous north, with its 'steep coves, goat-peppered hillsides and small fishing villages', still provided glimpses of 'a more traditional Pyros life'. It was famous for its endangered species: the European pine marten, and the Mediterranean monk seal, *Monachus monachus*, 'who lives in caves around the island's coast, especially on the parts that are inaccessible to humans'.

I looked out of the window. I had begun to feel nauseous. We were reaching Elconda – which I knew to my cost was all too accessible to humans. We lurched along the main street, with its run of 'cash bingo' joints and Irish pubs. I put down the guidebook and pressed my face to the window: none of it looked familiar. The bus turned a corner into a car park and shuddered to a halt. The Australian couple and the zipped-up youth got out, and a man with a shaved head carrying a roll-up bag swung on.

'You going to sunrise beach, mate?' he asked the driver. The accent was Geordie, Newcastle or thereabouts.

The driver nodded.

'Sweet. More action up there than down in Pyros town? We went last night. It was well quiet. We're looking for a bit of a party.'

The bus driver shrugged. 'Very nice beach,' he said.

'OK to camp?'

The bus driver made a balancing motion with his hands, which the shaved-head Geordie opted to take as consent. 'Sweet,' he said again, and gestured to his friends behind.

They clambered on, six or seven of them, and pushed on down the bus. Plastic bags clunked with bottles of Mythos. Rap music fizzed from one of their phones. A girl who looked like Rita Ora with red lips and white-blonde hair rolled tightly against her scalp in intricate plaits like ram horns stood in the gangway, complaining loudly about a broken flip-flop: 'You did it, you knob, you trod on it; you're going to have to buy me some new ones.'

'Sit down, Laura.' The boy with the shaved head pulled her on to his knee and she squealed. She stood up again. 'Fuck you,' she said.

I had craned my head to watch and she saw me. 'Hello,' she said, her tone overly familiar. 'You all right?'

I tried to close one eye in a cheery wink and slightly failed.

The man with the dirty toenails was muttering. He had taken against the music and the noise. I turned back to the window. On a lamp-post just by me was a large piece of laminated paper, with two photographs – the smiling thirteen-year-old Jasmine, and the twenty-three-year-old photofit. 'HAVE YOU SEEN THIS WOMAN?' The poster looked fresh. In smaller print was written: 'English girl missing since 2004. Light brown hair, blue eyes. Distinguishing mark: scar on right shoulder.'The mild nausea that had been toying with my insides soured. I had forgotten Jasmine. Now I recalled Alice's warnings. The anniversary. The parents. God – they weren't exactly going to be in a holiday mood. Poor them and all that, but after all the effort I'd put in to get here, I hoped they weren't going to spoil everything.

We stopped several more times on the way north. The scenery became greener and more wooded. People got off. I was aware of these details, though I drifted in and out of sleep – lulled by the undulations in the landscape and the glare of the sun. When I finally opened my eyes, the bus was empty but for me. We were driving downhill. Gnarled olive trees stood on either side, the ground covered in rolls of black netting. They looked like mummified bodies.

The bus stopped. The driver got to his feet, with a stretch of his shoulders. He pressed a button and as the door levered open, jerked his chin at me. 'Agios Stefanos,' he said.

I must have looked surprised. The bus seemed to have parked on a verge in the middle of nowhere. We were on a section of road edged by more olive trees, dappled shadows and a hot midday sun. No harbour. No boats. No cluster of tavernas. No obvious 'Agios'.

I grappled my bag and coat down from the rack and stepped out. The driver was leaning against the bus, talking on his mobile. On one side of the road was a small shrine: a collection of candles and icons. The photograph of a young man rested against a jar of dead flowers. On the other side of the road was a turning and a large sign, 'Delfinos Beach Club' – the place owned by the developers who had bought the freehold of Alice's land.

The directions to the house that Alice had texted me started from here, but there was no hurry. I lit a cigarette, waved farewell to the driver and set off down the hill in the opposite direction. I wanted to gather some independent knowledge, learn the lie of the land, find out where cigarettes could be bought, maybe locate the ideal spot for a sneaky nightcap.

I stayed in the shade as far as possible, which meant walking in a gully next to a low brick wall. The road was deserted and I enjoyed the solitude. The sleep had done me good. I was on holiday; nothing, no missing girl, was going to interfere with that. The air rang with the constant ratchet-noise of cicadas. On the road were coils of desiccated black snakes. And then the olives and the black netting gave way to more general trees and scrub, a patch of knotty grass containing four tethered goats, and then buildings: a couple of holiday villas, followed by several village houses, a brick and whitewash mish-mash of buildings, a run of vegetable plots, plants in pots, skinny black and white cats, a dog, tied to a post by a piece of rope, furiously barking.

I passed a dead kitten, splayed out at the side of the road, and, a little further on, an old woman sitting by an open door on a plastic folding chair. Chickens scuttled in a yard next to her. I smiled and said hello, imagining myself a cheerfully jaunty figure. She stared back. Shortly after, I left the main road and took a narrow pedestrian lane off to the right. My feet tripped down a flurry of uneven steps, between close whitewashed walls, heat bouncing, sun flickering in the cracks between buildings, flashes of blue sea. Smells of warm bread and sour milk, freshly fried garlic, roasting lamb. More cats, stretched out in corners of the steps, like basking fish. The passage widened, turned a corner and twenty or so steep steps led down to a narrow access road. A drainage ditch led me between two buildings and then an explosion of light, an expansion of sound – I had reached the water.

It was a pretty harbour, lined with shops and tavernas. I put my bag on the ground. Did any of it look familiar? Had our

boat, ten years ago, tied up on that very pontoon? I remembered gaps in the boards, oily water below, pitted barnacles
like rotting coral, the salty on-the-turn smell of fish. I'd seen
this before: the stillness of the sea, as if it were half set, and the
bulk of land visible on the horizon across the Albanian straits.
But how had we spent the day, Saffron and I? We swam, I was
sure of it. But where? Had we climbed across the rocks and
found a secret cove? Or had we waded out, from the tar-splat-
tered beach?

I remembered an argument, Saffron's voice raised, talk of
commitment, a bottle thrown. Another woman. A naked body
in a downstairs room, the shutters closed.

Or was that another day?

Fractured images.

I picked up my bag and walked past a row of shops, to the
other end, where the road widened. A man was selling live
chickens from the back of a van, advertising his wares through
a loudspeaker. Two women in shorts with straw baskets over
their shoulders were looking at something in the window of a
small supermarket. 'Such a shame,' one of them said, in a loud
English voice. 'Of course I've always thought the mother did
it.'

I stepped forwards. Between a rainbow-striped lilo and an
inflatable black shark was another Jasmine poster. One of the
women noticed me and gave me a funny look. I stepped back.

Nico's, the closest taverna, advertised 'Greek specialities,
family cooking. Breakfast. Yoghurty honey. Moussaka.
Calamari'. Beyond the dining area was a wide terrace built
out over the water where various groups were seated at square
white-clothed tables under a vine-covered awning. The sun
bounced through gaps in the greenery, the sea flashed
turquoise beyond. I prevaricated for a moment, wondering
whether I dared stop for a coffee and a 'yoghurty honey', but

an image of Andrew walking past stopped me. I could already hear the jibe he would make at my expense. 'You *deigning* to join us?'

Also – why spend money when I didn't need to?

I doubled back on myself, taking the main road this time out of the village, re-passing the old woman on the plastic chair, and the poor dead kitten, and the straggle of houses and veg gardens, to where the bus had dropped me. The small road leading to 'Circe's House' was just beyond.

It was narrow, and grubby. Hot going. Clods of earth cluttered the track and the bushes on either side looked battered, chopped at, as if heavy machinery had passed through. It was a good ten-minute walk, up through the olive grove, until the trees began to thin, the cicadas grew louder and the sky seemed more blue, the heat from the sun more intense. Oregano, warm and earthy, drifted on the breeze. Enormous bees buzzed.

I was almost at the brow of the hill when a gate loomed, and beyond it a churned-up field, a yellow digger with a red crane parked in one corner, and in the middle an oblong area of concrete, stabbed with metal poles. A dog, chained up out of sight, barked urgently. The construction site – I must be getting close. Here, the track took a sharp right and continued more steeply towards a huddle of buildings. A tall man in an orange T-shirt and a cap was cutting the hedgerow. I said hello, and he put his clippers over his shoulder and stared at me. He had blond stubble and very pale blue eyes. I walked on, trying not to look back.

There was an open gate at the top of the track and beyond it a grassy patch, a rough, uncared for, disorganised space, edged by dilapidated outbuildings: a ruined brick structure, overgrown with ivy, a grotty corrugated shed, and a long, narrow, low-slung bungalow, painted peach, hunkered down under a tiled roof.

My first emotion was disappointment. This wasn't what I was expecting. I felt a kind of homesick lurch, a feeling I often got on arriving somewhere new. (Then, of course, I was actually home*less*; I had no home to be sick for.)

The place was deserted. No car. The windows were shuttered, and the front door locked. I poked about a bit, trying to get in, and then I noticed a small passage leading around the side of the house which led on to a wide terrace, divided into sections with furniture – benches and wicker chairs and pots of lavender. It was in full sun – and there was the most breathtaking view. Outside again, the heat was white. The sea was closer than I'd realised – I must have climbed up and over a headland – and thick bands were laid out before me, in tie-dye colours of aquamarine, cobalt, sapphire, a dotted line of white clouds above the horizon, a frame of dark green cypress trees. I stood to drink it all in. So this was the point of the house. This was what made it special.

This side of the house felt more cared for. The walls were white, even if the paint was peeling in places. I peered through a window into a bedroom, a living room, another bedroom. Most of the rooms were locked, but halfway along I pushed a small blue door and it opened.

It took a moment for my eyes to adjust. I was in a kitchen, quite basic, with a stone sink and an old-fashioned gas oven. Saucepans hung from a circular iron rack. On a wooden butcher's block lay a bag made out of 1960s-style geometric fabric, a purse and a packet of tissues half falling out of it. Wet footprints led across the terracotta floor.

The fridge rattled.

'Anyone at home?' I called, standing up.

No one answered. I felt another crushing sense of disappointment, of anti-climax. I thought Alice would have been looking forward to seeing me, that something would have been made of my arrival. But no welcome party. No bustle and fuss, delicious lunch, cold drink. It's almost as if I weren't expected.

I walked through the door and stood on the terrace. The heat was white, almost blinding. The garden descended the slope in a series of rocky ledges, interrupted by bulks of lavender and white hibiscus and a pink-flowering shrub. And then beyond that, a plunge into emerald shadow, a glint of turquoise, and the bright corner of a cream umbrella.

I left my bag on the terrace and followed the path, part rock, part cement. CDs swung and clicked from branches – some sort of bird deterrent. The cicadas grew louder, a great wave of them, screaming in unison, as if they knew something I didn't. Under my feet was the crackle of small curled dead leaves. A breeze rattled and stirred; flies, on a mission, buzzed. It was *noisy*, that's the thing I remember, a constant noise that blocked out other sounds. A person could appear suddenly without notice. You didn't hear them coming.

Certainly, at this point, no one heard me.

I stood, when I got to the bottom of the steps, in the shadow of a fig tree, and studied the scene. I thought of those paintings by Hockney. The pool was a geometric arrangement of lozenges, white squiggles. Bodies lay motionless. I made out the two teenage girls, their narrow backs curving up above their bikini bottoms, hair across their faces, their thighs pink and exposed. Beyond them, furthest from me: two other figures. Andrew was leaning back on his lounger in a pair of dark blue swimming trunks, a Panama hat on his head, and a book in his hand. Alice was perched sideways on the edge of the next sunbed, a towel over her shoulders. Andrew's eyes were on his book but his chin was tilted and even now I am not sure if it was the reflection of the water on his face, the way it crinkled and distorted, which made me think he wasn't reading, but talking to her, quietly.

How long did I stand there watching? Longer than I should have. A leaf from the fig tree, detaching in the breeze, rustled on its descent through the branches. I stepped forwards. Alice looked up. There was a moment's delay. I saw her lips move and Andrew lowered his book. The teenage girls shifted. For a second or two, no one moved.

I rubbed my hands together, soothing the marks where the straps had dug in, and called roundly, as if welcoming myself, 'Hello!'

Alice leapt to her feet, the towel falling from her shoulders. She was wearing a bikini – the Topshop one she had showed me in the cafe, the one that was supposed to be Phoebe's – and she quickly fiddled with the straps at the back of her neck, prised her fingers under the band beneath her bust to rearrange it. Behind her Andrew, still seated, raised a hand in greeting, elbow taut, palm straight, as if stopping traffic. Daisy flipped on to her back and sat up. She was topless and I saw her breasts, small and pert, with nipples as pink as raspberries, before I turned my head.

'Well!' Alice said, coming towards me, her arms out. 'You made it!'

I was aware suddenly of feeling almost tearful with relief. My body was flooded with endorphins, so powerful it felt like a release. She *was* expecting me. She *was* pleased to see me. There was a broad smile on my face that was out of my control.

'You've brought your coat!' she said. 'You're mad.'

She took it from me, threw it on a chair, and slipped her arms around me. Her face met mine and I kissed her properly on the lips, knowing Andrew was watching as I pushed her mouth open with my tongue, my right hand pulling her towards me, thinking perhaps about Daisy's nipples while scrunching her bikini strap under my fingers. But also wanting her, wanting to hug her close.

She laughed, pulling away. 'You stink,' she said. It's true I was catastrophically hot, my forehead beaded with sweat. My linen suit was crumpled and the polo shirt underneath bore evidence of the 'gyro' kebab I had eaten the night before.

'Thanks.' I laughed.

'You're welcome.'

'I didn't know anyone was here,' I said. 'No car.'

'Tina's gone to the big supermarket in Trigaki with the boys to get food. If you'd rung earlier, she could have picked you up. Did you get a taxi? Was it easy enough to find?'

'Easy peasy,' I said.

Andrew had got to his feet and was waddling down the side of the pool, bandy-legged, his toes splayed. 'Hello, hello, hello!' he said, with enthusiasm. 'How wonderful that you made it. Bet you're itching to dive into that water. It's gorgeous. Lightly salinated, perfect temp. What do you say?' He slapped me on the back. His semi-nakedness was disconcerting: pale calves, freckly lower arms, a surprisingly round belly, hitched over the trunks, for such a small man. 'Quick swim and then we'll crack open a couple of beers? Tina will be back soon with lunch.'

'Maybe in a while,' I said.

'Oh no, go on. Have one now. It's glorious, I promise.'

'It'll help you relax,' Alice said. 'Wash the plane off you.'

I nodded, feeling cornered, and the two of them accompanied me back up the path to the house so I could 'get sorted'. Andrew, whistling tunelessly, disappeared into the kitchen while Alice showed me our room, at the far end of the house, accessed from the terrace by its own door. With the shutters drawn, it was hot and dark but I could make out a chest of drawers, an ornate wardrobe, and a large plantation-style bed, enveloped in a mosquito net.

Alice said, 'I expect you'd like to shower first.'

I grabbed her. 'I expect *you'd* like me to shower first.'

She pushed me away, laughing. 'Go on.'

She opened a smaller door on to a dingy bathroom and left me there, telling me she'd wait for me outside. I undressed and washed as thoroughly as I could. The water came in spurts, now frantically hot, now piercingly cold. A few nasty insects droned around my ankles. There was a smell of drains. I used the Jo Malone shower gel on the shelf and afterwards dried myself with the only thing I could find: a tiny linen hand towel hanging by the sink.

Naked, back in the room, I searched my bag and realised with horror I had forgotten to pack trunks. Not cool. Not the capable, organised, perfect house-guest image I was after. This was just what Andrew needed to get one over on me. I looked in the cupboard – maybe there might be a spare pair of Harry's here. But no – just slithery dresses and flowery tops, curled fragments of underwear. I fondled a pair of Alice's knickers, flimsy black lacy things, and cheered myself up momentarily by imagining myself peeling them off her later. I put them back. At the bottom of the wardrobe was a pile of empty blue Ikea packing bags. On top of them several thick stacks of leaflets, tied up with elastic bands – more Finding Jasmine stuff. I closed the wardrobe.

Nothing for it. I poked my head out of the door, concealing my naked body behind the frame. Alice, Andrew and Daisy were sitting at the table on the terrace. They all turned.

'Slight problem,' I said. 'I've forgotten my bathers!'

Andrew gave a satisfied laugh. 'Trust you, Paul! Daisy – get Paul a pair of mine, will you? The pink turtle ones? They should be in our room.'

Daisy slipped off her chair and wandered to the opposite end of the house. She had tied a flowery sarong around her neck. The fabric fell in a loose fold and ended at the top of her legs. I watched the muscles in her thighs flex.

Alice said, 'Oh, Paul. Bad luck. No trunks!'

'You can buy some down in the port,' Andrew said. 'The shop there does a nice range in tight Speedos.'

'Thanks,' I said.

I stood at the deep end, toes tense, arms upstretched, for what felt like a long time, watching a breeze flicker in a wave across the surface, before summoning every last muscle memory, and plunging head first into the water.

It wasn't perfect as dives go (a stinging pain on my thighs, a slug of water up my nose), but it wasn't embarrassing. I swooped to the bottom, pulling up Andrew's trunks, which had come loose, and absorbed the silence, the sense of being apart, alone in this white dappled world. I stretched out my arms, propelled myself across the base of the pool, watching the jagged lines of light flicker, feeling the crossed edges of the tiles rough along my torso.

When I broke the surface, Alice was at the shallow end, smiling at me. 'Nice?' she said.

I shook my head, like a dog, swept my hair back with one hand, and in a few strokes reached the side. 'Glorious.' I pushed myself out, flexing the muscles in my leading arm, hoping Alice would notice the difference between Andrew's physique and mine.

The trunks were too baggy, clinging almost to my knees; I pulled them tighter and sat on a free sunbed, aware that I was wet and soaking the cushion. Alice brought a towel over and put it around my shoulders.

She sat down next to me. 'How was your meeting?'

I had water in my ears and was screwing up the corner of the towel to get to it. 'Meeting?'

'Yes. The American editor. What did she say? Did she like the book?'

'Actually, yes,' I said. 'She did.'

'Did she offer for it?'

Alice sounded so eager, I didn't feel I had a choice. 'Yes, she did.'

'Oh Paul, that's wonderful.'

It was one of those moments when, basking in her attention, I got carried away. 'In fact,' I said slowly, 'she offered a very generous pre-empt – a high offer to stop my agent taking the book to auction.'

Alice put her hand to her mouth. 'How generous?'

Andrew was lying on the other side of the pool. I didn't know if he was listening, but there was one way to find out. 'High six figures,' I said.

I felt the lie grow and fill the air and settle. I tried to ignore a plunging sense of dismay.

Andrew sat up. Pearls of sweat collected between the sparse curly hairs on his chest. 'So the Milky Bars are on you!'

His hands were gripping the sides of the lounger.

Chapter Eight

I didn't hear Tina and the others get back, but suddenly there they were, at the pool: the two younger boys – Archie and Frank – stripping off their tops, kicking away trainers, plunging in.

Tina arrived more slowly, flashes of blue fabric through the bushes. When she emerged at the bottom of the path, she came the last few feet towards me with her arms outstretched. I stood up. 'Paul,' she said. 'You made it! Clever, clever you. You found us and everything.' She hugged me, recoiling at my wetness, and laughed, as the force of our greeting propelled an enormous straw hat backwards off her head. I was surprised by her warmth, and yet pleased. She was wearing a voluminous blue linen dress that covered her body like a tent. I never worked out why she was so unaware of her beauty. She was all about concealment – the only one among us who had no need.

'You've got the same trunks as Andrew!' she said.

'They are Andrew's.'

'Ah . . . well,' she bent forwards conspiratorially, her expression mischievous, 'they look better on you.'

Andrew looked up from his book. 'There's loyalty for you. My loving wife.'

She had made lunch, she told us, and even persuaded Frank and Archie to lay the table before they came down.

'Did Louis help too?' Alice asked.

'He was feeling a bit hot and tired.'

'Where is he now?'

'In the house.'

'Gaming?'

'I think so.'

The two women looked at each other and something ponderous and painful passed between them. I was vaguely aware that Louis had been becoming a problem. Alice shook her head; Tina smiled ruefully. Andrew, seeing it, stood up. 'Listen,' he said, walking over. 'I'll talk to him. We'll sort it.'

He crouched down at Alice's feet, so he could look into her eyes. Ugh. The self-importance of the man. The arrogance. Who was he to play parent to her children?

I remembered a snippet of wisdom I had picked up from Michael's wife. 'The conservation of gloom,' I said.

'What do you mean?' Alice asked, looking up at me.

'The rule that there always has to be one member of a family in a bad mood. Life would be too easy otherwise.'

Alice half laughed and said, 'Oh, that's quite good.' She stood up, treading carefully around Andrew, and hugged me. 'The conservation of gloom. I like that.'

'As a parent, you're only ever as happy as your least happy child,' Tina said.

'Yes,' Alice said. 'But in my case it's always Louis.'

Andrew stood up from his crouch and awkwardly rubbed her shoulder, half pat, half massage.

Tina was still smiling: nothing about his behaviour or body language seemed to concern her. 'Right then, you lot,' she said. 'Lunch. Paul – you must be starving. These days they don't give you anything to eat on planes.'

'You have no idea,' I said.

She and I had reached the bottom of the path when she squeezed my arm. 'I'm glad you're here.'

'New blood?' I said.

'Maybe. Or maybe I enjoy your company.'

We ate lunch on the long table in the shade. Tina had made a salad with tomatoes, onions and olives, and plated up a selection of cheese and spinach pastries from the bakery in Trigaki. It wasn't a particularly appealing spread (for all her qualities, cooking turned out not to be Tina's strong point), but it was a perfect opportunity to gauge the dynamics of the group. Andrew took the head of the table. He had clearly taken on the role of patriarch, 'organising the troops', as he put it, telling everyone where to sit, making sure Tina and Alice were on either side of him like vestal virgins. In my pique, I almost stropped off to the far end, but Alice meaningfully tapped the seat next to her. Her feet rested on the bar of my chair, her hand on my thigh. She clinked her glass and made a toast to my success: 'To Paul – for finally getting what he deserves.' I couldn't help smiling after that. Suck that up, I wanted to say to Andrew. Eat *my* shorts.

For all the beauty of the view, the mood was fractious. Family life: my idea of hell. Wasn't that what Ann had said? She might have had a point. There was an edge to the proceedings. We were under attack from insects – tiny black ants moving in formation on every crumb, larger red ants creeping up chair legs, and wasps. Who knew Greece was home to so many wasps? The teenage girls were sulky, 'not hungry', either fiddling with their phones or leaping hysterically from the table ('it's a fucking hornet!'). The two younger boys, Frank and Archie, both pale and etiolated in their colourful board shorts, all pointy bones and pent-up energy, ticked off for throwing olives, kept asking what we were doing that afternoon: 'Could we go to the beach? Could we go windsurfing? Could we go to the water park at Elconda?'

'For goodness' sake just enjoy this,' Tina snapped eventually. 'Don't keep going on about the next thing.'

It was Louis, though, who cast the biggest cloud. He had bulked out recently; in one of those sudden growth spurts that seem to affect children, his jaw had jutted forward, and his brow had become heavier. He sat at the end opposite Andrew, shovelling food into his mouth, his fork in his left hand. He was wearing black tracksuit bottoms and a black hoodie, which he was refusing to take off. I knew Alice worried about him – he had been in trouble for bullying at school. Perhaps I should have been paying more attention. Perhaps I should have been doing something to help.

'Why can't I have a beer?' he grunted. '*He's* on his third.'

Alice laughed. 'Paul's an adult,' she said. 'You can have one this evening. I'm not having you drinking at lunch.'

He rolled his eyes. 'It's just stupid,' he said. 'You have these insane rules. It's just irrational. You don't know what you're talking about.'

'Don't talk to your mother like that.'

Andrew's tone of voice was pompous. Louis glared at him, eyes dark, and then threw back his chair and walked into the house.

'Do you want me to get him?' Andrew said.

'I don't know.' Alice looked unsure, both defensive and apologetic.

'He's on the Xbox again.'

'I know. Oh dear.' She looked over her shoulder, twisted her face from Andrew. 'He's very . . . I know he's rude.'

'It's a difficult age,' I said. 'Everyone always goes on about your school days being the happiest time of your life, but it's hard being sixteen.'

'Thank you,' Alice said softly, turning back.

Of course I thought Louis was a little fucker, but I was

happy to stand up for him if it meant putting Andrew back in his box. 'Don't you remember,' I said, turning to address him with a sanctimonious smile, 'how angry you feel at that age? How frustrated. All those hormones surging round your body and nowhere to put them.'

'Yes,' he said. 'Yes, I suppose I do.'

'It gets so much easier,' I added, 'when you find an outlet.'

'An outlet?'

'When you start having sex. That's what Louis needs. Sooner the better.'

Alice went to our room for a rest after lunch. I planned to join her but I helped Tina with the washing-up first and then had a quick cigarette at the far end of the terrace on an Indian day bed. It was peaceful. I watched a group of swallows swooping in and out of a nest in the eaves, a multitude of small white butterflies bother a geranium, a line of ants leading to half a dead beetle. I felt oddly anxious. At lunch I had said some of the right things, but also some of the wrong things. It was all much harder than I'd anticipated. I cared more too. It was disconcerting. It made me feel out of sorts, not quite myself.

Alice was lying on the bed, reading *The Great Gatsby,* when I went to find her. The main shutters were still closed, but she had opened the smaller window on the side of the house and a triangle of sunlight slanted on to her pillow. It was hot and sultry in there; the air thick with itself, with the scent of jasmine and quince. Alice's bare limbs were pale against the silky grey bedcover.

She was stroking her neck absent-mindedly.

'Oh, don't,' she groaned, as I slipped under the mosquito net and pulled her towards me. 'It's too hot. Isn't it? I mean. Don't you think?'

'It's never too hot.' I ran my hands under her kaftan, felt the

warmth of her stomach, the damp of her bikini. I buried my
face in her neck, toying at the drawstring with my teeth. '*You're
too hot.*'

She laughed, pulled gently away. 'I can't believe you said
that thing about Louis having sex.'

'I'm sorry,' I said. 'Was it awful?'

'Just a bit off colour, maybe – in front of the younger boys.'

'Oh God. I'm crap. Sorry.'

'I forgive you.' She groaned. 'I don't know what to do with
him. I've tried jollying him along. I've tried being cross. I'm
running out of ideas. He's obviously driving Andrew mad. He
doesn't get him. Archie is such a different sort of boy . . .'

'And younger,' I said, working out what she wanted me to
say. 'And a bit goody two-shoes if we're honest – a bit lacking
in character?'

She laughed, and then bit her lip as if she shouldn't have. 'I
think Louis misses his father, or misses *having* one. Andrew
means well, but . . .'

'I'm sure it will be fine. Maybe you just need to stop worrying and think about your own needs for a bit.'

'Do you think?' she murmured, closing her eyes.

'Yes. Beginning now.'

I lowered my head again, taking her closed eyes as encouragement, kissing her neck and working down. She moved her
hips, bringing her pelvis to meet mine, and for the next half an
hour, as far as I was aware, neither of us thought about Andrew
or Louis while we concentrated on our own needs. Or certainly
on mine.

Alice slept afterwards. I tried for a while, but failed. She was
snoring very quietly and I was restless, in need of further stim-
ulation, as one often is at the start of a holiday, so I slipped out
of bed, careful not to wake her, and went down to the pool.

Tina was painting on a stool in the shade, the skirt of her tent pulled low over her knees. Daisy and Phoebe were on sunbeds, apparently asleep, and Frank and Archie were huddled in the barbecue area, heads together over an iPhone. No sign of Louis. Or Andrew.

I lay on my stomach, my eye on the girls, drawing comparisons for my own pleasure. Phoebe was more voluptuous than Daisy, but too plucked and dyed for my taste. She didn't like me: I'd worked that out. Daisy, with her hazel eyes and olive skin, had a sort of gamine grace. (Did I stand a chance there? An idle, but enjoyable question.) Mostly they both lay supine in the sun, though they roused themselves now and again to cool themselves in the pool, stepping past me, tiny bent shadows dancing at their feet, and on their return, re-anointed themselves with sun cream. It fascinated me, their relationship with their own bodies, the way they studied their limbs as they rubbed in the lotion, an intense look on their faces that conveyed either love or disgust, or perhaps both, combined with a potent curiosity as if they were noticing every inch of themselves for the first time.

Alice joined us after an hour or so. She lay down on an empty bed next to me. 'Hello, you,' she said under her breath. And then, more loudly, 'Construction hasn't started again, then?' to no one in particular.

'Siesta,' Tina answered. She held her paintbrush out to judge a distance. 'Maybe still too hot.'

Nobody was in the mood for talking, too languid and somnolent. I dipped into the pool once or twice, when the heat overcame me, rescued a giant bee I found drowning in the shallow end, read a few chapters of *In Cold Blood*, and at about 5p.m., volunteered to climb up to the house to fetch some drinks.

Andrew was sitting on the terrace with his glasses on, poring over some papers, tapping on a calculator. 'All right, old chap?' he said as I passed him. 'Hot, isn't it?'

He didn't seem to need an answer. I found beer and cans of Diet Coke in the fridge and a tray and carried it past him down to the pool, where I made a show of hand-delivering each drink to each person, with a small obsequious bow.

When I reached Phoebe, she didn't bother to raise her head so I laid the cold can carefully in the scoop of her naked back. She jack-knifed with a squeal and jumped to her feet. 'You fucker, Paul.'

The can rolled to the ground and she picked it up and shook it. I leapt backwards and darted away. Daisy and the boys were laughing. Frank shouted, 'Push him in, Dais!'

'Oh, leave him alone,' called Tina.

'Poor Paul,' Alice cried.

Phoebe was grappling with me now, arm-to-arm combat, her right leg twisted around one of mine. I was so much stronger, I had to tense up in order not to flip her over and throw her in.

'You're a fucking fucker,' Phoebe said in my ear.

I let her gain her advantage, my hands slipping down along her arms. I felt my balance begin to go and released a war-cry, vanquished, defeated, but as I did so I tightened my grip, hooked my feet through hers. She toppled after me, power-less, and we met the surface together. As the water rushed and surged, seething and gurgling in my ears, as I was brushed and kicked by her legs and hands and face, I felt a swell of pure happiness.

When I surfaced, Alice – rich, glorious, fuckable Alice – was at the edge of the pool, ready to pull me out.

It was all right after all. I was on a roll, unbeatable. No one here was going to get the better of me.

Chapter Nine

The plan was to eat out – as they had the night before. (Neither family was wary of spending money.)

Alice had a call to make and, as I was ready, I waited in the front yard by the car. It was close; the air stuck to your skin. A wood pigeon cooed in a dark copse of trees. A strange transparent lizard darted across the wall of the house, reached the rafters and hung there, motionless. I was watching it, to see if it would move, when I heard a noise, a small clatter and a rustle behind me. I turned and saw a man emerge from the shed with the corrugated roof. It was the blond man with the pale eyes whom I had seen earlier. He crossed the yard and walked past, not looking at me, with slow regular strides, adjusting a bag across his shoulders.

Tina came round the side of the house.

'Who's that?' I asked, as he disappeared down the drive.

'That's Artan,' she said. 'The gardener-cum-handyman. Looks after the house during the year.'

'He's not very friendly.'

'He doesn't speak much English. He's Albanian. He's worked for Alice for years. We first met him in the port the night Jasmine went missing. He had only just arrived, but he was unbelievably kind and helpful, spent days searching the hillsides. Alice gave him a job out of gratitude, and also pity. Someone told us his wife and child had died in a fire.'

'Oh dear. I feel guilty now.'

'So you should.'

The car was one of those van-like vehicles, silver in this case, with seven seats and sliding doors down the side. It would have been a squeeze even without me, but Andrew said pointedly: 'We'll have to squash up. We're nine, *with Paul.*' I offered to walk, but Alice wouldn't hear of it. 'No, no: we'll make it work. Come on, Louis, hop in the back. It's not far. Make life easy.'

'I don't want to go in the back. Why can't Paul go in the back?'

'Don't argue with your mother,' Andrew said.

If I'd been Louis I'd have found it grating, the way Andrew kept saying, 'your mother', as if her children needed him to remind them of their relationship.

'It doesn't matter,' Alice muttered. 'Leave it.'

At the bend in the lane, by the gate to the building site, the car scraped over a rock. Tina peered out of a rear window and called: 'I think we're all right. No smoke!' Alice twisted round from the passenger seat and said: 'For once in our lives we've got a genuine mechanic on board.'

'A genuine mechanic?' Andrew said.

'Yes. Paul's good with cars.' She smiled at me. 'Aren't you, Paul?' She twisted back. 'He's going to have a look at Hermes. If he gets the truck going pronto, we can all bomb around in that – ride shotgun.'

'Oh yes,' I said, realising what she was talking about. 'Of course.'

'Go Paul,' said Phoebe.

'Do you think you'd be able to put your hand on the key after all this time?' I asked.

'It's stuck in the ignition. Has been for years.'

'Great stuff.' I did a miniature drum roll on my knee with my index fingers.

Andrew parked in a small lay-by close to the centre of Agios Stefanos and we tumbled out. It was dusky and warm. Bats darted and dived from roof to roof in the darkness above our heads. Tiny insects flickered in the glow from the street-lights. Wine and good food lay ahead of me. I felt another surge of optimism, of confidence and hope: the sort of things you feel when a holiday stretches out before you like a naked woman waiting to be explored.

Alice was already marching ahead, a small, defiant figure in a clingy T-shirt dress, and a pair of high espadrilles which made her calf muscles bulge. The village had come to life: people and lights, music and cooking smells. Skinny-ribbed ginger and white cats mewled in corners. Children darted between legs. Alice kept stopping to hand out leaflets: a tourist, a shopkeeper having a cigarette, a man touting roasted nuts, a woman selling friendship bracelets. I felt a tug of tenderness, of both admiration and pity.

Tina was walking along beside me. 'Do you think it makes a difference?' I asked her. 'Seriously?'

She made a face, weighing up the options. 'It doesn't matter. The brilliant thing about Alice – she won't give up either way. She does this every year.'

'Does anybody ever get in touch with information?'

'Sometimes.'

'Is it ever useful?'

She shook her head. 'Sightings . . . or . . . but no, nothing concrete, not yet. Alice is so determined. The ten-year anniversary, the fact that it's the last summer at Circe's, all the money she's raised . . . You just have to admire the force of her energy and commitment.'

Andrew had caught up with us. 'She's determined to find her,' he said.

'If she's here to be found. I mean, even if she were alive, wouldn't she be long gone? I mean if I were going to snatch a teenage girl, I'd . . .'

'What?' Andrew was looking at me strangely.

'Come on. We're in a port.'

'Yes. So what would you do?'

'I'd find a boat. If I didn't already have one. I'd escape by sea,' I said. 'It's not rocket science.'

We ate not at Nico's (where they had eaten the previous evening), but at Giorgio's, the taverna next door. A large table was waiting for us on the platform by the water's edge, and a big fuss made: Tina and Alice received hugs from the elderly owner, the boys had their heads ruffled, the girls their palms kissed, and Andrew's hand was energetically pumped. I tried to stand back, but Andrew pushed me forwards. 'This year we are joined by our dear friend Paul Morris. A very famous writer. Remember his name, if you don't know it already. He's just sold his latest novel at auction. Six figures! You're going to be hearing a lot more about him.'

'A pre-empt,' I said under my breath. 'Not an auction.'

The owner, a stooped man with thick black hair and a grey moustache, clamped his arm around my shoulder. 'Is it your first visit to Agios Stefanos?'

'Yes,' I said, without thinking.

'Don't forget you've been here before,' Andrew said. 'Ten years ago.' He turned to Giorgio. 'In fact, he came to this very taverna, though I'm not sure he had a chance to sample your delicious fare.'

Fare: it's one of my least favourite words.

The others had sat down by now, but Andrew made everyone stand up and sit where he wanted them. This time, he placed me at the head of the table. 'Better view,' he said

– though I had my back to the water. I felt on show, and for a horrible moment wondered if that was what Andrew intended.

A young waiter with a faint moustache swept up. Wine was ordered and beer and Coke and Fanta, numerous starters – taramasalata, calamari, fried cheese, fried courgettes – as well as lamb, and chicken and fish. The casual profligacy astounded me. Both Louis and Frank ordered the steak, double the price of anything else, without seeking their mother's approval. 'What about you, Paul?' asked Tina, noticing I'd been quiet. 'I'm fine,' I said, worrying about my share of the bill (would it be split according to what we ate, or according to the number of heads? If the latter, I was in trouble).

'Oh, go on,' Tina insisted.

I'd only pretended to study the menu. Now I racked my brain for the cheapest thing I could think of. 'Some hummus, I think.'

'Hummus. Oh no, they don't have that here.' Andrew let out one of his laughs, three regular short snorts, which didn't convey much amusement. 'Oh, Paul. No, you don't get hummus in Greece.'

'Yes you do.' I could visualise the Cyrillic script on the plastic pot in the continental delicatessen on Lamb's Conduit Street. I added, more pompously than I intended, 'It's a Greek speciality.'

Andrew studied me. He'd noticed the pomposity and didn't like it. Catching the attention of an elderly lady by the till, he called: 'Sofia – hummus?' He flapped the menu in the air. 'I can't see it anywhere, but for a special customer, our famous author here, do you have hummus?'

Sofia shrugged and shouted something in Greek into the kitchen. Giorgio re-emerged, wiping his fingers delicately on a napkin. 'Giorgio,' Andrew continued loudly, 'settle this matter for us, will you? My dear friend Paul says hummus is Greek. A Greek speciality, he insists.'

Several people on other tables were looking at us, at me. Giorgio bowed his head obsequiously. 'My dear friend,' he repeated, 'is mistaken. Hummus is from the Middle East. But if he would like, I can bring something very similar, very delicious. Fava bean.'

Alice said, 'Oh, for God's sake, Andrew.'

'It doesn't matter,' I said. 'I'll have tzatziki.'

'We've ordered so much anyway,' Alice said. 'We can share.'

I smiled, but internally I continued to fume. I wish I hadn't said 'speciality' but of course hummus was Greek. Andrew was bullying me, deploying Giorgio in his little game. It's how I used to feel sometimes at school. I remember arguing about the spelling of the word 'desiccate' with a boy called Jeremy de Beauvoir who rallied a group of fellow trust-funders to support him, even when a dictionary proved me right. People with privilege always think they control the truth.

Alice clearly felt bad on my behalf, which was good. She tried her hardest to make things better, laughing loudly, throwing back her head, her white throat flashing in the light. Under the table, her hand rolled tantalising circles on my thigh. She said to Andrew, 'Did you know Paul did crosswords?' ('I'm more of a sudoku man,' he answered.) 'Paul – tell the others about Kate Boxer. He's got this wonderful picture by her in his flat. What's it called it again?' 'Twiggy Bird,' I said. ('*Twiggy Bird?*' repeated Andrew, his intonation expressing contempt.) She wanted everything to be all right. She wanted us to be friends. She had no idea how much I had begun to dislike him.

'I'm thinking of selling the flat,' I said.

'Are you?' Alice looked surprised.

'I feel like a change.' I put my hand across her back, slipping it under the fabric of her dress to fondle her shoulder, and as I did so, I brought my mouth to her ear. 'I want to live closer to you,' I murmured softly.

A secret smile played on her lips. She looked at me sideways, eyes narrowed, like a cat. 'Let's talk about that after the holiday,' she said, her voice full of promise.

I looked at Andrew to check he was watching.

It became noisy, hard to hear. The music, an electro dance track, was turned up loud and a rowdy group took over the next table – four English couples, the men in short-sleeved shirts, the women with plunging necklines. ('Delfinos,' Alice mouthed at Andrew, rolling her eyes.) Most of the kids had wandered off, Alice and Tina were sharing a slice of baklava and I was surreptitiously feeding some cats who had gathered under the table. They were worryingly thin, with jagged haunches; two of them had gammy eyes.

Tina was complaining about Archie, his tendency to get his own way. 'Not that I can talk,' she added, 'being the youngest of three.'

'Boys or girls?' I asked, dropping a piece of lamb kebab on the ground, and then another quickly as the cats began to scrap for it.

'Three girls.' She laughed merrily. 'I'm the baby, typical youngest child: spoilt, spoilt, spoilt; used to getting away with murder. What about you?'

'An only child,' I said. 'Like Alice.'

It was one of our late-night topics: the pressure of parental hope, the difficulty with relationships, the sensitivity to criticism – one of the subjects I used to accelerate intimacy. I wiped my hand on a napkin and put my arm around Alice's shoulder.

'You and me both,' she said. Her hand still lay on my thigh and I shifted slightly so that it would move higher. 'As fucked up as each other.'

'Get a room,' Louis said loudly.

Andrew picked up the glass salt cellar and shook it into in the v-shaped crook between his thumb and finger, his lower lip jutting. The cellar rattled, full of rice. Nothing came out.

He put the salt back down on the table and breathed in deeply. He turned to gaze out over the harbour, so intently that I twisted my head to see what he was looking at. There was nothing there – just the gleam of reflected lights, and the water stilled and darkened.

I looked back at him, as Tina carefully lay her arms around his neck. She kissed his cheek, then, arms still in place, drew back to study him. He continued to stare ahead, his mouth a grim line. He was trying to get attention. Personally, I'd have ignored him.

Alice took her hand away from my thigh. She leant across the table. 'Poor Andrew,' she said. 'I miss her so much too.'

'I'm sorry, Al,' he said. 'It's nothing like losing a husband, I know. It just occasionally comes back and hits me. It's the guilt, really. Maybe she'd have been with us here now, married, with kids. She'd have loved it here.'

'Poor Andrew,' Alice said again. The hand that had fondled my thigh took his hand. At the same time, Tina removed her arm from his shoulders. 'It's not about comparisons. In many ways it's worse – she'd been at your side nearly your whole life. As an older brother, you felt responsible for her, that's probably why you feel guilty, but you shouldn't. It wasn't your fault. It's just a bugger. An absolute bugger. And it is so unfair. Why your sister? Why my husband? They both died too young.'

'It's stupid, isn't it?' He thudded his fist against his chest where his heart was. 'But she's in here. Always will be.'

An image of Florrie, his sister, came into my head, or I think it was Florrie. It might have been Daisy: boyishly short hair, feathered around her face, a full mouth, a sweet smile. Was it another sister or was it Florrie who was dead? Florrie: could she be dead? If it *was* her, why had nobody told me? Was it a recent death or an old one? Had I known and forgotten? Was this the sort of thing that could feasibly slip your mind?

'Dear Florrie,' Alice said. She tapped her hand on her heart. 'Me too.'

So it *was* Florrie. How could I not have known? When had she died, and how? An aggressive cancer – leukaemia, breast – whatever type it is that takes the young? I wanted to know, but I couldn't think how to ask without sounding insensitive. It looked bad not to have known, or worse to have forgotten. I was peculiarly disturbed. We hadn't been that close. A Sunday afternoon on the Backs with a bottle of wine; jazz at the Blue Boar; a party – someone's birthday (was it hers?). Sex, probably – yes, I think we had slept together. A blue tinge to her skin in her student room light, goose-bumps, the rough thinness of her duvet. So yes, just a few dates here and there. So my reaction wasn't about her; it was more selfish. Death throws you, even if you didn't know the person well. You sense your own mortality, feel the devil's breath on your own cheek.

'She was a wonderful person,' I said. 'I'm glad I got to meet her.'

The three of them looked at me, as if I'd said something unexpected. Tina said: 'You knew her?' She looked at Andrew. 'Did I know that?'

'Yes. At Cambridge,' I said. 'She was the year below.'

'Two years below,' Andrew said.

'Yes of course.'

'And you dated,' Alice said, smiling strangely. 'You knew her well.'

'Really?' Tina asked.

'It depends on your definition of "dated",' I said. 'It was more casual than that.'

One of the women on the next-door table let out a scream of laughter.

Tina looked at Andrew. 'I didn't know.'

He ignored her. Raising his eyebrows, he said: 'I think Florrie thought you were dating.'

'Oh.' I laughed sheepishly. 'I suppose what I mean is, to use the current parlance, we weren't "exclusive". Which is not to say I didn't think she was a super girl.' A super girl: why did I say that? It wasn't even language I used. Possibly because I hadn't really got to know her. It had been a casual thing, and I couldn't admit to that now. 'Special, actually . . . Really a lot of fun . . . The kind of person you don't forget . . .' Though of course I had. *Shit*. Death makes one nervous, does odd things to one's tongue.

'She liked you,' Alice said, still with that unreadable expression. 'She used to write to me about you, talked about you all the time.'

'How come I didn't know any of this?' Tina asked.

Alice was sitting back in her chair rather stiffly and it struck me that perhaps she wasn't wild about the thought of me with another woman, that she was jealous.

I smiled back reassuringly. 'It was a long time ago,' I said.

Andrew insisted on paying the bill. 'No, no, no, my turn,' he said. He held the plate out of Alice's reach.

'You're very bad,' she said,

'You paid yesterday,' he replied.

He batted away the ten-euro note I was holding between my fingers. 'My shout, Paul. You can do another night.'

Another night? Please God, tell me I wouldn't have to pick up the whole tab?

He took his credit card over to where the old lady was hunched at the till. Daisy and Phoebe returned from the bathroom where they had been reapplying their make up. Daisy looked the same, except with red lips, but Phoebe had ramped it up a gear, with heavily lined eyes and a layer of foundation. If she'd been aiming for Egyptian goddess, she'd landed on Soho tart. They stood at the table to discuss their curfew.

'Come on, honestly, we're on holiday, this is Agios Stefanos, it's *safe*,' Daisy argued.

'Midnight,' Alice replied.

'That's insane. You're always so ridiculously stressy.'

'I'm not *always* anything.'

Tina said, 'Oh, Alice. Let them stay out a little later. They're eighteen now.'

'OK. 1 a.m. No later.'

'And me,' Louis said, looming into view. 'You know I'm going.' He was still in his black hoodie, with a purple baseball cap worn backwards ('Supreme' was written across the visor), and a thick silver chain hanging from his belt.

'Really?' Phoebe said. 'Does he have to? Mum? Tell him he can't come.'

Louis took a step forwards. 'Tell them I can.'

Phoebe pushed him slightly, her hand flat against his chest. He jostled her, jerking his shoulder in her face. The silver chain whipped against her bare leg. 'Ow,' she said.

'Of course he can go,' Alice said, her hands out to calm them. 'You'll be sensible, won't you, Louis? You've had one beer already. No more drinking.'

'I don't know why he even wants to come.'

'I can come if I want. It's a free country.'

'Well. You can't drink. You won't get with anyone.'

'I might.'

'Well, don't expect me to babysit.'

It seemed as good a time as any to have a quick smoke, so I pushed my chair back and walked out to the street.

I lit up, leaning against one side of the restaurant's awning. Andrew was talking to Sofia. 'How's your grand-daughter?' he was saying with fake interest, pushing his numbers into the machine.

'She is in Elconda, working in the tourist office there.'

'Lovely,' Andrew said, taking his card back. 'Excellent.'

I looked away. By the supermarket opposite, three English lads with tattoos across their necks were horsing around, trying to put ice down the tops of their female companions. 'You knob,' one of the girls yelled.

'OK then.' Alice had joined me. I threw my cigarette on the ground and stubbed it out with my shoe.

Phoebe and Daisy stalked off towards the far end of the harbour, where lights flashed and music throbbed. Louis followed, a few feet behind, a rolling motion to his walk that showed he was trying to be cool. I recognised the bulge in his back pocket as a packet of fags.

'Do you think they'll be all right?' Alice said.

Tina said, 'Of course they will. They've promised to stick together.' She looked at Alice in the face and continued pointedly. '*Nothing* is going to happen. Just because ... We mustn't ... you know.' She squeezed her shoulder. 'They'll be fine.'

'Right, we can go home now.' Andrew was standing by us, too, slipping his wallet into his back pocket. 'I'm ready for my bed. Where are those boys?'

'I think they're looking for crabs on the jetty,' Alice said. 'Wait here, I'll get them.'

The group of lads had crossed the road now, waving their arms and singing. One of the girls with them fell into me as she passed. She said, 'Hello! I know you!' She had a Geordie accent, a big red mouth and tight plaits. It was the girl from the bus, the Rita Ora lookalike with the broken flip-flops, though she was barefoot now so she must have given up on them.

I steered her to a standing position and she lurched off. Andrew raised an eyebrow. 'You know each other?' he said.

'I wish.'

Alice and the boys were coming towards us in the crowd. They were behind a group of girls – stupidly high heels, tiny cropped tops, sheets of hair, chattering away in German. How old were they? Fifteen, sixteen, at a shove, though they looked older. I glanced across at Andrew. He was watching them as they tottered towards us, his expression heavy, blank, torpid.

He saw me and shrugged sheepishly, his chin tucked in, and then looked not to Tina but to Alice to check she hadn't noticed.

I had planned to have sex with Alice but I fell asleep before I had a chance to take off my own clothes, let alone hers. At one point, I was aware of hearing her in the bathroom, a splash and clink at the basin, but I couldn't keep my eyes open, and before I could wake properly, I was overtaken by that thick, heavy, gloopy unconsciousness that makes you wonder if you aren't drugged.

What woke me a few hours later? Thirst? The heat? A mosquito whining in my ear? I lay motionless, fully dressed, on top of the sheet. The ceiling fan droned. A dog in the near distance barked, stopped for a while; then barked again.

It was hot, pitch black in the room, so dark you could forget whether your eyes were open or shut. Alice was motionless. I turned my back to her, as quietly as I could, found a cooler section of the pillow. Something troubling had woken me and it took a moment to work out what. When I remembered it came as a renewed shock. Florrie – the revelation that she was dead.

I turned my body to face Alice, in need of human comfort, and stretched out an exploratory hand. I was awake now, alert. And I realised, a fist clenched, ready to uncurl, down low in my belly, that I was aroused.

My hand met nothing. I moved it, tried somewhere else, padded here, there – a wrinkled sheet, the smooth surface of the pillow, a space where her body, her hair, her face, her mouth had just been. She wasn't in the bed.

I sat up, stared into the darkness. I had been sure that she had been lying next to me. Could I have fallen asleep for a few seconds and she had slipped out then? Or had I imagined her breathing so quietly beside me? Had she never been in bed at all?

I rolled into the space where she should have been, buried my face in her pillow and breathed in. That slight scent again of fig and quince. The thought of her inner thighs. I groaned and fumbled for the light switch, couldn't find it and stood up.

The door on to the terrace was open a crack; a tiny sliver of night air lapping the curtain in the motion from the fan. I made my way across the room, jabbing my calf on the post at the end of the bed, and pushed it open. Outside was a fraction lighter; a nail paring of a moon, black shapes to mark the shrubs and trees. The dog was still barking, louder out here, a desperate bay. Impossible to imagine how a creature could keep going like that.

I strained my ears: other noises. A tinkle and a small splash. Laughter. Was she swimming? If so, who with?

I moved across the terrace, barefooted, past the long table and the shuttered door to the kitchen, and round the large gnarled tree where the CDs dangled, to the top of the path. I began to descend, but it was uneven and rocky and I stubbed my toe on a root, or a stone. Possibly I said, 'Ouch.' I hopped, lifted my foot to have a look, saw a blotch of blood on the crescent of flesh above the nail. Another laugh from the direction of the pool.

At the bottom of the path I stood as still as I could under the fig. In the water were Daisy and Phoebe. They were leaning against the side, elbows up, sharing a cigarette; I saw the gleam of it. Their naked bodies shimmered white, distorted, in the underwater lights. Shadows in the copse beyond. The crunch of leaves. Was someone else there with them? No, it was my imagination. They were alone. I watched, the muscles taut across their shoulders, waiting for one of them to turn so I could see their breasts. They were tipsy – tipsy enough to welcome me if I joined them?

No. Bad idea. I mustn't forget the longer view. Ignoring my throbbing toe, I turned and crept back up the path, resuming my search for Alice.

All the lights were off in the house. I went back to the bedroom, pushing open the door quietly, half expecting to see her asleep. I checked the bathroom. It was empty, but I took a piss while I was there.

The small bathroom window opened onto the front yard. The glass was loose and it rattled very slightly. I moved to look out and picked up in the distance the growl of an engine, getting closer, rearing up the track, and then silence as it was cut. A car door opened.

I got myself in a position to see out.

The silver people carrier was parked close to the house, the passenger door open, and two figures – Alice and Andrew – bent over next to it. They were both dressed, Andrew in his polo shirt, Alice in the T-shirt dress she had been wearing earlier that evening.

They were whispering. I couldn't catch what they were saying, but then Andrew moved to one side and Alice knelt on the ground. 'Come on, darling,' she said, in a louder whisper. 'Wake up. Come on. We've got to get you into bed.'

A groan, and an inarticulate semi-shout: 'Gerrof.' An arm flailed and Alice rocked backwards.

Andrew took over. He braced and leant in, then staggered back with the weight of his load.

Louis. Semi-conscious. Ill? No. Paralytic.

They battled for a few moments, struggling for purchase, and then managed to hoist the boy between them, Alice tiny, pushed down under his bulk. They half pulled, half dragged him out of sight, round the corner of the house.

I was torn. I didn't particularly want to help. I've always had a problem with vomit – the smell tends to set me off. Also I needed my sleep and we could be up all night. And yet, and yet. Was I turning down an opportunity to put myself further in Alice's good books? An opportunity to show Andrew up?

Leaving the bathroom, I tiptoed across the bedroom and pushed open the door. The terrace was empty. A few clatters and mumbles, an isolated moan, from the far side of the building. They must have taken him into his own room. I hesitated, took a step forward and then back. Maybe I was already too late. Maybe he was already asleep.

'Paul?'

Alice was standing in the shadows. A darker figure against the dark.

'What are you doing?' she said.

'I was looking for you,' I said. 'I woke up and you weren't there.'

'Well, here I am.' She was standing very still, in that ballet pose she had, shoulders back.

'I just woke up and heard voices,' I said, trying to make my voice sound sleepy. 'Everything all right?'

'Yes.'

I took a step towards her so I could see her face. She was

frowning, as if she had caught me doing something I shouldn't. 'Why are you dressed?'

'I never *un*dressed,' I said. 'I fell asleep with my clothes on. And then when I woke up a minute ago you weren't there.'

'I got up to check Louis was back safely.'

'And is he?' I said.

'He's fine. Fast asleep. I'm going back to bed now. You coming?'

She walked past me, taking my hand as she did so, and I followed. Clearly, she didn't want me to know about Louis. She was embarrassed. This could only be a good sign. It showed she cared more about my opinion of him than I realised.

Chapter Ten

I slept late. Alice was already up. I put on Andrew's trunks and a T-shirt, found my book, and wandered out on to the terrace. The air was seriously warm, the sun dappling through a vine from which grapes hung almost indecently heavy. The table was laid for breakfast – cups and plates, a jug of coffee, butter and honey. One of the glasses had been upturned to trap an insect. I studied it carefully; a prawn with wings. A still, silent cicada.

I lifted the glass to free it, but it didn't move. It looked mournful, one leg crooked at an angle. I wondered if it were dead. Using the cover of *In Cold Blood* as a stretcher, I carried it over to a pot of lavender and gently scooped it on to the earth. It sat there, still motionless.

'What's that?' Tina was standing in the door to the kitchen, wrapped in a pink linen dressing gown.

'Oh. Nothing. Just rescuing one of earth's precious creatures.' I sat down at the table, and flapped a napkin on to my lap. 'This is rather lovely. Have you seen Alice?'

'Gone to get bread.'

She stepped out on to the terrace and pulled out a chair. Her breasts were heavy and loose beneath the slubbed fabric. Mascara was smudged under her eyes, and her hair, unusually, was loose and tumbling.

'Isn't this heaven?' I said, waving my arms at the view, at the laid table, at the pot of coffee. 'Aren't we lucky?'

She laughed. 'Someone's in a good mood. Yes, we are.'

'We should have got up earlier to make the most of it.'

'I almost did. I was woken by a crowing cockerel at dawn.'

'Don't exaggerate.' Andrew's voice from the kitchen. 'It wasn't dawn.'

I made a face, and said conspiratorially, 'Probably was dawn. It being a cockerel. It's in their job description.'

Tina let out a gurgle of laughter and I poured us both a cup of coffee from the jug. Andrew emerged from the kitchen and stood in the doorway, his head bent over his BlackBerry. He was wearing khaki shorts and a navy polo shirt – brand new; it had two symmetrical creases where it had been folded in the packet. He let out an exasperated groan – and began to tap frantically.

Tina passed me a carton of milk, which I rejected with a wave of my hand. Long Life by the look of it. 'How did you sleep?' she asked.

'Fine.' I looked at her carefully. Did she know about Louis? 'I woke up a couple of times.'

Andrew put his phone in his back pocket and came to join us. He pulled out a chair. 'Did that dog wake you?' he said. 'It must have barked all night.'

'Don't exaggerate,' Tina said. 'Not *all* night.'

'I'm not sure,' he said. 'It made a pretty good stab at it.'

We talked for a bit about the Greek attitude towards animals, their lack of sentimentality. Tina, who claimed to have slept through it, wondered if the poor mutt were being fed, if it ever got a chance to sleep. I speculated on whether it took its responsibility as a guard dog seriously and was alert to every approach, or whether it was just barking desperately into the abyss, hoping someone would come. 'The problem,' Tina said, 'is that the noise isn't just disruptive, it's also distressing: that's probably what kept Andrew awake. It's like when the neighbours are having a late-night party. The noise wakes you but it's the lack of consideration that keeps your mind whirring.'

'The emotional component of noise,' I said. 'Discuss.'

Andrew put his coffee down and stood up. He tapped his phone in his palm with an air of self-importance. He said he might try and find out whoever was responsible for the dog – the contractor, perhaps – and have a word with them. 'It's not on really, is it?' he said. 'It's bad enough that they're digging up our land in the day. I don't see why they should ruin our nights, too.'

Our land: I noticed, but only idly.

My arm was caught in a shaft of sun and I could feel the heat of it, the skin burning. It was going to be a scorcher. I bent to scratch a bite on my ankle, and then was immediately aware of others, on my neck and arms and face. 'Damn,' I said, inspecting with my fingers. 'I've been eaten alive.'

'It's only the females that bite,' Andrew said. 'Did you know that? The males settle for nectar. It's only the females that go for blood.'

'Tell me about it,' I said, one man to another, and he laughed.

We heard the car bumping up the drive, the high rev of the engine as it negotiated the last steep bit of hill. Then silence, the slam of the driver's door, and Alice rounded the side of the house. She was in shorts and a vest top over a bikini. She was frowning.

'Hello, darling one,' I said, hoping to make her smile.

She didn't answer, just walked towards us very quickly. When she reached the table, she put down the paper bag and said to Andrew, 'The police are all over the port. Something happened at the club last night. A girl was attacked.' She was gripping the back of my chair, but not looking at me. 'Where are Phoebe and Daisy?' she said to Tina.

'They're still in bed,' Tina replied. 'Asleep. How awful.' She had emptied the paper bag, and laid the contents, nine nectarines and a flat, rather grey, loaf of bread, carefully on the table. 'Sit down.' She patted the chair next to her and reluctantly Alice perched on the edge of it. Andrew was standing on the terrace, his arms crossed behind his head, staring at Alice.

'Was it a sexual attack?' he said.

A muscle twitched in Alice's jaw but her voice was calm. 'I don't know the details, only that there are police everywhere. The woman in the bakery said they've been there all night. She didn't know much either. Just that it was a young girl. She was found in the water, covered in bruises, incoherent – upset, drunk, her clothes ripped. I think she might have been raped.'

'Poor thing,' I said. 'I hope they find the bastard who did it.'

I reached for the bread. It didn't look much, but it smelt delicious, yeasty, still warm. As surreptitiously as I could, I tore a corner off and popped it into my mouth.

'The girls didn't say anything, did they?' Alice said to Andrew. 'They didn't see anything?'

'I haven't spoken to them.'

'I wonder,' Tina said, 'if they'll have to give statements.'

'What about Louis?' I said, finishing my mouthful.

Alice turned to face me, frowning. 'What about Louis?'

'I just wondered if he'd seen anything, that's all.'

She shook her head, looked at Andrew and then back at me. 'He wouldn't have. He came back early, much earlier than the girls.'

'Oh.' So that's how she was spinning his little misadventure. 'If you say so. OK.'

Andrew was fiddling with his phone. 'Shall I ring Gavras?' he said. 'See if I can get a heads-up.'

'I don't know.' Alice looked at him and then away again. She was flicking her fingers, as if trying to dry them. 'Yes. No. Don't. It would seem as if we were interfering.'

'Who's Gavras?' I asked.

'He's the head of the police in Pyros,' Andrew said. 'Number two when Jasmine went missing. He speaks good English. We've rubbed up against him quite a lot over the years.'

I took Alice's hand, to try and still it. 'I would have thought definitely keep out of it. At least Daisy and Phoebe are safe.' She smiled gratefully, and gave mine a squeeze. 'I'm sure the whole thing will have blown over by the end of the day. For all we know, she knew her attacker. That's usually the case, isn't it?'

A grim silence settled.

'They'll catch whoever did it,' I continued. 'And lock him up.' I was just trying to put Alice's mind at ease, to reassure her that her own daughter was not at risk, but then I began to *enjoy* the sound of my own voice. I didn't self-censor. 'You know, the kind of girl who gets herself in trouble, swanning around in a different culture, dressed inappropriately, drinking too much, flirting probably, flashing her body.'

Tina said, 'Oh dear, Paul. Are you saying this girl was "asking for it"?'

'No. Of course not.' God, it was so hard negotiating this stuff, at the best of times. 'I just mean . . . it might not be what it seems. More complicated. Less complicated. We're all jumping to conclusions. Was she *actually* raped? Come on, Andrew? You saw the kind of girls I mean, the ones parading themselves at the port last night.'

He looked at me sideways, out of the corner of his eye, like someone approaching a dangerous animal. 'No,' he said slowly.

'Oh come on, I saw you watching them! The ones in tiny skirts. The ones that were dressed like slappers even if they weren't.'

'I don't know what you're talking about.'

'Yes you do.' I glared at him.

'Slappers? It's not a word I'd use. Er . . . I don't think so.'

Alice stood and crossed the terrace to where a towel was hung over the back of a chair. She picked it up and walked down the steps in the direction of the pool.

Neither Tina nor Andrew looked at me.

Tina said, 'I'll get the kids up and then I ought to get dressed. I can't believe it's almost eleven and I'm still in my dressing gown.'

Andrew said something about putting on a wash.

I cleared the table and then took my book and my cigarettes over to the ornate bench I had begun to think of as my 'fag seat'. The dog had shut up at last. My forehead was beaded in perspiration. I knew I had gone wrong there. I was livid with Andrew for not backing me up, but I was also aware that I had said things I hadn't meant, or that were, at least, easily misunderstood.

I lay as far back as the wooden bench allowed, closed my eyes.

When I opened them, Alice was standing in front of me. I hadn't heard her coming. The sound of her bare feet, up the steps, across the terrace, must have been swallowed by the ticking of the cicadas. She was wearing a swimsuit, a functional navy Speedo with racer straps. Her hair was wet and pulled back. My coat was dangling between her finger and thumb, like a damp rag. 'You left this by the pool,' she said. 'Artan hosed it by mistake. It's soaking.'

'Oh,' I said. 'Damn.'

'It'll dry in seconds in the sun.' She spread it over the arm of the bench and sat down next to me. Her expression was unreadable but she moved her knees quickly together and apart and together again and I took the gesture, along with her decision to sit down, as conciliatory.

'If it doesn't shrink,' I said.

'I don't know why you brought it with you. It's 35 degrees.'

I looked at her, gazed deep into her eyes. 'Insecurity,' I said. I told her how kids from the local Dr Barnardo's children's home used to come and spend a day at my primary school every year, and how they never took off their coats. 'That's how I feel here,' I said. 'A Dr Barnardo's boy.'

She studied me seriously. 'I don't understand. Do you feel insecure?'

'That stupid comment earlier. Yes, maybe in this company I am a little out of my depth.'

'*Do* you feel out of your depth?'

Suddenly, I had an urge to tell her the whole truth: to admit I had lied about my life, my novel, my flat, to tell her I was a fake, that I wanted to be a better person, that I wanted to change. Things might have worked out differently if I had. The course on which we were set could have changed. But the moment passed and was gone.

In the distance, behind Alice's head, the sea gleamed silver. A couple of sailing boats leant sideways. I stretched, with a small yawn, rested my hand on her neck. I wanted to say something to make her happy. 'I'll have a look at that van of yours today,' I said, ignoring her question, 'when it cools down a bit. If all goes well, perhaps I'll even get it on the road by tonight.'

She turned her head and kissed my arm. 'Kind,' she said.

I took her hand and turned it over gently to kiss the palm. Two livid red scratches ran across her wrist. Had she got them when Louis lashed out? I traced them with my fingers. She pulled her hand back and got to her feet, with an air of completion. 'I'm going to have another swim. Coming?'

'In a minute.'

About to turn, she picked up a sleeve of the splayed coat,

then dropped it. 'Paul, I'm sorry, but it's gross. It's like a flasher's mac.'

'It's tweed,' I said, pathetically.

Construction started up shortly after that, the sound of large amounts of earth being moved, and of even larger pieces of machinery cranking and grinding. It wasn't just the noise, which was loud, or the vibrations, which were strong enough to make the ground tremble, it was the sense not of construction but of *destruction* that was disturbing. It made you feel watched, encroached upon. It put your nerves on edge. I left my bench, no longer a relaxing place to be, and walked across to the main part of the terrace where I found Louis sitting at the table. He was wrapped in a towel, but naked from the waist up; his chest pale and spotty, with red stretch marks just above the line of the towel and patches of sunburn over his shoulders. His head was resting on one hand, sweat on his forehead, his hair damp. A bowl of cereal sat untouched on the table in front of him.

'You look a bit rough,' I said.

His eyes were glassy, with dark rings beneath. His mouth was hanging open, but he didn't answer – even words were too much effort.

'Late night?'

He made an incoherent sound, a semi-grunt, lifted his cereal spoon and then, thinking better of it, put it back down.

Down at the pool, Phoebe and Daisy were asleep on loungers, their arms crossed above their heads, each naked back as smoothly curved as a musical instrument – a violin, say, or an expensive guitar. Artan was sweeping the pool area with large regular movements of a rubber broom, turning his head to look at them. Daisy lifted her head and saw him. 'Artan, chuck me my suntan oil, will you?'

He picked it up from the table and brought it over to her. 'You're a doll,' she said.

Alice and Andrew were standing on the far side of the lower terrace, gazing at the sea and talking quietly.

'Louis's up,' I said, walking over to them.

They both spun round at the sound of my voice. 'Yes,' Andrew said. 'I woke him, but perhaps that was a mistake. He's still a bit tired.'

'He can have an early night,' Alice said.

Andrew looked at his phone. 'I'll check on him again,' he said. 'Make sure he's had something to eat.'

'Good luck with that,' I said.

'Thank you,' Alice said to Andrew. 'Maybe encourage him to have a shower?'

'Wilco.' Andrew gave a small salute and lolloped off, back up the path.

The racket, which had stopped for a few minutes, started up again. 'Oh God,' Alice said, facing the sea again. 'It's awful, awful. They're much closer than they were yesterday. They're practically *on* our land. They'll be up to the copse tomorrow.'

'You'd have thought they'd have the courtesy to wait until the end of our holiday,' I said.

'You would.' She half smiled.

'What's worse? The digger or the dog?' I said, trying to make her laugh.

'They're both bad.'

'I think the digger is better. At least you don't have to worry about it feeling hungry or abandoned. At least the digger isn't digging desperately into the abyss.'

She smiled again, swept a strand of hair away from her mouth, and then walked to the barbecue area and sat down on a metal chair. She stretched out a leg and bent to inspect her ankle – a mosquito bite, or an ingrowing hair.

I found a spare bed and lay down with a sigh. I would ignore the noise, I decided. I opened my book.

Time passed. Frank and Archie appeared, dive-bombed into the pool, and then raced up and down, turning the water to foam. Tina arrived with her box of paints and finally, taking the steep part of the path very slowly, Louis. He stood under the fig tree at the bottom of the steps, not looking at anyone, and then shuffled slowly towards the other end of the pool, head bowed. He lay face down on a sunbed, his arms trailing.

I fell asleep. I don't know for how long. When I woke, the diggers were still churning but I was alone: the sunbeds were empty, the pool a sheet of glass.

Tina was standing at the foot of the steps. I could see her mouth move. 'Paul!' she was repeating. 'Paul.'

I jumped to my feet, the world black and white, dizziness swimming, my ears buzzing.

'Paul,' she said again, walking towards me. She was wearing another tent: this one made out of a faded 1960s-style fabric decorated with boats. 'Didn't anyone tell you to get ready?'

'Get ready?'

'We're going to hire kayaks and have a picnic. We promised the kids we would this year. Alice wanted to get out, to escape from the noise. We're all in the car waiting for you.'

'Oh, OK.' I made a rueful face, tugging down the corners of my mouth. 'No one told me.'

I put my shirt over my head and we walked together up the path and round the terrace to the front of the house. Faces at the car windows. The engine already running. It occurred to me that maybe I had been forgotten; someone had remembered me as they were just about to leave. No. Alice wouldn't do that. Tina opened the boot, looked at me expectantly – 'Sorry, it's all that's left' – and I climbed in, folding myself up between two large canvas beach bags. I was doubled up on myself, my knees in my face, my neck rigid with the effort of keeping my head down.

'Sorry for keeping you waiting,' I said cheerfully to the car. 'I was asleep.'

Alice was just in front of me, in the middle of the last row of seats. She turned round. 'You sleep through anything,' she said.

'I have a clear conscience.'

She stretched out her hand, managed to touch my shoulder. 'I should be so lucky,' she said, and then mouthed. 'Sorry.'

Andrew drove down the track to the main road and then almost immediately right at the sign for Delfinos Beach Club. I couldn't see much past the obstruction of the beach bags. 'Isn't this enemy territory?' I said as we pulled into a car park at the end of a long tarmac drive. 'Isn't this hell's mouth?'

Everyone was piling out. An agonising wait while they stretched and collected, car doors sliding shut. Finally, the boot was lifted. Andrew was standing there. 'It's the only place you can get kayaks,' he said crisply.

Outside it was all white – blindingly so. White walls and white-painted pavements. The hotel was modern and angular, channelling as much an Eastern as a Greek vibe, with turquoise-painted windows, pots of bamboo, small windows. A few spiky palms were planted in beds of white gravel. A youngish woman carrying an enormous sack of bed linen came out of one door and disappeared into another. I could hear a small baby bleating in an upstairs room. Otherwise, it was oddly deserted. No sign of the marauding hordes that filled Alice and Andrew with such horror.

Andrew took one of the canvas bags and handed me the other, then we trailed in a marauding horde of our own across the car park towards the end of the building, beyond which you could see a snapshot of beach: sparkling water with small, frolicking waves, rustic umbrellas made out of dried-palm matting, a strip of custard-yellow sand. Here's where the people were. You could hear their shouts and ringing cries, that particular beach acoustic that's like noisy birdsong. On the side of the building an arrow pointed to 'Reception' and Andrew, after telling the children to wait outside, pushed open a door, holding it after him for Alice and Tina. I hesitated, not for the first time unsure whether to ally myself with the adults or their offspring, but then followed.

Inside was a small room, freezing cold and smelling strongly of chemical vanilla. An air-conditioning vent in the wall hummed, and a candle was burning on a long desk. Three men had looked to the door when we came in – one sitting the other side of the desk; the other two standing, both dressed in thick navy trousers and crisp white shirts with the sleeves rolled neatly to above the elbow. Police. Guns hung from their belts.

Alice took a step forward. There was a catch in her voice, as if she had left it slightly too late to breathe in. 'Lieutenant Gavras.'

The older of the two policemen was tall and muscular with short salt and pepper hair, thick brown arms, and blue eyes within the tanned folds of his face. 'Mrs Mackenzie,' he said politely. 'Mr Hopkins. Mrs Hopkins.'

He put out his hand and shook theirs, one after the other, then adjusted his waistband, tucking in his shirt in at the back and sides. Patches of sweat bloomed under his arms. He introduced them to his younger colleague, Angelo Dasios, who had the symmetrical good looks of a film star, and to Iannis, 'the hotel manager', a fat man sporting sideburns and a patterned Nehru shirt. No one introduced me, pressed up against a noticeboard on the far wall, and I didn't bother to push myself forward.

They exchanged awkward pleasantries, about the weather, and the busy-ness or otherwise of the resort. 'You got the new posters?' Alice said.

'I did indeed,' he said, turning back. He smiled, his jawline firm. 'We have distributed them to key points around the island.'

'I haven't seen any,' Alice said. '*I'm* the one who has been putting them up, handing them out everywhere I can.'

'Well, I can assure you,' he said, his smile tight, 'they have been allocated.'

How much he must resent Alice and Andrew, I realised. He had had ten years of this. All this fuss for a dead girl.

'I've seen one,' I said, before I could stop myself. 'On a lamp-post in Elconda.'

Gavras craned his neck and noticed me. 'There. An independent witness,' he said, clearly taking me for a random hotel guest. 'I assure you again, Mrs Mackenzie: no one wants to find Jasmine Hurley more than I do.' He gave her name a particular pronunciation: *Yazaminer Urley.*

A pause, and then Andrew said: 'So we heard about the attack in Agios Stefanos last night. A rape, was it? Terrible. Just not what you want.'

Gavras brought a finger up to an eyebrow and smoothed it. 'It is why we are here,' he said. 'Not good.'

Iannis, the hotel manager, let out a noise from somewhere between his nose and his throat, expressing agreement.

'What happened?' Tina asked. 'Can you tell us?'

'It was unfortunate,' he said. 'A young girl left her companions and went outside alone for some fresh air. It appears that, taking advantage of her inebriation, her attacker took her against her will into an isolated area and . . . well . . .'

'Our girls were at the club last night,' Tina said. 'They say they didn't see anything but if you want to talk to them, I'm sure they'd be happy to answer your questions.'

'That is useful.' The policeman pulled a small pad of paper from his breast pocket. 'I am trying to collect a list of everyone who was there. The girls' names . . .?'

'Phoebe Mackenzie and Daisy Hopkins.' Alice spoke before Tina could answer. 'You can contact them through me.'

I waited for her to mention Louis, but she didn't.

'Is that it?' I said.

'Yes.' She was standing very still, her hands behind her back, her fingers tightly laced together. 'Lieutenant Gavras: did the girl see her attacker?'

'That I can't say. What I can say is that we have a suspect we are hoping to take in for questioning.'

'Oh, do you? Someone staying here? Someone she knew, maybe?'

'I shouldn't say any more. It's why in fact . . . as I say . . .' He caught the eye of the receptionist and held it.

I saw Alice's shoulders relax a tiny bit. 'Anyway,' she said, picking up on his unspoken message. 'We'd better get on.'

'Yes.' Gavras gave a small bow. 'I have taken up enough of your time.'

But we still had to pay for kayaks as well as the 'day member-ship' that was required to access them. Gavras and his hand-some sidekick had to move out of the way while Andrew produced his credit card and Iannis brought out a dial-up machine from under the desk. Andrew input his number. It hadn't occurred to me to bring any money, so I quietly left.

Outside, there was no sign of Frank or Archie. Phoebe and Daisy had moved away and were talking to a couple of girls just in sight on the edge of the beach. Louis, however, had slunk to the ground and was slumped against the wall, his legs stretched across the path. His eyes were bloodshot and he had a greenish pallor; he was swallowing hard. 'Oh dear,' I said. 'Do you want some water?'

'No. Nothing.'

The door opened and the others came out. Alice made a small exclamation of dismay when she saw Louis crumpled on the pavement and put out her hands to pull him to his feet. 'I'm sorry, I'm sorry,' he muttered as he stumbled forward. 'I think I'm going to be sick.'

'OK. Hang on.' She looked frantically around and then seeing an arrow sign for 'Shop and Toilets' began to steer him back towards the car park. Over her shoulder, she shouted, 'Wait for us.'

'Don't worry,' Andrew said. 'It's probably just sunstroke.'

She put her hand up to acknowledge she'd heard and disappeared around the corner.

Tina and Andrew stood staring at the sea, with bored half-smiles on their faces. I told them I was going to have a quick smoke and I walked away a few feet, out of the shadow and into the sharp sun. I lit a cigarette and surveyed the scene. It's always odd when you discover another holiday that's happening only a few feet from your own. Not an isolated villa up in the hills, but a beach with activity, noise, organisation. The smell of coconut oil, and Nivea Factor 50. On the shoreline rows of Lasers and kayaks lay like beached whales. A mother was trying to help a toddler build a castle. Two girls in bikinis threw a frisbee back and forth. Shrieks of pleasure from a volleyball game; splashes from a pool, somewhere over to the right, set back perhaps behind those palm trees. *Other people*. Crowds. I felt a sudden pang of longing for Alex's Bloomsbury flat; for the primary school children's voices that were sometimes carried on the wind.

I turned, stubbed out my cigarette in the imported sand. I was almost near enough to Phoebe and Daisy to be able to hear their conversation with the two strangers – girls with long wet hair wrapped in matching blue and white striped towels. I took a step closer.

'She was like really, really drunk,' one of the girls was saying. 'She'd been like drinking all day. That's why she went in the sea afterwards – it was stupid because the salt water got rid of all the evidence.'

'I don't think she even really knew what was happening,' the other girl said.

'And who do you think did it?' Phoebe asked.

'Everyone thinks it was Kylie's brother, Sam. He really fancied her and he was following her around all night.'

'Which one was he?' Daisy asked.

'He's kind of young looking, bit spotty, long brown hair, bit over his eyes.'

The child with the sandcastle began wailing and hitting the bucket. I missed what Phoebe said next, and then the girls suddenly moved apart. Andrew, Tina and Alice, with Louis trailing, had emerged from the side of the building. The girls slipped past them, eyes averted.

Alice watched them go. 'Who were they?'

Phoebe threw her hair over her shoulder. 'Just friends from Club 19. We were arranging to meet them tonight.'

'I don't think you'll be going to Club 19 tonight,' Alice said.

'I doubt it will be open,' said Andrew. 'And even if it is, you must do what your mother says.'

'That's not fair. *Their* parents are letting them go out tonight,' Phoebe protested. 'And they actually knew the girl who was raped. I'm not even joking. They talked to her.'

Andrew said: 'We have your best interests at heart.' God, he could be pompous.

Phoebe said, 'It's not going to happen to us. We're not going to get raped because a) we're not stupid enough to split up, b) we're not going to get drunk and c) we wouldn't flirt like she did, lead some weirdo on.'

I mused for a moment on the self-absorption of the teenage mind. In order to be allowed to go out, Daisy and Phoebe were laying as much blame on the victim as they could. They were presenting many of the same arguments I'd caused offence with that morning. And then Daisy said, 'I mean, she was obviously coming on to him – she was wearing his shoes because she'd broken her flip-flops.'

I'd had my back to them for much of this discussion, but I turned.

'Where was she from?'

'Newcastle, I think.'

I turned back to face the sea. Broken flip-flops. Newcastle. It sounded like it might be the girl from the bus who'd been raped. The one who looked like Rita Ora. *'You knob.'* What was her name? Laura. I'd taken the attack lightly, with no real thought for the victim, but now it felt horrible and real. Anxieties I had been suppressing rose to the surface. *Was* Louis involved? Was Alice covering for him?

'Excuse me.'

I turned round. A bald, thickset policeman was approaching from the other direction, trudging across the sand in his big shoes, the flash of a gun at his belt. He was holding a young boy above the elbow. The boy, who was only about fifteen, was wearing board shorts and a baggy vest, his feet bare, his arms long and thin. It was hard not to notice the difference in their sizes, not to imagine the thumb-print bruise being pressed into his arm. He had a long narrow face, with hollow eyes. He was biting his lip.

I was blocking the path and I stepped out of the way. They

passed me, the man still gripping the lad's arm. The boy looked once over his shoulder, clumsily rubbing the palm of his hand in his eye, and then they headed back along the side of the building, towards Reception.

We had all stopped to watch. No one spoke for a moment, then Tina turned, her mouth dropping. 'Surely he isn't a suspect?' she said. 'He looked about twelve.'

'I know,' I said. 'God. Poor kid. I mean, I suppose they know what they're doing?'

'Of course they do,' Alice said. Louis had slunk down again on to the sand and she gave him a nudge with her foot. 'Come on, stand up. Let's go.' She seemed unaffected by the boy's arrest. In fact, if anything, she looked relieved. She gave me a perky smile and set off towards the kayaks without a care in the world.

Chapter Eleven

The water beneath me didn't look cobalt blue as it had from a distance, but black and threatening, full of danger. Beneath me were crags, jagged pumice with snags and dips, sudden patches of darkness.

I worried about tipping over, sinking down into the abyss. I tried to concentrate on the paddle, on the angle of the blades. It was hard work and I was out of breath, that nasty hot feeling scouring the back of my throat. The big yellow life jacket they'd made me wear was chafing beneath my armpits.

The hotel receded, two white cubes above the swell. To my left was a small island – 'Serena's rock'? Alice had left me to my own devices: 'You don't mind, do you? I need to keep going or I'll capsize.' She was way ahead, paddling side by side with Andrew. Tina had volunteered to drive Louis round, but Phoebe and Daisy, Frank and Archie kept doubling back to taunt me, weaving back and forth to show how easy it was, and then setting off again at mocking speed. 'Got the hang of it now?' Frank yelled at one point, and then added something that made Archie laugh.

I battled round the chain of rocks at the mouth of the bay. It seemed to take ages. I kept hacking at the water, not cutting through it. By the time I had got round them and then fought the current to change course, I was alone. The others I could see had reached the small cove, and were pulling their boats out of the water. Tina was standing at the edge, a hand shielding her eyes. She waved, and I raised an elbow in reply. Salt stung the corners of my mouth. I ploughed on. Alice and Andrew were bent down over the boats, heads close. Louis was sitting on the other side of the inlet, throwing stones into the water. Why hadn't Alice told the policeman he'd been at the nightclub? Did she think he might be involved, or worse *know*? No, it was more likely just a natural instinct to keep her son out of trouble. But still – Andrew should have encouraged her to tell the truth. It was the right thing to do – whatever Louis's involvement. It didn't surprise me he hadn't. There was something unsavoury about Andrew, something *off*, a discrepancy between his actual physical standing and how he wanted to be seen. I kept coming back to the way his eyes had followed those young German girls, and then how he had lied about doing so this morning. At least, for all my failings, I was honest. I was the one she should be listening to, not him. I felt a twinge of something unfamiliar, and realised it was what it might be like to occupy the moral high ground.

I reached the shallows to cheers and cries of congratulation. Archie and Frank had been despatched to help me out of the water: 'One, two, three, yank,' Frank shouted, heaving the kayak with exaggerated effort. As I divested myself of my yellow straitjacket, a small smile played around Phoebe's lips. 'Nasty bit of chafing there, Paul,' she said. 'You might need some cream.'

She was lying on a towel. I let my eyes run over her body. 'Are you offering to rub it in?'

'Fuck off.'

Alice separated from Andrew and came over. She put her arms around my shoulders and held me, laying her head briefly on my shoulder. I felt the damp swell of her Speedo against my chest, causing me to stir, even through my exhaustion. 'Poor Paul,' she said, kissing my sunburnt shoulders.

'You should have said you'd never done it before,' Andrew called. 'Though how you could have reached forty-four without once rowing a kayak, I'll never know!'

He laughed to hide the jibe. A little knife, that was his weapon of choice.

Tina was kneeling on a threadbare tartan rug, laying out rolls and tomatoes and unfolding greaseproof packets containing ham and a plastic-looking cheese. She reached into a coolbox for a bottle of beer and thrust it into my hand. A rash of freckles had sprung up across her nose and cheeks; she'd caught the sun. 'There you go,' she said. 'Cure for all ills.'

I thanked her and rummaged among the bags on the ground until I found my cigarettes. I perched on a rock to smoke while the others milled around on a patchwork of rugs and towels, picking at the food. It wasn't much of a beach, small and pebbly, but we had it to ourselves. A path led through a sharp incline of trees to a strip of road, a silver stripe across the hillside. Most of the stones, white and oval, were stained with black tar. The air smelt unpleasantly of sulphur. In a crack between rocks, litter had collected, including a rolled-up nappy.

'Everything always tastes so much more delicious when you eat it outdoors,' Tina said after a bit.

No one bothered to say anything, though Alice, who had hardly eaten a thing, made a noise of agreement at the back of her throat.

'Paul – are you going to eat?' Tina called.

I waved my cigarette in the air, gestured to the beer lodged between my knees. 'I'm fine. Maybe in a minute.'

'That's why you stay so slim,' she sighed. She had made herself a sandwich, and she opened her mouth around it and took a messy bite. 'I'm going to start the 5:2 diet when I get home.'

'It works better for men,' Andrew said.

'Are you saying I'm a lost cause?'

'I think you're perfect the way you are,' I said.

'Bless you, Paul,' she said.

Phoebe and Daisy had laid out towels and were sunbathing in matching swimwear – hot pink strapless bikinis. They were talking quietly to each other. I began to concentrate on the shapes of their mouths. The subject was Kylie's brother, Sam, the young lad we'd seen being taken by the police at Delfinos and whether he could possibly be guilty of rape.

'He didn't look the type,' Phoebe said.

'What *is* the type?' Tina, who had been eavesdropping too, said. 'It's an important lesson, you two. Appearances can be deceptive.'

I looked across at Alice. She had picked up a pebble and was studying it. 'Anyway,' I said. 'They might just have wanted to talk to him as a witness, not a suspect.'

Alice looked up at me, and then away. She threw her stone high into the sea and leant back, eyes closed, face up to the sun.

'I think he went home early anyway,' Daisy said, propping herself up on her elbows. She called to Louis who was sitting in the shade of a tree, picking delicately at a ham roll. 'You talked to him, didn't you? He left about the same time as you, long before us. Weren't you going to walk up together?'

I watched Alice. She didn't move.

'I don't know,' Louis muttered, looking down. 'I got a bit lost.'

'I didn't hear any of you come in,' Tina said. 'I was dead to the world.'

I waited. Surely Alice or Andrew would tell the truth now? When neither of them said anything, I opened my mouth to speak – I could quite innocently just say what I'd seen – but then thought better of it.

Tina said, 'Anyway, that poor girl. I hope she has a good support group and she isn't in hospital in a foreign country on her own. I hope her parents have flown out, or if not, she has a nice friend to look after her.'

'She was with a big gang,' Phoebe said carelessly. 'I'm sure she's fine.'

I thought about the people Laura had been with: the bottles of beer, the shaved heads. 'Her friends didn't look much cop to me,' I said.

Alice turned to look at me. 'How do you know anything about her friends?'

I had spoken without thinking. I stubbed out my cigarette carefully and said: 'If she is the girl I'm thinking about, she's called Laura. She was with a load of skinheads on my bus up from the south yesterday.'

'I thought you got a taxi?'

I felt the heat rise into my face. 'Um . . . I got a bus in the end.'

She looked at me with an odd expression. 'But I thought you said . . .'

'Yeah, silly me – I don't know why, but I lied.'

I climbed down off the rock and picked up a tomato to eat. Warm juice spurted down my chin. I wiped the liquid with the back of my hand and sat down on the pebbles, making a show of getting comfortable next to Alice. I was aware of her shifting very slightly away and of Andrew's eyes on both of us. How typical. They were the ones behaving reprehensibly, but I was the one who now felt in trouble.

I would get tar on the seat of the trunks, but it didn't matter. They weren't mine. Nothing here was mine, I realised unhappily, no matter how hard I pretended.

★ ★ ★

After lunch, as Louis had rallied, we swapped places. I took a lift back to the house with Tina, leaving him to paddle by kayak back around the headland. I watched them all push off from the shoreline, and shouted ironic advice and encouragement – 'that's it; well balanced, nice clean strokes' – trying to use humour to wrest back control of the situation.

The car was reached by a climb through trees, along a rough path, half stones, half pine-needles. The air was sharp with eucalyptus. Above us, a bird of prey circled, a hawk maybe, its shadow curling and slanting. Tina clambered a way ahead, though I could hear her exhaling loudly, letting out small cries of astonishment at the gradient. I was carrying the bags and paced steadily behind, glad to have a few moments alone with my thoughts. I had a lot to think about.

When I arrived at the road, Tina was leaning against the car, fanning herself with her hand. 'Phew. Hot work,' she said. 'I'd have died if you hadn't offered to be my pack horse.'

A convoy of quad bikes, topped by teenagers in vests, snarled by, like chainsaws on wheels.

I waited until they had rounded the bend, a skirt of dust in their wake. 'At least I'm good for something,' I said. I'd meant to sound flirtatious rather than self-pitying, but Tina took a step forward. 'Don't worry about Andrew,' she said. She made a strange darting movement with her hand, curling it into a fist and pressing it into my cheek. Sympathy in a lunge. A feint retreat. If I'd been a child I wonder if she'd have squeezed my cheeks, pushed her face into mine. She took her hand away and sat next to me on the barrier. 'He feels responsible for Alice and sometimes he gets carried away.'

I said: 'Thing is, I wouldn't mind being responsible for her myself.'

Again I must have misjudged the tone. I'd been wondering on the way up whether to tell her about Louis being drunk, about Andrew and Alice covering for him. I knew I wouldn't now. Tina looked at me for a long time. I half laughed under her scrutiny, felt the prick of tears, bit the side of my lip, looked away.

'You've fallen for her, haven't you?' she said eventually.

It was a peculiar moment. I had had no idea until that point of the truth of it. Perhaps I was feeling over-sensitive because of the rape and the worry about Alice. Or perhaps it was the delayed trauma of the kayak trip and relief that it was over. My insides weakened and for a second I found it easier not to speak. I gave a nonchalant shrug and eventually managed to say, 'I'm not good enough for her. That's the problem.'

She said, 'Was that why you lied about taking a taxi? To make yourself sound more suitable?'

'Probably. Yes.'

We were leaning in, facing the road. But she spun round to face the view. 'I'm sure you are good enough. I'm sure you're just what she needs. She just needs to realise it, to relax into it. She's not quite herself this week. She's worried about Louis. And losing the house isn't easy. On top of everything.'

I turned round too. The prospect before us was of trees and sky and the large dark body of Albania, but on a triangle of sea, a few small shapes wriggled slowly towards the headland. 'On top of *what*, though?' I said. 'Aren't we supposed to be on holiday?'

She sighed lightly. 'You wouldn't understand. It's never completely a holiday here. It's almost like a duty. Alice has always carried Jasmine's disappearance on her shoulders.'

'But why?'

She sighed again, more heavily. 'Partly, I suppose, because she was there when it happened, lived through that night and the days that followed, the police interviews, the search . . . We all did, I guess. But Alice – it's just the kind of person she is

– took it more deeply than the rest of us. And now, the end of the lease, having to give up the house . . . Here's the thing about Alice. You don't know her as well as I do. Alice *has* to be in control. She always has. She doesn't trust anyone else to do anything; she is only happy if she has charge of it all. I love her dearly, of course I do, but she has this belief that unless she is at the centre of everything, nothing holds together. Without her in the driving seat everything goes wrong.'

I frowned. 'That must bring a few problems.'

'It's just the sort of person she is,' she said again.

We were both quiet on the drive back to the house. I was disarmed by drowsiness: a combination of physical exhaustion, upset, heat and the soporific effects of Mythos. Tina pressed in a CD, a compilation they brought to Pyros every year: a private joke in musical form. Through half-closed eyes, I watched olive groves rise and dip, the sea and sky merge and separate. I sang along sleepily to the second track, a haunting song about cruelty and betrayal.

'You're familiar with this one, then?' Tina said.

'Yeah. People used to play it a lot at college.'

Her face flashed towards me and then back to the road. 'Everything But The Girl. "Charmless Callous Ways". It was Florrie's favourite. Apparently.'

Florrie. I opened my eyes and sat forward. Was it the song that brought the memory back? An image of that oval pixie face, the slight overbite, flickering in candlelight across the table from me. The Maharajah Tandoori. Dancing wildly in the buttery during some party, a clumsy drunken kiss on the corner of King's Passage, and another physical memory: the slither of her sheets, the roughness of an over-washed cellular blanket.

'It's funny I wasn't aware you'd gone out with her,' Tina mused.

'It was very brief. I wanted to say . . .' I tried to judge the tone right – gentle concern with a smidgen of mortification. 'How sorry I am that she died.'

Tina blinked slowly; possibly she moved her head but so slightly I wasn't sure. 'It's awful, I know.'

'Was she ill?'

'Andrew doesn't like to talk about it. It's a bit of a taboo subject.'

'An accident?'

'Yes, I suppose it was: a terrible accident.' We had reached the drive up to the house and she changed gears sharply, indicating and checking her mirrors. I opened my mouth to ask more, but there was a look in her eye as if she might be about to cry.

I said: 'I'm sorry.'

I didn't want to upset her. There were other ways I could find out.

Chapter Twelve

The house was sun-baked; the walls trembled in the heat. A black swimsuit hung, bat-like, from a limb of the olive tree; a plastic bottle of Ambre Solaire stood upright by the leg of a chair: otherwise there was no sign of habitation. It was silent – the builders had stopped. The empty terrace dazzled.

Tina put the towels to dry and sat outside at the table while I tooled around in the kitchen, making us a pot of tea with the Red Label sachets I found in the cupboard. Several flies droned, spiralling in head-height patterns. The breakfast plates lay unwashed in the sink: a smear of butter, a crescent of crust. Someone had left a scrunch of money on the counter – a few coins loosely wrapped up in a five-euro note. Andrew's trunks only had a flimsy pocket so I slipped both the note and the coins into the cigarette packet I had rolled, James Dean-style, into the shoulder of my T-shirt.

I carried the tea out on a tray. 'Ah, lovely,' Tina said. 'Will you be mother?' and then, after I had poured and she had taken her first sip, 'I needed this. Isn't it funny how a hot drink can be so refreshing!'

I think about Tina quite a lot these days. She was a warm, interesting woman; wrong for Andrew. She could have been anything if she had followed her own instincts, if she had wriggled out from under the yoke of his control. I always liked her. Perhaps things would have turned out differently for me if I'd married a woman like her.

At that moment, she released her hair from the linen scarf that tied it back. It bounced free, springing in an auburn halo around her face. She ruffled her fingers in it and then raked it behind her ears, with an apologetic laugh.

'You should grow it long,' I said, smiling at her. For a moment, I let myself imagine her naked body rising above me, her hazel eyes half closed, the full breasts she liked to hide tumbling free.

She blushed, as if she could read my thoughts. 'Andrew likes it shorter,' she murmured. 'Easier to keep neat. And at my age . . .'

'What age?' I said, as charmingly as I could.

'Oh don't flirt, Paul. I gave that all up when I went through menopause.'

I raised my eyebrows.

'It was an *early* menopause,' she said, with a small smile. 'I'm vain enough to tell you that.'

I smiled back and, when a few moments had settled, asked after her painting. Was it something she wanted to do more of? She looked thoughtful: 'I don't really have the talent.'

'Those pictures in your kitchen – they're wonderful,' I lied.

'I used to have more time,' she said, 'when I was younger, before the kids . . .'

We talked about her various jobs then: how she had left the City for a better work/life balance, how she had struggled with the pressures of bringing up children, of being a good enough parent. She worried about them both – of course she did. The shop was a wonderful compromise and had brought her fulfil-ment. She loved a new delivery of yarn, took an almost sensual delight in organising the balls by colour or texture, how balancing the accounts was an oddly satisfying task, how a grateful customer made a hard day worthwhile.

I was enjoying listening to her, touched by the obvious pleasure she felt in her work, finding I was actually interested in what she had to say; questions sprung from me unbidden! Did she advertise? How did she attract custom?

'Word of mouth.'

'Does it work?'

'Usually, and when it doesn't, we lasso them with balls of cashmerino aran and drag them in off the street,' she replied.

Who was looking after the business in her absence? She stuck a sign in the window announcing annual holiday. No, she wouldn't necessarily lose customers, wool being a seasonal purchase. 'People knit in winter,' she said, 'and play tennis in summer.'

I laughed. 'I think you move in different circles to me.'

She looked at me, once again almost fondly. 'I expect I do.'

Now I'd brought it all to the front of her mind, she began to think out loud about the things she should be doing: re-orders to make, website designers to chase, course dates to finalise. This year, they'd be offering Starting to Knit, Beginners' Crochet and Learning Fair Isle. 'In fact,' she gulped back her tea and brought her hands together in a determined little clap, 'I might get on with some emails while it's quiet.'

She went into the house, leaving me alone. The bags from the car were still on the ground where she had dumped them and I rummaged until I found my phone. Signal was terrible on the terrace and I walked round to the front yard. It was strongest, three bars, over on the far side, and I leant against the door of one of the outbuildings, to write the text to Alex I'd been composing in my head since the car.

It was a little awkward. I'd only seen him once since he'd got back from New York. He and his boyfriend Zach had invited me to supper and the experience had been traumatic. Alex cooked a spelt barley risotto with kale, surprisingly delicious, and they were full of Alex's new job at the LSO, Zach's latest Bikram yoga business, their plans to redecorate the bathroom. I'd hoped their return was temporary; I realised, sitting on the sofa like a guest, Persephone kneading my knee, that I was wrong.

Alex had suggested a coffee soon after that, and then later a trip to a concert. I hadn't made the time for either. Looking back, I suspect that as a flat-sit was no longer an option, I'd lost interest in the friendship. But Alex was my only link to a certain aspect of my past. I sent him this text: *Hello. Sorry I haven't been in touch – madly busy with work. Couple of ?s. 1st off, do you remember Andrew Hopkins's sister – Florrie? Two years below us? Did you know she was dead?*

It whooshed off. I waited for a while. No reply. I peered, for something to do, through the filthy window that took up the top panels of the double doors. Beyond it, a crochet pattern of spider webs, the hulking form of a vehicle. Hermes. I considered this for a moment, then turned the handle, expecting it to be rusted stiff, but it turned smoothly.

I stepped in. The door, on a vicious spring, snapped shut. Inside was a smell of grease and hot plastic and rotting earth. It was gloomy; a grimy strip of glass near the roof let in a grey light. Against the far wall, a row of shelves held ancient bags of unmixed concrete, battered pots of paint, a few dirt-smeared plastic containers. The truck itself, a white Toyota, was an ugly rusty thing. I couldn't think why Alice was bothered with it. It looked ashamed of itself with its face to the wall, hidden away. I wondered how long it had been since anyone had sat in it. Years, probably.

Now I was here, a small thought wormed itself into my mind. Perhaps it was a simple thing that was wrong; to do with water, or oil. I had seen my father change those often enough on his old Morris Marina. The unscrew, the glug, the re-screw. The dip, the wipe, the re-dip. A fantasy grew: my macho credentials re-established; Alice's arm-flinging delight; grudging respect from the others.

To reach the bonnet I would have to go further into the shed. There wasn't much room between the vehicle and the wall, just enough for a person to squeeze through, but the walls were black with dust and I wouldn't be able to get by without getting dirty. I paused, fastidiously averse. And then my phone buzzed: a text from Alex.

Hello stranger. Course I remember Florrie. Poor girl. One of your conquests, wasn't she? Friend of Gillian's. Surprised you didn't know. Tragic.

I typed quickly: *How?*

This time his reply was immediate: *Suicide. Overdose I think.*

I leant back against the wall, felt the grit of the concrete against my head. An overdose. Suicide. Leukaemia or a car accident: these were the horrors I'd been imagining. Yet, in my mind, they hadn't really been horrors at all. I'd incorporated the thought of them into the narrative of her life without real upset. But suicide was different. I couldn't avoid the thought of Florrie in this – Florrie's thoughts and feelings, her state of mind, her problems at work, whatever had gone on in the life she had led.

Shit, I typed. *Wish I'd known.*

Of course, I knew why I hadn't known. I wasn't in touch with anyone who might have told me apart from Alex, and he had been abroad so much of the time. Gillian – she was a friend of mine too. She and Alex and I had lived together in our second year, but I'd lost touch, just as I'd lost touch with most people – unless, like Alex, they were of use to me. It was what I did. It was how I was. But the success of my novel, first the flurry of the bidding war and then my brief period of so-called fame, when there were literary festivals and award ceremonies and photo shoots ('Ten Young Writers to Look Out For') . . . it had all encouraged that aspect of me. Why trudge to Peckham to see Gillian when I could be having cocktails in Bibendum with the arts editor of the *Sunday Times*?

Standing in that dark shed, I had a moment of regret. My finger hovered over the ring icon. It would be nice to speak to Alex, just for a chat. Find out how the LSO was treating him. Ask after Persephone. I stopped myself: God knows how expensive a call would be. Instead, I quickly padded out another text: *Thanks.* I put the phone back in my pocket.

I had lost interest in the van now so I left the shed and walked back round to the terrace. I poked around the house a bit – abandoned bedrooms, clothes and headphones scattered. Only the teenage boys used the sitting room, and there were mugs abandoned on the floor, a glass on its side, a curl of corrugated paper from inside a packet of biscuits.

A door from the sitting room opened into Tina and Andrew's bedroom. It had been left ajar and, as it was so quiet in there, I peered in. Tina was asleep on top of the bed, laptop nudged to the side. One arm was thrown above her head revealing the dark crease of her armpit, her dress twisted tight across one breast.

I left the house quietly, grabbed a drying towel, and took the path down to the pool.

Artan was standing at the deep end with a long pole in his hand, scooping insects out of the water. Light flickered on to his face. His cheekbones threw shadows. I felt a moment of shock, seeing him. How long had he been there? How quiet he was. I greeted him and he put his hand up, fingers spread. 'Five more minutes,' he said.

'It's OK,' I said. 'No hurry.'

But I felt self-conscious now. How could I lounge, recumbent, as he toiled? So I left my towel on a chair, as if that had been my intention, and wandered into the scrubby wooded area just beyond the pool: eucalyptus and pine, saplings mainly, tiny dry leaves under foot. Sun splintered the shadows. I was at the edge of the property – beyond the copse was the field where the construction had begun.

A low white wall, half collapsed, marked the boundary and I decided, to give Artan time to finish, to do a loop, walk through the field, over the gate and back up the drive. I took a couple of steps forward and tripped. I looked down and saw the raised lip of an old well, too small to fall into, and thick with leaves, but I had hit the bony bit of my ankle and I had to rub it hard to stop it hurting.

The walk round was pleasant: the air still hot but the sun much less intense. Bees hummed in long-stalked yellow flowers. A thousand cicada clocks ticked. In the distance, a row of tall thin cypress trees, emblems of death, formed quills of dark green against the landscape.

The diggers had their noses in the ground as if grazing. No sound from the guard dog, though I was careful to keep to the edge of Alice's property and to tread as quietly as I could. From the gate, I could just make out, under a temporary tin hut, a black and tan shadow, prone, legs and tail flopped to one side. Smaller than I'd imagined from the depth of the bark, and painfully thin – you could see the curve of its ribs. 'Poor mutt,' I murmured as I climbed gingerly over the gate. The bar rattled as my weight sprang free, and the dog was immediately on its feet, rushing forwards, yanking on its chain. It began to bark and didn't stop. I heard it all the way up to the house.

★　★　★

I was asleep on a bed down at the pool and then suddenly I was awake.

The air was musky, and full of bugs. The sun had long slipped behind the hill. The pool was navy-black.

Up on the terrace I knew something was wrong. They were all back. Andrew and Tina were standing looking awkward and Alice was sitting between them on a chair, her face pale, her lips almost bloodless. Her dress was damp in places where her swimsuit underneath was wet.

'Oh God, are you all right?' I said, the moment I saw her face. 'Are you ill?'

I stepped forwards but Andrew put out his arm to stop me. 'She's fine,' he said. 'We've got it under control.'

'What?'

Andrew said: 'It's nothing. She's had a bit of a shock, that's all.' He spoke slowly, his voice calm. Someone was being patronised – and I thought it was me, but then wondered if it might be Alice. There was a tension in the air between him and Tina, as if they were scared of her, or worried about breaking her. Each word, each action, was being carefully chosen. Andrew turned and put his hand on Alice's shoulder. 'Take a few deep breaths,' he said. 'There. Come on. It's important that you're calm.'

'I know.' She patted Andrew's hand and kept it there.

'Poor Alice,' Tina said. She was standing by the kitchen door. The light was on behind her and mosquitoes buzzed above her head. 'I'm going to make some tea,' she said. 'I think we could all do with some.'

As she turned, Alice shifted her head a fraction and kissed Andrew's hand. Tina didn't see. But I did, and I didn't like it. I wanted to punch Andrew. Instead, I managed to say, 'Can you tell me what's happened?'

Andrew moved his hand away and took a step back.

'Alice saw somebody,' he said. 'Someone who looked like Jasmine.'

'We both did,' Alice said, twisting her head up at him. 'Didn't we? This time we both saw her.'

'Yes.'

Alice tipped back in her chair, tightly gripping the edge of the table. 'In the little supermarket. It was packed. And there was this guy behaving oddly – wasn't he?'

Andrew nodded.

'He kept going up and down the aisles and then going out of the shop and coming in. I was just curious. I left Andrew in the queue and went outside to see what he was doing, and there was this car there – what was it?'

'A Peugeot 205, pale blue. A hatchback, two-door.'

'It was pulled up outside, waiting for the man, with its engine running. He was running out of the shop and throwing the food he'd stolen through the window. And there was a girl in the driver's seat. I saw her. She . . . she was just there.'

She tipped her chair forwards again.

'Did you speak to her?'

'I went up to the car and I tried to talk to her through the window. I was calm, wasn't I? Andrew? I was calm, wouldn't you say? I was calm.'

Andrew nodded.

'I asked her what her name was, but she wouldn't answer. She put her hand on the car horn and the man came charging out, barged me out of the way, and then they just took off.'

'They probably thought you were about to call the police,' I said.

'Because I knew who she was.'

'Because of the shoplifting.'

'No, Paul. Not because of that.'

She looked at me, her eyes troubled. I didn't know what to think. Perhaps she had seen Jasmine. Perhaps she hadn't. But no one could argue with how much she wanted to find her. I felt an intense tug of tenderness, and with it an overwhelming desire to unbutton her damp dress, peel off the wet swimming costume underneath and take her to bed.

'What?' she said. 'What are you thinking?'

'Nothing. Did you get the number plate?'

'Yes.'

'Then you should ring the police.'

'I'm not sure . . .'

'Gavras doesn't always take Alice's sightings seriously,' Andrew said.

'But he could find out who the car belongs to.'

He shook his head. 'Pointless. It's bound to be stolen, or unregistered. They looked like they lived rough, to be honest. You know, druggy, hippy types.'

'Hippy types?' I turned to Alice. 'Didn't you tell me there was a big hippy commune on the island? Didn't you say you thought Jasmine might be there?'

'Yes,' she said doubtfully.

'Well, maybe we should go and look.'

'It's quite a way.'

'I know, but if there is a chance . . .?'

Of course the woman wasn't Jasmine, but this was what I needed, a day alone with her. I wanted to get her away from Andrew. We could bond. I could talk to her about Louis, *help* her do what was right, make her fucking mine. 'Why don't we go tomorrow, you and me, and ask around?'

Alice pressed her fingers to her forehead. 'Show me the photograph again, Andrew.'

'You got a photograph?' I said. 'Can I see it?'

Andrew fiddled with his phone, and passed it to me. I sat down at the table to study it. The picture was poor quality. It was shot through the windscreen so the face was blurred, but I knew immediately it wasn't Jasmine. She looked too old for one thing. This woman was in her late twenties with a long oval face, and two curtains of mousy blonde hair; a black stud in the side of her nose and another in her chin, below her lip. Thin arms stretched to hold the steering wheel, a dark cavernous gap between her armpit and her vest top. I stretched my fingers across the screen to zoom in on her face. There was a look about her – not of the photofit older Jasmine, but of the thirteen-year-old wearing the flowery bandana in the family snap, the same defiance, the same twist of vulnerability. It must have been that that Alice had recognised.

'See?' Alice said. 'See?'

'Yes. I see,' I said. 'This is useful. We can take it with us tomorrow.'

I flicked my finger across the iPhone's screen. The next photo was also of the girl, but of the back of her head; the next a close-up of the car's wing, at an angle; the next, the rear view of the car as it disappeared up the road. I flipped backwards, the way I had just come: car's wing, back of head, blurred girl. I did a further flick with my finger. The previous photograph was not of the girl at the supermarket, or the car. The previous photograph was of me.

I looked more closely. It had been taken earlier that day on the beach. I was standing on shingle, tall trees visible just to the right, the sea in front, and in front of me the others were getting the boats back into the water. But my eyes were on Daisy, at the bright pink triangle of her bikini bottoms, as she bent over.

Lord, I'd been caught.

'Thanks,' Andrew said suddenly, at my shoulder. 'I'll have that back, if that's all right.'

And luckily, before Alice could see, he took the phone out of my hands.

It was a tense supper. Alice and Tina were quiet, Andrew hectoring, and the children, fractious. Phoebe, furious at not going to the club, picked a fight with Louis about his table manners. Archie made a mildly negative comment about the spaghetti bolognese and Andrew suddenly exploded with anger, leaping to his feet and violently yanking his son out of his chair. 'Go to your room and stay there,' he hissed.

'Calm down,' Tina said carefully.

'He's got to learn.'

'Now is not the time.'

'I was trying to help.'

I was grateful when it was time to clear away and made a big point of doing it myself. 'Everybody stay where they are. My turn.'

'You're kind. Thank you,' Alice said. 'I don't think I have the energy.'

At the kitchen sink, I could hear snippets of conversation: chopped phrases. They were still at it. Alice's voice now, almost tearful: 'It's different this time, Tina.'

'I know. Be careful . . . I'm thinking about your own health.'

Tina brought some more glasses in.

'She's done this before, I gather,' I said.

'Yes. Poor Alice. It's hard to know how to deal with it. And each time, of course, she might be right, so . . .'

She grabbed a tea towel, but I took it off her. 'Leave the drying-up,' I said. 'I'll do it.'

When I came out, Alice was nowhere to be seen. The teenagers were playing cards on my fag seat. Only Tina and Andrew were still at the table, nursing their wine glasses, talking quietly. They stopped when they saw me. In the distance the dog barked.

'Everything all right?' I said.

'Yup. Humid tonight, though, isn't it?' Andrew replied.

'And that bloody dog.' He stood up, teeth clenched. 'I CAN'T BEAR IT.'

'Do you know where Alice is?' I asked Tina.

'I think she's gone to bed.'

She was lying face down, still in her clothes, tearful, and compliant. I'd played the evening well, it turned out – washing up, keeping out of arguments. Sometimes, it transpires, a low profile is all you need. I pulled her round to face me, kissed the salt from her face. She didn't demur as I wrinkled her dress over her head, rolled her Speedo down across her breasts, laid my mouth along the line of her tan.

Her arms were above her head, her face turned into the pillow. 'Tina thinks I'm mistaken, I know she does. Maybe we shouldn't go to Epitara. Maybe it's just foolish.'

I lifted my mouth. 'It's worth investigating,' I said. 'And you promised Yvonne that you'd do everything in your power to find her. Just imagine if the woman *did* turn out to be Jasmine – how amazing that would be.'

She moved her hands to my head, cupping it, drawing me up so she could look with a peculiar intensity into my eyes. 'Andrew says he'll come with me. Why are you so keen?'

'If it is Jasmine I want to be there when you find her.'

She half smiled. 'Why?'

'Because I care about you more than I understand.'

She looked at me for a long moment and then said, 'I wish you were one thing or the other.'

'None of us are that,' I said. I brought my mouth up to stop her from talking and miraculously it worked.

★   ★   ★

I woke again in the early hours. The dog again, pitiful, but barking over and over: an unbearable sound, hacking the night into pieces. Mosquito bites, like a crawling under my skin. I thought I had heard a noise; Alice moving about the room, but I checked and she was asleep next to me, a bundle of heat, and hair.

Chapter Thirteen

I woke before Alice, had a quick shower, trying not to wake her, and dressed in long trousers and button-down shirt: the kind of clothes I felt were appropriate for driving to a village on the other side of the island to confront a shoplifting hippy.

Alice slept on, her hair damp across the pillow, her mouth slightly open.

Outside, in the heat, the construction workers were back with their churning and drilling. Various teenagers had stirred. Phoebe was sitting on the top step of the path, wearing a cotton sarong and chewing on a hunk of bread. At her feet, ants were collecting, slowly tugging at crumbs. In the kitchen, Frank was flapping hysterically at a large orange insect with a tea towel, while Louis was holding open the fridge door and staring in. He was a better colour today, though he might have been spottier. Hard to tell. I watched him take out a jar of peanut butter and unscrew the lid; he was about to dip in his finger when he saw me, and turned away, flushing red, to find a spoon. He was just a boy when it came down to it. Awkward and troubled, raging with embarrassment. Alice's son. Not a rapist.

When I came out on to the terrace with a cup of coffee, Alice was standing by her bedroom door, talking to Andrew. She was dressed now, in a summer dress, high espadrilles and a floppy straw hat; he was barefoot, in a short towelling dressing gown. I heard her say, 'No, he's adamant.' Her face changed when she saw me. 'Here he is now. You want to come, don't you, Paul? Andrew is offering, but I was just telling him he wasn't needed.'

I put the coffee cup down on the table with a decisive clink. 'I'm your man,' I said.

Andrew walked towards me, shoulders back, chest braced. His chin was bristly this morning, but patchily, like an old man's. 'I'm not happy about her doing all the driving,' he said, through gritted teeth.

Alice had turned away to talk to Phoebe. 'She's not a child,' I said.

His mouth came close; his breath was stale and smelt faintly of chicory: 'She's in a delicate state.'

Behind my back, my fists clenched.

'I tell you what,' I said, 'give me the paperwork and I'll ring the hire company. I'm sure they'll add me to the insurance.'

A pause in the churning of machinery; the air suddenly sweet.

Alice looked up. 'How clever,' she said.

Andrew looked like he was going to be sick.

'Panic over,' I said agreeably.

A delay, then, for Andrew to find the right phone numbers, and for me to wander out to the front to where I had a signal in order to deliver my driving licence number and payment details to an operative I pretended to call, but didn't.

It was a two-hour drive on poor roads. We passed through a few scattered villages, where old men played dice under trees, but then began to climb steadily uphill, the scenery becoming barer, less cultivated, with bare rocky outcrops, sudden lurches of green below. We played the compilation tape – Pulp and Oasis and The Beautiful South – singing along sporadically. I pressed the button to roll down the windows.

'Andrew's obsessed with keeping them closed for the air-con,' she said, turning her face to catch the hot breeze. Her hair fanned away from her face. 'But this is nice.'

I nodded in time to the music.

It was a big car with bad rear visibility and I needed to concentrate, particularly on the mountain pass, which had sudden hairpin bends and dizzyingly vertiginous drops. At one point a lorry hurtled towards us out of nowhere, and I braked so suddenly Alice shot forward in her seat. 'Sorry,' I said. 'I don't want to kill us.'

'I don't want you to kill us either.'

She was calmer today, in a much better mood than she had been; hopeful, relieved to be in control again, I suppose. I felt a sense of affection from her, and wondered if I had passed some sort of test. I had planned to talk about Louis but I changed my mind now we were alone. I was desperate to please her. She seemed already to be accepting the possible disappointment of the trip. 'You're probably just humouring me,' she said at one point. 'You all are. It's only that I am so desperate for an answer, for Yvonne to have closure. Otherwise, she'll never be able to move forward with her life. The thought of picking her up from the airport tomorrow with *nothing*, seeing the emptiness in her face.'

'Tell me about the night Jasmine went missing,' I said. 'If you can bear to.'

She grimaced. 'It was horrible. Just awful. We'd only arrived that day. Tina and Andrew had organised the trip. They'd done everything, taken me under their wing, were doing their best. But Harry had been dead two months and I was a mess. Sorry—' She shook her head. 'I'm talking about myself. This shouldn't be about me.'

'No. Go on. I'd like to hear it.'

She sighed. 'Grief can feel like panic. You need people around you, but when you're with them you can feel this overwhelming urge to get away, to be alone. I'm telling you this because it's tied in somehow. I was all over the place. It was a difficult evening. We had dumped the bags and come down to Giorgio's for supper. We were drinking too much – well, not Tina. She kept it together and took the kids home; they were little then. Andrew and I had got into conversation with a French couple who were sitting on the next table. Then you burst in—' She gave me a look.

'Ah. Yes.'

'You were much drunker than us, shouting and singing, and being generally objectionable.'

'We were all in the middle of our own private dramas that night,' I said.

'Andrew got rid of you but it all became too much for me. I had to get away from everyone, be on my own, so I left, leaving Andrew to it. But I got halfway home and realised I'd forgotten my cardigan on the back of the chair, so I drove back and ended up having another drink with Andrew and the French couple. It wasn't much later that Yvonne arrived in the street, shouting that she'd lost her daughter. All these Greeks and other tourists were clustering round, but none of them spoke English, which is why I became involved. I was trying so hard to calm her, telling her everything would be OK. And then the police came and search parties were sent out . . .'

She broke off.

'You did everything you could,' I said after a while.

'I didn't. We didn't *find* her. She had just vanished into thin air. She'd stormed out of their apartment after a fight with Karl – he'd told her she couldn't go out dressed as she was. Yvonne had been in the shower during the row but as soon as she heard what had happened, she was out looking for her, determined to bring her home. They were staying in an apartment block, where Delfinos is now, and they'd gone along the beach, up the road, down to the port, to the club, searched the bars. They'd looked *everywhere*. That horrible feeling – I once lost Phoebe in a department store, when she was a toddler, and there is this moment when rationality is taken over by panic, and you don't know what to do with yourself.'

'Presumably the police thought she'd gone off with the boyfriend you mentioned and would be back in the morning?'

'Yes. But no boyfriend ever came forward and Jasmine was never seen again.'

I said: 'Well, you never know, we might find her today.'

She turned her head away from me to look out of the window. 'Yes.'

The road began to flatten out after that. Alice seemed keen to change the subject. She asked me why I didn't like Andrew. I looked straight ahead and told her that I felt he had designs on her body. She laughed.

'Am I wrong?' I said, trying to sound cool and unemotional. 'I feel like there's something between you.'

'Are you jealous?'

'Yes. I suppose I am.'

'Well, that's just daft.'

She flicked at my shoulder with her finger, then looked out of the window. I felt awkward, exposed, and to cover it I told her how much I liked Tina. 'Yes, she's perfection, isn't she?' She asked me how I 'found' the Hopkins children, a question I rose to magnificently, telling her that *her* kids were so much more alive and interesting, that Archie was insipid, and that Phoebe's charm and beauty put Daisy's in the shade.

'And yet Daisy does so much better academically . . .' she said leadingly.

'It's emotional intelligence that counts,' I said.

'Yes,' she said with satisfaction. 'And Daisy can be a little pert sometimes.'

'She can be quite over-confident.'

Out of the corner of my eye, I noticed her smile. It always surprises me how competitive parents are, how they love to hear even their friends' children *put down*.

'Listen, about Louis,' I said, thinking it was a good moment.

'What about Louis?'

'The other night. I saw you bring him back in the car. He was back later than you told the police.'

She laughed. 'Poor Louis. He was paralytic. I promised him I wouldn't tell anyone. If the girls found out, they'd make his life a misery. But that was early – don't you remember? We woke you up; the girls were still out.'

'I thought the girls were back . . . I thought they were . . .' I stopped. I couldn't admit to knowing they were back, because that would mean admitting to spying on them in the pool. 'Oh yes,' I said.

A tiny pause and then she added: 'It's interesting what you just said about emotional intelligence. Florrie was always cleverer than me at school. That's why she went to Cambridge and I went to Bristol. But she was very impractical. She had no sense of direction, or spatial awareness. I was always having to lend her things, or help her look in lost property. She found it harder to make friends.'

I felt myself tense. I had remembered a few more details about Florrie. She'd written me a letter. I couldn't remember the contents. I'd only skimmed it, before throwing it in the bin. 'Poor Florrie,' I said. 'She was very sensitive if I remember.'

'Yes.'

'She never married or had children?'

Alice looked at me and away again. She frowned. 'No.'

'Did she have a job when she died?'

'No, she had moved back home.'

'That's sad,' I said, thinking, *fuck, it's me. No wife, no kids, no job, living with your old mother* ... 'I'm sorry. Suicide is a terrible thing for the people who are left behind.'

'It is. I know.'

She looked out of the window, quiet now. I tried to think of something more cheerful to talk about, though it seemed insensitive to move away from Florrie completely. 'Did you go to a birthday party she had?' I said, after a few moments' thought. 'It was in the Fellows' Garden.'

'I did.'

I glanced at her. 'Maybe we met.'

'We *did*.'

The tyres hit a patch of rough gravel, and I looked back at the road. 'Surely I should remember.'

'One thing I have learnt about you, Paul Morris,' she said – not without affection – 'is you only remember what you want to.'

Epitara was on the west coast; it was windier there and the sea was different – waves broke a distance from the shore and rolled in. The sand was a darker yellow, almost grey.

A scrappy, spread-out village, it consisted of a run of buildings and tavernas set back behind a long scrubby beach. The place had an itinerant feel, with signs everywhere advertising 'Rooms, Chambres, Zimmer'. One end of the beach, closest to where the main road came in, was dedicated to conventional tourism, with rows of fold-up sunbeds and tatty yellow umbrellas, but at the other, a makeshift campsite had been erected – mismatched tents, rubbish bins spilling their contents and a couple of vans with awnings under a group of trees. It felt hot and grubby. Toddlers played in the water, and brown naked bodies sprawled here and there like basking seals. A few of the women had laid out towels and were selling jewellery and hair-braids.

We parked in a small car park off the main road, and headed for a taverna where Alice said she knew the owner, an English woman who'd lived on Pyros since the 1980s. She walked round the back to see if she could find her and I sat on a narrow shady porch overlooking the beach and ordered coffees from a young waiter with sleeked back black hair and a neat moustache. It was windy – the plastic tablecloth kept flapping out of its metal clips.

Alice came through a door with a blonde woman in her fifties. 'Paul – this is Niki Stenhouse,' she said. 'She used to live in Agios Stefanos – she was a rep with CV Travel when we first met her – but then she married Theo and they moved down here to run his family business.'

I stood up to shake the woman's hand, appraising her: a combination of Sloane and hippy – a sensible bob and shirt dress, but also big dangly earrings, jangly bracelets and a necklace made of shells. Her face was wrinkled, and over-tanned, but there was a looseness in her movements, in the way she stood with her legs apart, that suggested she might be rather good in bed.

'Well done for coming all this way,' she said, her voice more Home Counties than I was expecting. She was still holding my hand and looking intently into my face. 'I know Alice is grateful.'

'Niki thinks she knows the girl I saw,' Alice said. 'But she says she's newish here – only arrived this summer.'

Niki dropped my hand, and looked at Alice. 'I have to say I had assumed she was German,' she said.

'But you don't know that.'

'It's only that she's shacked up with Gunter – he's been here a while. The car isn't his. It was dumped last summer and one of the longer-term residents spent the winter doing it up. They share it down there, I think.'

'Drink your coffee,' Alice said to me. She hadn't sat down. 'They're living in the last camper van, so I think we should go.'

I downed the dregs and stood up, swaying my hips while clicking my fingers to show I was galvanised. It set slightly the wrong tone, a little too frivolous. Sometimes I forgot myself.

A smell, of pot and paraffin, of cooking oil and burnt cinders, became stronger the closer we got to the camp. A woman with white dreadlocks and a Mancunian accent came off the beach to ask Alice if she would like a foot massage. 'No thank you,' she said, staring ahead. She was tense, out of her comfort zone.

The last camper van was less retro and more of a mobile home, square and white, with an extending roof and three plastic chairs arranged around a table outside. Balls of screwed-up paper-towel were scattered around a grill on the ground. A couple of thin cats lay sprawled next to the wheels.

It was sheltered, less windy here. There was a heady smell of rotting vegetation and dope.

A door at the front was open but Alice knocked anyway. 'Hello,' she called. 'Anyone in?'

The van rocked slightly, the sound of footsteps, and a woman came to the door and peered out. She was wearing a clinging faded brown T-shirt dress, no sleeves, no bra. Hairy legs and armpits. Her hair was pulled back in a long plait, and there were two black studs on her face – one in the side of her nose, one in the middle of her chin. She was probably the woman from Andrew's photograph, but I wasn't sure.

'Hi,' she said.

Alice stared at her. She swallowed hard. 'Jasmine?'

The woman took a step back. Her face closed and her mouth tipped down at the corners. 'What you want?' she said.

Alice put her hands out. 'I'm here to help you,' she said under her breath. 'Do you know who you are? Do you know your name?'

The woman laughed. 'I don't need your help. None of your business,' she said, 'what my name is.'

Her accent wasn't English and, close up, I could see faint traces of lines on her forehead, and at the sides of her mouth. I was right. She was older than twenty-three, maybe even in her early thirties.

'I saw you at the supermarket,' Alice said. 'Across the island. In Stefanos.'

The woman put her hand on the door and pushed it hard. It began to close.

Alice let out a small groan and I saw a chance to show my mettle, to demonstrate my commitment, and I stepped quickly forwards, getting to the door just in time and slamming my palm hard against it. It was propelled backwards, and the woman let out a cry.

She was on the floor, holding her forehead. Blood was dripping from her nose.

'Oh God,' Alice cried. 'Is she all right?'

I bent down, tried to touch her, put my arm out to reassure her, but the woman pulled away from me, disgust and fear on her face. She was screaming now, obscenities in English and another language – possibly German, possibly Dutch – kicking out at me.

A man came running up from the beach, tall and rangy, bare-chested, in nothing but shorts; knees slightly bent and feet splayed, to get purchase on the sand. 'Greta,' he shouted, speeding up when he reached the van. He began to pummel me with his fists. 'What the fuck you doing?'

I put my hands up, tried to push him off.

'I'm sorry. I'm sorry!' Alice shouted. 'It was an accident. He didn't mean to. It was the door. We just wanted to ask some questions.'

'I didn't mean to hurt her,' I said.

The woman – Greta – got to her feet, pulling her dress down. She grabbed a tea towel and held it to her nose. 'You crazy?' she said.

'I'm not crazy,' I said. I put my hands out, a gesture of peace, and took another couple of steps forward. 'We're just looking for an English woman called Jasmine. We thought it might have been you. We just wanted to talk. I'm sorry. I'm sorry.'

The man shoved past me and climbed into the van. He put his arm around the woman's shoulders, moving the towel to inspect her nose. 'I get the police on you. You animal.'

'No you won't,' Alice said calmly. 'Because you are thieves.'

'No Jasmine here,' he said. 'Leave us.'

Alice had begun to walk away, but I had one last chance to impress her. Remembering a detail I had read on the poster in Elconda, I darted back up the step. 'Can I see your shoulder?' I asked. 'Do you have a scar there? The Jasmine we're looking for has a scar.'

The woman simply stared at me. Without really thinking about it, I began to extend my hand towards the neck of her dress. Even as I was doing so, I felt two firm arms grab me around the chest and the man in the shorts hurled me sideways out of the van. I reached out to break my fall and took the skin off my palm.

'Crazy man,' the woman said as the door slammed.

A police car was parked outside the house when we got home.

Alice, her hand on my thigh, had fallen asleep against the window. I'd been as careful as possible not to jolt her, slowing right down on the bends, and avoiding the rougher patches of road. She'd woken as we'd bumped up the last section of track and I'd been about to capitalise on the closeness I felt between us by suggesting we went out for dinner alone. But she was out of the car before I could say anything.

I followed her round to the terrace where Gavras was sitting at the table between Andrew and Tina. The two girls were there, too, in their swimming costumes, their feet up on the seat of their chairs, fiddling with their toenails. No sign of the boys, though a sound of Xbox combat, of muffled explosions, was audible from the house.

'Don't get up,' Alice said.

'Mrs Mackenzie.' He had got up anyway, with a half-bow. He was wearing a dark grey shirt today, the sleeves rolled up to the elbow. 'I hear you have been for a nice drive.'

'Yes. We went to visit an old friend in Epitara . . . I . . . We . . .' She was faltering. I knew why: it was embarrassment at having embarked on another wild-goose chase, of having once again been wrong.

I stepped forwards, shielding her with my body. 'Alice was kind enough to show me some of the island.' I stretched out my hand. 'Paul. Paul Morris. I am not sure we've met.'

He raised an eyebrow as he shook it. 'You look familiar.'

'I was in the hotel yesterday,' I said.

'Ah.' He nodded, craning his head to see Alice. 'Which brings me to why I am here. Mrs Mackenzie, you were kind enough to mention that members of your party were at the club on the night of the rape. I am following it up. I have just been asking Phoebe and Daisy for anything they recollect.'

Alice was doing that thing at the back of her hair – nervously running her fingers along certain strands. 'Yes. Yes,' she said. 'Was there anything useful?'

Andrew was tapping his BlackBerry into his palm. 'Nothing much,' he said.

Phoebe yawned. 'We left too early. But we did say there was no way that boy Sam did it.'

'But you should ask Louis,' Daisy added. 'He talked to him, I think.'

Gavras gave an impatient flap of his hand. 'The boy you mention has been released. He has an alibi, his sister who came to take him home. So – a misunderstanding. And this Louis . . .?'

'Phoebe's brother.'

'Oh.' Gavras looked suddenly more alert. 'He was at the club? The night of the rape?'

Alice looked quickly towards the house, where gun battle continued, and back. Before she could speak, Andrew said: 'Louis left even earlier than the girls. I'm happy to disengage him from his video game for you to ask him more, but there's little point. We only let him go for a drink at the beginning of the evening and we brought him home long before midnight.' He laughed and lowered his voice. 'He's only sixteen. Don't think he got much out of it. Spent most of his time playing Candy Crush on his phone in the corner.'

I looked from Andrew to Alice and back. She had flushed slightly. Was she happy that Andrew was persisting with the lie? Did it matter? If Louis had been that drunk he wasn't exactly a useful witness. Or a likely suspect for that matter. But still. It would have been better to have told the truth.

'I see,' Gavras said. 'In that case let us not disturb the boy from his killing machine.'

Everyone laughed, except me.

'How is she doing?' I said.

Gavras looked at me, confused. 'Who?'

'Laura, the girl who was attacked. Is she OK?'

He narrowed his eyes. 'Are you familiar with Laura Cratchet? Is she a friend of yours?'

'No. I just overheard her name, that's all.'

'How kind of you, Mr Morris, to show concern.'

Andrew smiled. 'Our guest is always attentive to detail when it comes to young ladies.'

Gavras bowed his head. 'She is receiving the best possible care and is assisting us as much as she can. Mr Morris – were you at the club the night she was attacked?'

'No.' I shook my head, laughing. 'I'm far too old.'

'I see,' he said again.

'What do you mean, "assisting"?' Alice said. 'Did she see her attacker?'

'No she did not.'

'Do you think it was planned?' Andrew asked. 'Or heat of the moment?'

'It is impossible for me to say.'

I said: 'Did the girl get any sense of how old her attacker was?'

Gavras looked at me. 'Enough questions.' He made a rotating movement with his shoulders, stretching out the muscles. 'None of you must worry. He will not get away.'

There was to be no intimate dinner *à deux* after that. Tina made another pasta dish – this one with tinned tuna, seriously worse than anything I ever ate at college. It was supposed to have olives in it, but Alice had bought the wrong sort at the supermarket – uncured, raw and hard as bullets. 'Never mind,' she said, closing up the jar. 'We'll find some use for them.'

We all sat down together on the terrace. The atmosphere was tense. I was sure Andrew and Tina had rowed again, and Alice was in a state about the imminent arrival of Yvonne and Karl. I was troubled by Louis. I studied him across the table, a great lumpen man-child, his body too big for his developing mind, his face still undergoing that teenage seismic shift. He shovelled in his food, holding his fork in his right hand, as if showing he was *beyond* conventional manners, too macho. But then Daisy asked him to pour her a glass of water, which he did clumsily, spilling some on the table, and he blushed, as bashful as a small boy.

It was still hot, as humid as it had been, and there was talk of a 'midnight swim'. Alice insisted she do the washing-up; 'Go on,' she said to me, caressing my shoulder, 'you've done enough today.' Andrew volunteered to dry, and the rest of us went down to the pool and switched on the underwater lights.

Tina was in a mood. 'I'm sorry it didn't work out in Epitara. But I could have told you.'

'Yes, it was a shame. Still, we had to try.'

'We missed you both today. Well.' She flicked a leaf off the table towards the pool. 'Andrew did.'

I watched Daisy as she swam aimlessly, her hair dripping, her nubile body flickering white in the LEDs. For once it left me cold.

'What's keeping Andrew and Alice?' I said.

'I'm sure they'll be down in a bit.'

But I couldn't stay still. I told Tina I'd forgotten my cigarettes and climbed back up to the house.

They were on my fag bench where they must have thought they were safe, out of sight. Andrew's arm was around Alice's shoulder, his fingers clasping her upper arm, his chin resting on her head. The thought of his bristles against her soft hair made me shudder.

They didn't see me. Alice was looking down. His eyes were closed. They were talking quietly; her lips moving. They hadn't heard me approach – to be honest, I'd crept up from the pool as quietly as I could.

This was a stolen moment; not the intimacy of friends, but something darker, more dangerous.

My teeth clenched, my fists coiled.

So I was 'daft' to feel jealous, was I?

I felt as if I had been kicked in the groin. I didn't know what to do with myself. I wanted to scream, to fight. But in the end I turned away and went quietly back the way I had come.

Chapter Fourteen

I hardly slept, what with the dog and the heat and the yearning for Alice. Perhaps if I hadn't been so far from home, if I had been in London, with Michael to talk to, I'd have kept my perspective. But instead I lay there, veering between violent jealousy and a pathetic humility. One minute I ached for the feel of her skin on mine, longed to stretch my palms across the hot crumpled sheet, to run my hands over her ribcage; the next I imagined getting out of bed, finding Andrew, kicking him all over the house.

With daylight came a new rationality. Perhaps I had imagined it? Alice was still lying in bed when I came out of the shower, and she put her arms out and pulled me down next to her. 'Thank you for yesterday,' she murmured, her fingers slipping under the damp edge of my towel. I searched her face. 'It was nothing,' I said. 'I was happy to.'

She kissed me on my nose, and then on my mouth, her tongue seeking mine. 'Come back to bed,' she said, her hands slipping lower and cupping my buttocks.

I had turned my back on her the night before to read my book, or pretend to, but now I succumbed – of course I did. I forced her legs apart more insistently than felt right, caught her lip between my teeth, and pinioned her hands above her head. I was trying to possess her, trying to exert control – over my own emotions if nothing else. She moaned in pleasure, though she didn't come. Could I have misread the situation?

Would she have initiated this, would she have enjoyed it, if she was in love with Andrew?

We joined the others, late to breakfast. The construction work had re-started; there was a sound of drilling. Tina in her pink dressing gown was sitting a distance from Andrew, painting the view, tubes of paint and a pot of water arranged at her feet. Andrew was perched fully dressed on the table, looking at his watch. 'Cutting it a bit fine, aren't we?' he said irritably to Alice. Yvonne and Karl were due to land at lunchtime; there had been discussions at supper about what time he and Alice should set off to collect them.

'We'll be OK,' she said. 'They've got to get through security. Anyway, I'm ready.'

She tore herself off a piece of bread, holding it to her nose, breathing in the yeasty scent, her eyes closed.

'Of course, now I'm insured for the car,' I said, sitting down and pouring myself a coffee, 'I could drive.'

I put the cafetiere back on the table and watched them both carefully. Alice looked thoughtful, as if considering it: 'Well, that's a suggestion,' she said. 'Andrew, what do you think?'

'The airport is quite hard to find.'

On the other side of the terrace, Tina put down her sketch pad. 'I'm sure Paul can manage.'

'No, it is difficult.' A'   reed. She stretched over me for the butter and wip'   r bread. She finished speaking with her mouth   e it as is.'

I waited until I could no longer hear the car, until it had reached the end of the drive and bumped around the corner, until the engine was a distant rumble. And then I went back round the house to find Tina.

She was in the kitchen, having abandoned her paints and got dressed – another linen sack, this one an over-washed, faded green, a few inches shorter at the back than the front, revealing the dimpled blue-white curves above her knees. Her eyes were red – a tiny mesh of broken veins in the corners – and I wondered if she had been crying.

'You all right?' I said.

'Yup.'

I took a deep breath. Should I ask her what she thought about Andrew and Alice? Did I dare I put it into words?

'I'm planning a picnic in Stefanos. We can walk down. It will do us good. Plus get us away from the noise.'

She pushed past me and started picking up towels from various chairs on the terrace. 'We can buy cheese pies for lunch and eat them on the beach,' she said, stuffing the towels into a large canvas bag. 'Snorkel. Swim. I'll take my paints.' She shouted: 'Kids! Hurry up! Let's go!' and then to me again, 'Maybe write some postcards. You coming?'

I stopped her in the doorway by putting my hand on her shoulder. She was agitated, I could tell. She needed to know I was on her side. 'Would you like me to come?' I said with meaning.

'You must do what you like,' she said.

'Yes. But do you *want* me to come?'

Shit. Thinking about it now: yes. Maybe I did sound needy. I didn't mean to. I was just trying to be kind.

She looked at my hand, and then up into my face. Her voice was steady, as she said again: 'You must do what you like.'

There was something in her expression that I resented. I took my hand back. 'Maybe I won't, then,' I said.

I sat on the terrace after that, smoking, and watched them fussing about, coming and going, searching for and finding and losing again what they needed (trunks, balls, rush mats), collecting useless props for their useless lives. Nobody wanted me, I thought to myself with self-pity; nobody needed me.

'You staying here?' Frank said before they left.

'I thought I might, yes.'

'To do what?'

'I'll find something to do, some use for my time.'

'Like mend Hermes?' he said, and behind him, Phoebe laughed.

When they were safely out of the way, I went back into the house. There were two doors into Andrew and Tina's room – one from the terrace, which was locked; the other from the lounge, which wasn't. I went straight in and looked around. It was a combination of messy and scrupulously tidy, as if a sergeant major lodged with a whore. The chest of drawers was littered with make-up and jangly nests of jewellery, but the bed was neatly made. Andrew's side was clear, but Tina's book, a bestselling romance, was open, face down with the pages scuffed, on the other side. A half-empty glass of water sat on the small wooden stool next to it, and a blister pack, which I looked at closely. It contained sleeping pills – Ambien. So that's why she slept so soundly. I helped myself to a couple just in case – you never know when a good night's sleep might come in handy.

I opened the wardrobe and looked through his clothes. Emptied his pockets: nothing. On the bottom shelf, tucked under a towel, was a small leather washbag, which I emptied onto the floor: a tube of Kiehl's 'Ultimate Brushless Shave', Tom Ford 'Noir' and a jar of Macho-man MAX vitamins for 'increased health & vitality and sharpened mental performance'. I was about to return the items to the bag when I realised it had an internal compartment. I felt inside and took out three gold-wrapped packets. Condoms. I held them in my hand, feeling suddenly sick. Why would Andrew need condoms? An early menopause, Tina had said. He certainly wasn't using them to sleep with his wife.

I put everything back into the washbag and replaced it under the towel in the wardrobe. But the condoms I put in my wallet. Maybe Andrew would think Tina had found them. But I hoped he'd know it was me.

Back on the terrace, I turned my head, holding my breath. Above the distant drilling, I could hear voices, and a girl's laughter. It was coming from the pool. I slipped quietly to the bottom of the steps and stood under the fig: two people entwined in the water. One was Daisy; and the other was a blond man with broad shoulders. He turned, saw me. Fuck. Artan.

I waved.

Daisy leapt out at the side closest to me, and grabbed a towel. 'I thought you'd gone with the others.'

'I thought you had,' I said.

'Don't tell,' she said. 'It's not what it looks like. We're just friends.'

Artan had got out at the far end of the pool, and was pulling on his trousers with his back to us.

'He's a bit old for you,' I said.

She gave a sarcastic smile. 'Really, we're going to go there?'

I considered her for a moment, weighing up the options. Was I supposed to be outraged? To yank her up to the house? *Wait until I tell your mother, young lady.* Is that how someone with a normal moral compass would react? To be honest, I didn't care. I had too much on my mind to worry what she did. She was an adult. Or almost. 'OK,' I said. 'Deal. I'll be up at the house if you need me.'

'Doing what?' she said suspiciously.

I shrugged. 'Mending the van.'

This time I wedged the shed door open, using a large plastic container that was sitting by the wall. The label was in

Greek, but showed a skull and crossbones – the international sign for poison. The lid was tightly closed, but to be on the safe side, I wiped my hand on my shorts after I'd moved it. A shaft of dusty light streamed in and I saw that where the wall had been thick with dirt two days before, now a smear ran along it, in a wide curve, as if it had been wiped with a towel, or as if someone else had squeezed past.

The stuff on the shelves at the back of the shed looked like old rubbish – half-finished paint tins, empty containers. I couldn't think why anyone would have ventured in. And then I remembered Artan closing the door behind him. Maybe this was where he kept his tools, though I couldn't see any. Or perhaps he came in here to change into his work clothes. Or to fuck Daisy? *Was* he fucking Daisy? Who cared?

The car had been parked almost up to the shelves, but with just enough room to stand at the front of it. I fiddled under the bonnet and found the release hook in the middle under the front. It popped quite easily, and I secured it open with the metal support. Easy so far. But inside – I recoiled. It was like looking at innards, intestines – coiled and dirty. I didn't have a clue. I couldn't even locate the water tank let alone the oil stick. An old spanner was resting on what might have been the fan belt. I took it out, weighed it in my hands. It was heavy, rusted up, the hinge like a parrot's beak. Then I moved round the bonnet to try the driver's door. It opened – not fully, because of the wall, but just wide enough for me to wriggle through and up on to the seat.

I sat there for a few moments in the cool half-light, with the bonnet open. I tried to imagine I *was* a mechanic, or maybe just a regular guy somewhere in the American Midwest who knew what they were doing, a man a woman like Alice would have no choice but to respect. I lit a cigarette and rolled down the window to stick out my elbow. I leant back. It wasn't particularly comfortable; the seat was a flat bench with a padded plastic cushion. But the interior was clean, apart from a few pieces of twig and road-grit and an old handkerchief lying scrunched in the footwell. Hell – I smiled ruefully to myself – if Alice left me for Andrew, I could move out here.

I finished the fag and stubbed it out with my shoe. The key was in the ignition, just as Alice had said. A surprisingly stunted key for such a mighty machine; no fob. It seemed an unwise thing to do, get a car going in an enclosed space. Carbon monoxide fumes, all these bottles of liquid.

I bent my head to twist the key but it was stuck tight. I tried to pull it out but it wouldn't budge. My fingers were slippery with sweat and it was almost impossible to get a purchase. I mopped them on my shirt and tried again. Still no joy. The key couldn't have rusted completely; I just needed something to help my grip. I looked around, and spotted the old hand-kerchief on the floor. That would do. I reached down to pick it up and then wrapped the dusty cream cotton round my fingers and tried again. This time, my grip was secure enough to provide sufficient friction. The key turned. The engine coughed, died. A second go: same deal. One last time, my hand sore already, the metal digging deep into the meat of my forefinger through the cotton. A rattle, and then a throaty whirr and the beast began to vibrate, the propped-open bonnet rattling on its support. I took my hand off the key and marvelled. I *had* mended it. Perhaps it was as simple as removing that spanner.

I switched the engine off and the shed fell quiet again.

I felt an extraordinary sense of achievement, and with it a lift in my self-esteem. What could Alice possibly see in Andrew that she didn't see in me? Clearly he provided her with moral and emotional support, but were they having an affair? Could the gold condoms be old? Or confiscated from his son? I lit another cigarette and took a deep drag. Fact is, if they had been sleeping with each other, was Andrew *really* any match for me? I had to prove my worth, was all. I had to find a way to get rid of him.

I remember this thought process in detail. What I don't remember is what I did with the spanner. I don't know whether I dropped it on the floor of the shed – but it was heavy and would have made a resounding clank and I don't remember that. Or whether I took it with me into the cab and left it there.

Chapter Fifteen

Alice and Andrew were back at about 5 p.m., long after the others. I was lying on the bed, pretending to read, when Alice breezed in as if nothing were wrong. The plane had been delayed, their car had got stuck behind some goats – 'we had to switch off the engine and wait for a man to come and shoo them through a gate' – and they'd stopped for a drink before dropping Yvonne and Karl at the hotel. 'Anyway,' she said, throwing off her shoes and plonking herself down on the side of the mattress. 'They're here.'

'Are they OK?' I said. 'It must be traumatic coming back.' I was reaching for the intimacy we'd shared in the car. But Alice was in a different sort of mood. Her gestures were over-generous. When she reached over to kiss me, her mouth loose and moist, her breath smelt of ouzo. 'Yes. Actually, yes, they're both fine. Under the circumstances.' She was drawing out her words. 'I'm not sure it's hit them. What have you been up to?'

'Well, actually,' I propped myself up on my elbow, 'I've had an interesting day.' I was planning to tell her about Daisy and Artan and about mending the van. I was expecting both pieces of information, in their different ways, to draw us closer.

But she had got to her feet, and was peeling off her clothes. 'Tell me later,' she said, standing there naked. 'We're meeting Yvonne and Karl at Nico's in half an hour and I'm desperate for a shower.'

★   ★   ★

Nico's was smaller and prettier than Giorgio's, with gingham tablecloths and a cascading vine over the terrace. Yvonne and Karl were sitting alone at a long table over by the water when we got there. Alice wended her way round the chairs to reach them, holding my hand to make sure I followed close. Yvonne stood up and Alice pushed me forward. 'Darling Yvonne, this is my friend Paul, whom I told you about in the car. He's staying with us for the week.'

Yvonne put out her hand and I stood for a moment, clumsy and awkward, staring at her. She was small and slight, with a thin face and long hair; the skin under her eyes was rough like sandpaper. Her dress was a floral cotton one with cap sleeves – it was an old one of Alice's; I recognised it from a photograph – and it hung off her, gaping at the neck. She was smiling, showing stained teeth.

I bent down and hugged her, feeling the rub of the crucifix that lay around her neck. The damp of her lipstick brushed my cheek.

'I'm actually here for a fortnight,' I said, pulling away, 'unless she's forgotten.'

Yvonne stretched her mouth into a wider smile and Alice laughed. 'Sorry. A fortnight. And this is Karl.'

He was smaller than Yvonne, an ancient pocket-rocker with grey stubble, sunken cheeks and a faded blue tattoo of an elaborate lizard behind one ear. When he shook my hand, a square gold ring on his forefinger jabbed the flesh at the base of my thumb. 'Delighted, I'm sure,' he said.

Around me I was aware of the others greeting Yvonne, Tina embracing her, Louis knocking over a chair, Daisy sitting as far away from me as possible. I pulled out the empty chair next to Karl. The waiter brought us menus. Andrew ordered wine: 'Or Karl, would you prefer beer?'

'Wouldn't mind,' Karl muttered.

'And a beer for my esteemed friend,' Andrew said.

Alice, who had taken the head of the table, was talking with animation to Yvonne, asking her about her hotel room, was it cool enough, did they have mosquito nets, were the pillows comfortable?

I thought Yvonne began to look a little irritated. 'It's fine,' she answered shortly. 'It's what we expect. It's all fine.'

Karl leant into me. 'Alice wants everything to be perfect,' he said. 'She's like this every year. None of it makes any difference.'

'Where is it that you're staying?'

'It's up there somewhere –' he gestured with his chin. 'It's got a nice pool, and some of the rooms have sea views, though ours hasn't. The first year we came, the year we lost Jasmine, we stayed at the Barbati Beach Apartments and after that they used to give us a discount. But they bulldozed it to build that big posh hotel—'

'Delfinos.'

'Same manager, but . . .'

'People forget,' I said.

Karl shrugged. 'Yeah. People forget a lot of things.'

The teenagers were sitting at the far end of the table. I looked over just as Daisy looked over at me. Her face suffused red. I smiled and gave a very small nod. It turned out it felt nice to have something on her.

'Is there any point?' Karl said.

I turned back to him. 'Sorry?'

'In the car, Alice said you were on holiday in Pyros, actually in Agios Stefanos, the night Jasmine went missing but that you don't remember anything about it so there was no point asking you.'

'No, she's right, I'm afraid. That night is a bit of a blank.'

He nodded. 'One too many shandies, was it?'

I was beginning to feel disordered. 'Absolutely. Several too many, in fact.'

'I recognise you, though.' He narrowed his eyes, biting the side of his lip. 'Yes, definitely. You were out in the street.'

'I don't think I was. I think I'd already gone.'

'Are you sure?' He tapped the side of his head with his finger. 'I've got a head for faces.'

My brain reared wildly back in time, trying to recall past conversations with Alice. I thought she had said I'd left the village in a taxi long before Jasmine went missing. I racked my brain for a genuine memory of my own – nothing.

'I don't think so,' I said again. 'It's certainly the sort of thing I hope I'd remember.'

At the head of the table, Alice was telling Tina and Yvonne the story of the goats – making vigorous gestures with her hands as if trying to propel the anecdote along, filling it with life and air. I imagined the narrative sinking to the floor without her efforts, limp and shapeless, and felt a welling of sympathy. What a pact with the devil she was engaged in, pretending Jasmine was still alive, pretending there was still hope. And I noticed how Alice was the woman here I felt most sorry for, not Yvonne, and how odd that was.

Karl tapped my arm to get my attention. 'You're a writer, Andrew told us.'

'Yes, I write novels.'

'I'm not really a reader, though one of my mates down at the local has published a book about philately – I say "published". He paid for it himself. Ah, thanks.' His lager arrived and he took a long slug.

'And what do you do?' I said.

He put the glass down. 'Work-wise I'm at B&Q, on the replenishment side of customer services, but I began as a roadie. Big Tallulah? Steve and the Sunshine Boys? The

Krooks?' He looked at me enquiringly. 'None of them ring a bell?'

I shook my head apologetically.

'That's how me and her met, back in 1995. She was a lovely singer, sang like a bird, though she gave it all up. She hasn't sung a note since Jasmine left us.'

He stopped and looked across the table at Yvonne.

Alice was leaning over to point at items on Yvonne's menu. 'I think you should order moussaka. You like that.'

'It's a good thing I have you to tell me what I like,' Yvonne said, putting the menu down. She seemed exhausted, letting her arms drop by her side as if she didn't know what to do with them.

'I don't suppose anything has been the same since then,' I said, turning back to Karl.

'It's a fucked-up world,' he replied. 'I can't tell you what a hole she's left. I don't know. It can make you angry.'

'What was Jasmine like?' I said, after a beat.

He folded his napkin into smaller and smaller squares. 'She was a handful, I won't tell a lie. Had a lot of tonsillitis and missed a lot of school, got a bit behind. But she loved her rabbits, though Yvonne was always having to nag her to clean out the hutch. They were at each other a lot, those two – fighting all the time, but it was just the age, you know? Jas had just got into Eminem, boys, doing everything to wind her mother up. Flashpoints.'

I looked to the other side of the table, where the younger members of our party were all on their phones. 'Teenagers can be trying,' I said. 'I realise that.'

Karl pulled his wallet out of his back pocket and removed a photograph. It was a picture I'd already seen of Jasmine – the one with the ginger cat held up to her cheek. But this picture wasn't cropped and in shot was a table piled with dirty takeaway cartons, a half-eaten pizza, a spilt bottle of beer, a different kind of kitchen tⱺ the one you might imagine – filthier, more out of control. *Flashpoints.*

Karl's voice seemed to get stuck at the back of his throat. 'She had a wicked smile. *Has.*'

Food arrived and Andrew snapped to it, bossing the waiter around, directing lamb kebabs and swordfish steaks. Yvonne and I had both ordered the moussaka, though I noticed she only picked at hers.

Andrew was squeezing lemon on to his calamari with one hand while gesturing at Phoebe to pass him the jug of water. 'Big excitement here this week,' he said. 'Poor girl was raped after a night at the club.'

Louis muttered something.

'What did you say?' asked Alice, her eyes on him.

'I said silly slapper.'

'Louis!'

'It's what Paul called her.'

My feet jerked forwards so violently, my chair legs scraped. 'No I didn't.'

Andrew stood up. 'Louis. That's not a good thing to say.'

He shrugged, and Alice put her hand on Yvonne's. 'I'm sorry,' she said. 'I shouldn't have mentioned it.'

Yvonne moved her hand away. 'Have they found the rapist?' she asked.

Alice exchanged a glance with Andrew. Her lips downturned slightly at the corners, and she gave a small shake of her head. Her earrings reflected the candlelight. 'No,' she said. 'Not yet.'

I went to the bathroom after the meal, stared at my face in the mirror, tried to make it look relaxed, normal. I had a cigarette and was gone longer than I intended. When I got back to the table, only Tina was sitting there. The others, she told me, had wandered off – some to buy ice creams, others 'to get some air'. Yvonne was feeling emotional, she admitted. Alice had offered to walk her home.

'Did she want Alice to walk her home?' I asked.

Tina smiled, raising her eyebrows very slightly. 'I don't think she felt she had a choice.'

The waiter brought the bill over and asked if we were ready to pay, or whether we would wait for our companions. I threw my head back and stared at the roof.

'My turn, I suppose,' I said, straightening up. I took my wallet out of my pocket and eased out my credit card, careful to shield the condoms as I did so. 'I think I said I would get this one.'

Tina turned the bill over and winced. 'Let's go halves,' she said. 'It's quite hefty.'

'Thank fuck,' I said, settling in my chair once our cards had been accepted and returned.

She laughed, studying me. 'Poor Paul,' she said.

I sat back, expecting another of our cosy chats, a comfy corner carved out of our mutual isolation, perhaps a nightcap. The restaurant was emptying out, and a song that I liked was playing – a jazz standard that made me want to click my fingers and sway. I had an aggression or a sadness in me that needed releasing. But Tina didn't seem to share my mood. Poor Tina. I wouldn't have told her about Daisy, even if I hadn't promised not to. She had enough worries of her own. She breathed in sharply and stood up. 'I think I might join the kids in an ice cream,' she said. 'Do us a favour and nip to the supermarket? We need mineral water and toilet paper, and more coffee for the morning. I think that's it, don't you? Unless you can think of anything else we're out of?'

I shrugged, having no clue about what the house needed or didn't need.

'OK then,' she said. 'I told the others we'd meet at the car in fifteen minutes or so.'

She left the restaurant, waving at the owner who was drinking with a friend by the door. I downed my glass of wine and finished what remained of hers, and after a few moments, I followed suit.

The village was busy, as it always was at that hour, that tide-turning moment when families were starting to leave and young people were streaming in. From the nightclub across the bay, music throbbed, a heavy bass, with the intermittent high shriek of a whistle. Coloured lights flashed and strobed.

I wandered slowly up to the supermarket. It was bright in there, and hot. Three men hovered by the alcohol. In the bakery section, the pastries looked shrivelled. I bought what we needed, and walked out into the square, idly looking around. I was about to walk up to the car, when on the other side of the street, I caught sight of Andrew going into Nico's. I crossed over quickly, assuming he was returning to pay the bill and looking forward to telling him that I had dealt with it, but inside there was no sign of him. I scanned the street, and again I thought I saw him, heading in the direction of the nightclub.

It was hard work to pass with any speed through the meandering holidaymakers. I managed to keep his head in sight until my foot caught the back of a sandal, and the person wearing it, a large man with bulbous calves, turned to glare. I apologised but, in that fraction of a second, I lost concentration. When I reached Club 19, at the end of the strip, Andrew had disappeared.

Four teenage girls in tight skirts and heels were pausing at the entrance, to pull down their skirts, to shake out their hair, before going through the door.

I was curious. I followed them in.

The club, dimly lit and still quite empty, had a bar and a few tables. A young boy in wide jeans and a tight white shirt was standing behind the decks, big metal watch dangling from his wrist, headphones strung around his neck. Several teenage girls were swaying self-consciously against the walls. Up close, their skin flashed blue, and yellow and red.

I stood for a moment, shopping bags dangling. Girls in hats and denim shorts, and tiny off-the-shoulder black dresses, legs and lashes, eyeliner, trembling clavicles. The music, the thump and grind, the ear-aching drone. And I knew, with sudden clarity, that I'd been here before. I'd met a girl that night after I'd split from Saffron and gone back with her to her rented room. And if I didn't remember much else it was because she was just one girl in a stream of girls. And how old I felt now, how *beyond* all that. All I wanted, I realised, was to leave it all behind. Now I'd met Alice, it was within my grasp. I could be *that* person.

I leant against the wall, exhausted by my own life, by the *fucking snare* of it.

I didn't hear him enter. Who could have, above the noise? The room had filled anyway by then. What was one more person, one more body?

How long had he been there? Not long. A few minutes, seconds, before I turned and saw him.

He raised his eyebrows at me, tilting his chin. I let a beat pass, trapped, and then I crossed the room.

'Mr Morris,' he said, when I reached him.

'Lieutenant Gavras.'

He bent to speak in my ear. 'This reminds me of that famous English chat-up line. Do you come here often?'

I pulled away, smiling. 'Only once or twice.'

He fixed me with his gaze, his brows heavy. 'I thought you said you were too old for places of this nature?'

'I am, but I'm looking for Andrew. I thought I saw him come in.'

'You weren't looking for a date?'

'No. Of course not. I've got a date.'

He nodded a couple of times, sticking out his lower lip. 'Mrs Mackenzie?'

'Yes.'

'Delicate woman. Needs looking after.'

'It's funny – you're the second person to have described her as delicate. But yes.'

'So make sure you do.'

Chapter Sixteen

The others were waiting in the lay-by when I got there. Bats swooped above their heads. Fireflies flickered. I apologised for being late. I didn't mention my encounter with Gavras. I told them I thought I'd seen Andrew heading into the nightclub and followed out of curiosity. 'Not me, mate,' Andrew said, slapping me on the shoulder. He seemed to have picked up some of Karl's mannerisms, in that irritatingly chameleon-like way of his. 'Sure it wasn't some hot piece of skirt? Time to get the old eyesight checked out, if not. It starts declining at your age.'

I squashed up next to Alice in the back of the car. She kept sighing on the drive up to the house. 'Glad that's over,' she said to everyone; and more quietly to me, 'Thanks for making so much effort with Karl.'

Andrew let out a guffaw from the front. 'Did you hear him tell Paul he was "on the replenishment side of customer services"? You know what that means, don't you?'

'What?' I said.

'Shelf-stacker!'

'I liked him,' I said.

Alice put her hand on my thigh and gave it a squeeze.

'I can understand why the police might have been suspicious at first,' I added. 'Because of the way he looks, I suppose – but he'd known Jasmine since she was a baby. I think he genuinely loved her.'

'To be honest,' Alice said, 'he did most of the parenting.'
I looked at her, surprised. 'What do you mean?'
'Yvonne wasn't particularly maternal.'

I thought about this more the next morning when Yvonne and Karl arrived for an early swim. Karl was wearing shorts and sandals, both of which looked brand new, but Yvonne was swamped in a wrap-dress, which might have been another of Alice's cast-offs. Her hair was loose, hanging in curtains on either side of her narrow face, and Alice fetched her a flowery hair-clip, standing back to admire how it looked. She seemed to be peeling off bits of herself and giving them to her. I think if she could have given Yvonne slivers of her own skin she would have done so. She would have flayed herself alive.

Yvonne didn't thank Alice for the clip, and I saw her pull it out a bit later, yanking out a piece of hair. She wasn't grateful for her beneficence; she was *bearing* it. And of course this was understandable. Here was Alice so desperate to make things right, when Yvonne must be thinking nothing – none of Alice's silly little offerings – would ever make it right. But I didn't like Yvonne much. I felt guilty even thinking it. But there was something cold, and beady, about her. I know it seems a bit unfair to judge her on this – she'd lost a child, she should have been allowed to do what she liked for the rest of her life – but she didn't laugh at people's jokes, or even try to laugh. Not remotely. And most people do, whatever has happened to them, so it was just odd.

It was a humid, slightly overcast day – thin white clouds were layered across the sky – and in the dull uniform light, the terrace and the pool looked grubby and grey. It wasn't just the presence of Yvonne and Karl that ruined the atmosphere; it was also the weather. You get used to the sun and when it goes it leaves everyone feeling flat.

I volunteered to help Tina make coffee and, alone in the kitchen, I heard myself say: 'Did anyone ever look at Yvonne for Jasmine . . . I mean was *she* ever a suspect?'

Tina bit her lip, almost laughed. 'Paul. Sssh. Don't.'

'No, but seriously,' I said. 'All those press conferences we've seen with weeping parents when it turns out one of them did it. Wasn't there that poor kid in Wales? Jasmine and Yvonne were always at each other, Karl says. Perhaps it was a fight that got out of hand.'

'I thought it was Karl who was always fighting with Jasmine.'

'He says it was her.'

Tina poured hot water on to the coffee grounds. 'I don't know. I don't know either of them very well. It's always been Andrew and Alice who had the relationship. You know, I was up at the house with the kids when it all kicked off. I slept through it. It wasn't until the next morning I even found out what had happened. By which time, the police were everywhere. God. It was all so awful.' She shuddered. 'Of course Yvonne didn't have anything to do with it. She's her mother. Alice wouldn't have stood by her all this time, fought so hard to find Jasmine, if she had had the slightest inkling or doubt.'

'I'm just not sure. I've got this funny feeling about her.'

Tina smiled. 'OK, Inspector Morse. Why don't you bring it up with Lieutenant Gavras next time you see him?'

Down at the pool, Karl and Yvonne were sitting, fully dressed, in the shade. Daisy and Phoebe were sunbathing, in tiny bikinis. Alice was ploughing up and down the pool in her Speedo and Andrew was standing at the edge of the small copse, on his phone. The builders hadn't started yet, but the dog was barking.

I laid the tray down on the metal table next to Yvonne and

handed out the cups. 'Ta,' Karl said. He was looking tired, his eyes bloodshot. 'Butler service. Very nice.'

Yvonne dropped sugar cubes in her cup and stirred it with a spoon, round and round. Karl put his hand on hers to make her stop.

Alice swam to the end of the pool and rested her arms on the side. 'You wonder if that poor animal ever sleeps.'

'Maybe someone should put it out of its misery,' I said.

'You're nice.' Phoebe lifted her head to scowl at me. 'Maybe someone should put *you* out of your misery.'

Andrew returned his phone to his pocket. 'It's unliveable with,' he said. 'I'll ask Artan to deal with it, tell him to get a bit heavy. He speaks their language.'

'Does he?' I said.

Daisy looked up, caught my eye and then looked away.

'I meant metaphorically,' Andrew said. 'Gosh.' He looked me up and down. 'You're certainly getting good wear out of my trunks. We never got to buy you a replacement pair, did we?'

'Sorry,' I said.

He waved his hand dismissively, as if it was of no consequence. But he'd mentioned it on purpose, in front of an audience, to make me feel small, and it worked.

'Now, listen up everyone, I've booked us a treat.'

He stood there in his crisp black polo with its crisp white piping, his over-long pressed shorts, his legs apart, his chin disappearing into his neck, waiting for one of us to ask.

Tina spoke first. 'Do tell,' she said.

'I've made some calls and . . . well, I've booked us a yacht – a thirty-footer with skipper. We'll do some fishing, have lunch on board, swim. Would you like that, Jasmine?'

A ghastly moment in which he realised what he had said.

'Yvonne, I mean.'

She looked over to him. There was nothing in her face to show she had noticed. 'Yes. It would be something to do.'

Both teenage girls had sat up, suddenly perky, and even Tina was nodding in an appreciative way.

'I think that sounds perfectly heavenly.' Alice pulled herself out of the water and grabbed a towel, wiping the chlorine out of her eyes. She laid a wet hand on his shoulder. 'What a clever man you are to think of it.'

What a clever man you are to think of it.

I felt a surge of anger. It was her subservience that triggered it, but it had been building: the cheap comment about the swimming trunks, Phoebe's sarcasm, the humidity, the dog, the fact that I was feeling sex-*starved*, Alice having turned her back on me the night before. At some point I'd tell him what his daughter had been up to, watch him squirm. But in the meantime, no way was I setting foot on his yacht.

'I'll get the boys up and sorted,' Tina said, heading for the path.

'Tell them not to forget suntan lotion,' Alice called. 'Cloud cover is deceptive.'

No one had asked my opinion. No one had asked if I wanted to go on a boat trip or if I wanted to do something *different*. (By no one, of course, I meant Alice.) I might just as well have not existed.

I returned to the bedroom and got Michael's guidebook out of my bag.

I was lying on the bed, flicking through it, when Alice walked in.

'The builders are back,' she said. 'We're leaving at the right time. You ready?'

I put the book down on the bed, cover up. 'For what?'

'The boat trip.'

'Oh, that. I'm not coming.'

She had opened the cupboard door to find a dry swimsuit, but she stopped and turned, the costume, a strip of rainbow-coloured Lycra, hanging off her fingers.

I picked up the guidebook and opened it at random. A folded newspaper cutting fell out; I slipped it back in. 'I'm going to visit some ruins today.'

'What ruins?'

'Ruins of the early Helladic Settlement at Okarta. Maybe if I have time –' I consulted a page '– the Spring of Exoghi, where, according to legend, Odysseus's swine-herder Eumaeus used to bring his pigs to drink. There's a bus from the top of the road. I asked in town last night.'

I was hoping she would lie down next to me, wrap her arms around me, beg me not to go off without her. It was a test of sorts.

She had bundled the swimsuit in a towel and now she held it to her chest, resting her chin on it. 'Don't sulk.'

'I'm not sulking.'

'You are. It's because of what Andrew said about the trunks. He was only joking.'

I shrugged.

'Come on. It'll be fun.'

'Why?'

Because you'll be there with me, I wanted her to say.

'It just will be. Andrew's a brilliant sailor.'

I am my own worst enemy. I wanted to be with her more than anything on earth, but now she had mentioned Andrew's sailing brilliance. Fuck. I was too riled.

'I could do with a bit of time on my own,' I said.

They were doing their hopeless milling when I left – moving round in frantic, ineffectual circles like flies trapped in a room.

'Jesus H Christ,' I heard Andrew say to one of the boys. '*Shoes.* What is wrong with you?'

'I'm off,' I said, to no one in particular. Aiming for a cultured air, I was wearing a lilac shirt with my linen suit (I left Andrew's wet trunks on the kitchen table), and I was armed with certain props: Michael's guidebook, an old bus timetable I had found in a drawer, and a bottle of water from the fridge. I crossed the terrace, cutting a swathe through their chaos. I wanted them to watch me go, to witness my independence, my defiance. Nobody owns me, said my swinging arms. Look, said my tilted chin, this is what freedom looks like.

'Bye then,' Alice said. 'Have fun.'

I blew her a kiss. 'I will.'

At the end of the drive, I stopped at the gate and peered over. A new area the size of a football pitch had been levelled in the upper reaches of the field. Several men were standing around a concrete mixer, which was churning hungrily. The fence on this side had been dismantled and several trees felled, undergrowth cleared. The larger of the two diggers had moved up the hill several metres towards Alice's land and was tugging at the earth with its claw.

The dog was under its temporary shelter chewing a bone. It couldn't hear me above the racket. Or maybe it knew not to be on guard when the machinery was actually in use.

I pulled myself up on to the gate and jumped over. To the left was a small patch of untouched rough grass behind a chunk of hedge thick enough to hide me from the lane. Checking the dog was still oblivious to my presence, I slunk down and lit a cigarette, noticing the packet was nearly empty. While I waited, I opened the guidebook and found the newspaper article that had fallen out earlier. Michael must have cut it out for me. It was from the *Daily Telegraph* – his journal of choice – and was headlined 'The Dark Side of Paradise'. I read it through. In a nutshell it described Pyros as a hotbed of crime and corruption, exacerbated by the euro crisis. The practice of bribes or 'fakelaki' underpinned its entire infrastructure, being rife among 'lawyers, doctors, customs, the judicial system, the police'. There was guff about prostitution and illegal immigrants, and a whole paragraph on the abuse of the disability allowance. Ten times more people were signed off with eye problems on Pyros than anywhere else in Europe. Its nickname on mainland Greece was 'the Island of the Blind'.

At the bottom of the article, in his lawyer's spider writing, Michael had written: 'Enjoy!'

What a wag. I scrunched it up.

I didn't have to wait long before they left. Vibrations along the earth, a jolting flash of silver through the branches. I waited until the people carrier had disappeared down the track to the main road and then stood up. A short, squat man in a short-sleeved pale blue shirt, an orange hat shadowing his face, was looking in my direction. I stubbed out my cigarette with my foot and raised my arm in greeting. He didn't respond, so I turned away, pulled myself back over the gate and set off up the track to the house.

The key was where I knew Alice kept it – under the lavender pot on the terrace. I let myself into the kitchen, which was a mess. No one was bothering to keep it clean any more. Cupboards yawned open; tea towels lay on the floor. An open tin of honey was attracting an army of suicidal ants. Next to the kettle was a pile of loose change, which I took. I snooped around the house a bit – finding a ten-euro note in the middle of the rumpled folds of Louis's bed. Nothing much to look at in the girls' room, apart from underwear, and a couple of the plastic gusset-protectors they put in new bikini bottoms. Phoebe had left her credit card propped on the keyboard of her laptop, which I looked at regretfully, but even I wouldn't be that stupid.

I took a cold beer from the fridge, and drank it down by the pool, enjoying having the lower terrace to myself. I smoked the last cigarette in the packet and at 2 p.m., found the remnants of Tuesday's picnic in the fridge and made myself a sandwich with what was left of the bread. Overcome by the exertion of that, I lay on the bed and slept for a while. When I woke up it was 3.30 p.m. – just the right time for a cup of tea. I brewed up and sat on the Indian bench, when I remembered I'd run out of fags. I left the bench to search my suitcase: nothing. Alice's bag too. Of course she didn't smoke, but I remembered the pleasure she had taken in a cigarette the first night we met (though I hadn't seen her smoke since). I looked in the boys' room – under Louis's bed. In the cupboard above the kitchen sink.

I felt restless. Nerves jangled, jaw on edge, fingers twitchy. The supermarket in Stefanos would be closed for the afternoon, but Nico's taverna sold Marlboro Lights and the Greek brand, Karelia Royal. I began to imagine the weight of the packet in my hand, the scrunch of paper in my fingers, the loose strands of tobacco between my teeth, the sweet woody smell.

And then an idea hit me: Hermes. What was to stop me driving down? Alice didn't know I'd mended it – I'd never had a chance to tell her. I could make up for this morning by surprising her off the boat.

The van started on the third try, and I reversed carefully out into the yard, managed to turn round, with some grinding of the gears, and then proceeded down the drive, past the building site, along the narrow lane, and down to the main road. The engine was by no means smooth. The bite was high and I stalled several times. But the road was quiet at this time in the afternoon, and there was no one around to watch. I drove carefully into the village, looking for the people carrier; when I saw it parked in the lay-by, I drew up behind.

I bought cigarettes – Karelias, the cheapest – and smoked one walking back to the lay-by. To my surprise, when I got there, the people carrier was gone. I climbed back into the truck, completed a clumsy three-point turn, and roared back up the hill. I wondered what they would think when they saw the garage empty. I was looking forward to seeing their reaction when I drove up – Andrew's annoyance, and Alice's delight.

I stalled only once in this section of the drive, at the turn-off. It took me a few goes to re-start the engine. An elderly woman dressed in black was working in the scrap of field to one side to the road. She leant on her hoe and watched me. The window was rolled down and I said, 'Kali spera.' She nodded.

It was harder going up the track than coming down. A couple of rocks crunched on the undercarriage. I stayed in second gear after that, the engine throaty, wheels erratically spinning, dust on each side as thick as smoke. It was a rabbit-hop of a journey and at the bend, where the lane ended and the track up to the house began, I changed down to first in preparation for the sharp turn and promptly stalled again.

I waited a few seconds to give the engine time to recover. It was silent out there, the air liquid; the construction workers had stopped work. Bees droned. The sound of a sheep's bell, ringing miles away. A distant shout, the splash of water.

The engine turned, but didn't fire.

I opened the door and got out. I stood up on the second bar of the gate, my hands gripping the top, to see if there were any labourers around who might help. The sun had slipped out in a crack in the clouds and the makeshift shelter was in the shade, the long knife shadow of a cypress slanting over the awning and the patch of ground it covered. I wasn't sure if I could see the dog or not. There was a dark shape under there, but it might have been a small heap of clothing. It wasn't moving, or making a noise, so no – it can't have been. The dog must have gone. Perhaps Artan, instructed by Andrew, had got heavy and the contractors had agreed to do without their Cerberus.

My hands were wet, tacky. Assuming sweat mixed with dust, I wiped them absent-mindedly on my shirt and made to climb down, then noticed I'd left marks on the lilac – a dark pinky brown. And my hands were stained with something like rust. Puzzled, I rubbed my fingers together, had another look at the top bar. It was streaked and crimson wet.

I looked back at the shape motionless under the shelter. I swung my legs over the gate, clambered over and walked towards it, across the stones, spiky plants scratching my calves, with a horrible feeling of dread.

The poor animal was lying on its side – the ridges of its bony body soaked in blood. Its eyes were glazed, already misted, lifeless, its teeth bared in a horrible rictus, viscous saliva stretched between the open jaws. The knife was still in its throat, blood congealing around the handle. Beneath the blade was a gash of bone and sinew. Bile rose at the back of my throat, and I bent to retch.

I heard a shout and stood up. A man in a hard hat was walking down the field towards me. He was gesticulating, pointing at his car, a blue sedan, doors open, which was stuck behind my truck. He obviously wanted me to move it.

I shouted, 'Over here. Come quick! The dog! Someone has killed it!' I put my hands out to show horror and dismay. The palms were still bloody, and I quickly wiped them on my trousers.

The man began to run, and when he reached me, he started shouting even more, his face contorted. He was short and dark, arms thick with muscle. He pushed me a couple of times, hands against my chest. I stumbled backwards, had to stop myself from falling.

'It wasn't me,' I yelled. 'I just found him. I've just arrived. A second ago.'

He got on his phone, holding my arm in a vice to make sure I didn't move. His fingernails were ingrained with dirt. Behind him, another man had emerged from the car. He opened the gate and came down the field at a run. He was wearing a short-sleeved blue shirt, torn across the shoulder – the man I had seen earlier.

The two men started talking loudly, over each other, almost shouting. 'I had nothing to do with it,' I kept saying. 'Please understand.'

The first man pushed the poor animal with his foot. The earth beneath the body was dark, a cluster of white stones stained red. Then he made another threatening gesture with his fist, pointed at the dog, and pointed to my pocket, rubbing his fingers together, gesturing for money.

'I haven't done anything,' I said, 'and I haven't got anything.'

I turned the pockets inside out to prove my point.

They had started shouting at each other. Then the second man turned to me. 'You stay here,' he said. 'We get the boss.'

'Listen.' I tried to sound as persuasively honest as I could, putting everything into my expression. 'I didn't kill the dog. I don't know who would do such a thing. I just found it. I'm going to go now, but I'm not running away. I live up there.' I pointed beyond the corpse. 'I don't know who would do such a thing. But I didn't. It wasn't me.'

I decided to risk it and started to walk away, up the field, towards the open gate and the truck. They both followed, talking intently to themselves. I looked over my shoulder a couple of times, smiling in what I hoped was a helpful way.

They watched as I got into the cab of the truck. I said, through the open window, 'Let's hope it starts.' I was trying to sound relaxed, to behave as somebody who wasn't guilty would behave, self-conscious about it, even though it wasn't an act. *I wasn't guilty.* My wallet was in a pile with my phone and the Karelias on the long plastic bench-seat. I didn't want them to see it.

The engine turned and fired. I can remember fewer occasions when I have felt more relieved. I smiled again through the window and said, as I pulled the steering wheel sharply round, 'I'm sorry about the dog.'

'What on earth's happened?'

Alice had come round the side of the house as I drew into the yard and switched off the engine.

I opened the door and almost fell out into her arms. She reared back. 'Oh my God. Fuck! What's happened? Are you hurt?'

'It's the dog,' I said. 'I found it. Someone slit its throat. I was too late to save it.'

I leant back into the van and fumbled for my cigarettes. My hands were shaking.

'You're covered in blood,' she said. Her expression was one of revulsion. I lit a fag and took a deep draw on it.

'I know. It was horrible.'

She took a step back. 'You've got blood on your . . . on the cigarette.'

I held it up. She was right.

'Good God.' Andrew had rounded the house, wearing nothing but a towel around his waist. Fresh from the shower, he had swept his hair back; you could still see the comb lines. 'What the fuck has happened? What have you been doing with Hermes?'

'Yes.' Alice pulled her eyes away from me. 'What have you been doing with Hermes?'

'It was supposed to be a surprise.'

Gavras was at the house within half an hour. While Alice put the van back in the shed I held my hands under the hot tap, watching the blood stream, mix with water and disappear in swirls down the drain. I was still in shock. I needed to shower and to change but Tina brought me a cold bottle of beer and I sat down on the terrace to recover. 'What a horrible thing to witness,' Tina said. 'Poor you.'

'We thought we'd been burgled,' Andrew said. 'The van gone, all the doors to the house wide open . . .' He had got dressed and was wearing a Breton top and white jeans, a close-fitting outfit he looked uncomfortable in.

'I should have locked up.'

Tina topped up my glass. 'The kids think stuff is missing, cash, and that someone has been going through their things. But obviously they're mistaken.'

I sighed heavily. 'I should shower,' I said, looking down at my T-shirt and blood-streaked trousers.

'What have you been doing all day?' Alice said, putting her arm across my shoulder.

'We missed you,' Tina added.

I should have abandoned the Helladic settlement story. Sue me: I didn't. I told them I had gone to Okarta and visited the ruins – not a lot to see, most of the discovered artefacts being kept at the museum in Pyros town. I had returned to the house and, finding it deserted, had driven down to Agios Stefanos to meet them off the boat, didn't know how I had missed them. The rest of my account was the truth – driving back, stalling, looking over the gate, seeing the dark motion-less shape.

'So – when you decided to take Hermes, she just started?' Alice said.

'No. That was yesterday.'

'But you didn't tell me last night.'

'I tried to!'

That's when we heard the car.

Gavras was accompanied by two men: the stocky builder in the pale blue shirt, and a thin man with a wispy beard in a midnight blue rayon waistcoat, who, Gavras said, represented the contractor. The four of them stood, legs apart, while Tina and Alice offered beer or glasses of cold water. Andrew leant against the olive tree at the top of the path to the pool. Archie and Frank lumbered up, and Tina darted across the terrace and gestured at them to return to the pool. She went with them, so only Andrew and Alice were witnesses to what happened next.

'Oh dear,' Gavras said, looking with distaste at my bloody clothes. 'Hopefully –' he smiled briefly '– we can sort this messy business quickly.'

He took the chair next to me and leant in, elbows on each side, his feet hooking under the legs of the table. He was holding a large leather-bound notebook and he opened it on his knee, half under the table to conceal its contents.

It felt airless on the terrace; a light, ragged shelf of cloud had shuffled over the sun and the breeze had dropped. I dipped my head to wipe the pearls of sweat from my forehead on the bottom of my shirt, realised I might have smeared blood and put my hand up to check.

Gavras looked down at the notebook, perhaps to refresh his memory of my name. 'Mr Morris. A few boring administrative questions.'

'Sure.'

'I wonder if you could tell me when you arrived in Pyros?'

'When I arrived?'

'Yes. How long have you been a guest of Mrs Mackenzie?'

'Oh. I see. Oh right. Yes. I arrived here on – when was it? God, you lose track of time here.'

'Monday,' Alice said, sitting down on the other side of me.

'Yes, that's right. I got the early Thomas Cook flight.'

Gavras wrote my first lie down in his notebook and then looked up. 'And how long are we lucky enough to have your company here on Pyros?'

'Another ten days. With fair winds and a following sea.'

'Fair winds?'

'It's a quote.'

'I wonder if I might take your contact details. Obviously I have Mrs Mackenzie's and Mr and Mrs Hopkins's on file, but you are new to me.' Gavras's eyes were still on me. 'Your phone number?' he said eventually. 'Mobile will be adequate.'

'Of course,' I said and reeled it off.

He wrote it down, then looked up. 'Address?'

I shrugged. 'Well. Here!'

'In the United Kingdom?'

I felt the heat rise again, sweat collecting in my armpits. Alice was listening. I told him the address of Alex's flat in Bloomsbury. Gavras had trouble with the name of the road – I had to spell it out, letter by letter. Lie by lie.

When he had finished writing this down, he closed his notebook and leant his elbows on it. 'Mr Morris. I understand your emotions regarding the guard dog got the better of you today. I am not here to arrest you. A dog . . . is a dog. But I am sure like the rest of us you would like to secure a peaceful end to this business.'

'He didn't do it.' Alice leant forwards. 'He says he didn't and I believe him. Paul likes animals.'

'Mrs Mackenzie. Stravros here –' Gavras gestured to the labourer in the pale blue shirt '– saw him covered with blood. As he still is.' He looked at my T-shirt again, turning down the corners of his mouth. 'He was caught, is caught . . . how do you say, red-handed.'

I looked down. 'I know I have blood on me. I don't know how. I must have picked it up.'

'Stravros, as you see, does not have blood on him.'

'I think I got it from the gate.'

'Did you attempt to assassinate the dog earlier today, Mr Morris?' Gavras gave a wry smile, enjoying his own joke. 'A witness saw you in the field at about 11 a.m., staking out the land, shall we say. You were spotted and you ran away.'

'I was there this morning, it's true,' I said. 'I was just having a quiet cigarette. I wasn't staking out the land, and I didn't kill the dog. I'm sorry. I just didn't.'

'We all heard you!' Phoebe came out of the kitchen, followed by Daisy. 'You said it needed putting out of its misery. Didn't he, Daisy?'

Daisy slunk back against the wall. 'I dunno,' she muttered. She was caught. Keeping quiet had turned out useful after all; she needed to keep me on side.

'He said he had plans,' Phoebe said. 'That's why he didn't come sailing. Tosser.'

'Phoebe! Go back into the house.' Alice said. 'You're just making things worse.'

I waited until Phoebe had slammed the door behind her, and then I said quietly: 'I didn't go sailing because I went sight-seeing.'

Gavras was looking at me expectantly. 'Sight-seeing?'

I sat down. 'I went to visit the ruins at Okarta. I took the bus.'

'The bus?'

I nodded. 'From the stop by the shrine. Wonderful views up there,' I said.

Gavras nodded. He gestured to his sidekick who took a few steps towards us, holding a plastic bag which he laid on the table.

Gavras poked it. 'The knife. I could, if I wanted, have it tested for prints. But, for a dog, who could be bothered?' He laughed. 'Maybe we can sort this out between ourselves? Mr Morris – the builder needs to procure a new dog. You understand. Valuable machinery needs to be protected.' He said something in Greek to the man with the wispy beard, who answered. Then Gavras turned back to me: 'Two hundred euros – no problem.'

I began to protest.

'Two hundred euros and the whole thing goes away.' He waved wearily at the house, at the pool; at Alice, who had sat down, her hands cupping her face. 'It is nothing, no? And at least tonight you'll get a good night's sleep. And I can get back to the investigation of more serious matters.'

'I didn't do it,' I said. 'I don't see why I should pay anything.'

Andrew said, eminently reasonable: 'Come on, let's just do what he says.'

'I haven't got the money,' I said. 'Look . . .' I got up and went into the bedroom, grabbed my wallet from the bed and coming back out, handed it to Gavras. 'That's all I have,' I said.

He undid the clasp and pulled the leather apart. The ten-euro note from Louis's bed was in there, as was my credit card, a few random receipts, and – I realised too late – Andrew's three gold condoms.

'I see,' he said.

He drew out the ten-euro note, closed the wallet, paused, reopened it to study the gold condoms, and then re-closed it and handed it back. With a small, disappointed smile, he said, 'I was so hoping we could end this. Now I don't know. Paperwork.' He shrugged, and turned to the other two men who, seeing the ten-euro note in his hand, began waving their arms and talking angrily.

Andrew stepped forward. He murmured something softly to Gavras, who then gestured to the other two men and the four of them walked to the other side of the terrace. Andrew unlocked the external door to his room and went in for a minute, while the others waited. When he came out, he was holding a clear plastic wallet from a bureau de change, and he opened it. He handed several notes to the man with a wispy beard, and then peeled off a couple more for the blue-shirted builder, and a couple more for Gavras.

Gavras nodded and put his notes in his pocket.

A brief conversation took place, and then all three of them left.

Andrew walked back towards us with a sloping, apologetic gait. 'Sorry,' he said. 'It seemed the easiest thing.'

'But I didn't do it,' I said. 'And now you've practically accepted that I did. Paying them off is an admission of guilt.'

'Anything for an easy life,' Andrew said, opening the kitchen door and going in. There was a suck as the fridge door opened.

'I wouldn't be surprised if *they* didn't cut the dog's throat,' I said loudly so my words would reach him. 'They weren't even feeding it. It was half starved. We've been *played*.'

Alice pushed her chair back and dropped her head to rest her forehead on the edge of the table.

'Who did do it?' I said. 'Who would do such a thing?' I remembered something Andrew had said earlier. 'What about Artan? Andrew – did you talk to him? Did you ask him to get heavy?'

Andrew came back out, holding a bottle of beer. 'I did talk to Artan,' he said.

'Do you think he misunderstood what you meant?'

Andrew sighed. 'Yes, maybe. He doesn't speak good English.'

'Would he kill a dog?' I was aware of screwing my face up in horror.

Daisy was sitting quietly on the ground by the kitchen door, but she cleared her throat. 'He wouldn't,' she said, her voice husky.

'You sure?' I asked, making her look me in the eye.

She stared up at me from under her lashes, her mouth firm, and then she nodded. 'He's a friend,' she said eventually.

Alice said, 'I think when you have watched your own family die, you tend to be less sentimental towards animals.'

Andrew rested his spare hand lightly on her bare shoulder. I felt, in the tightness of the air, the rigidity of their stance, a kind of electricity, of mutual understanding, and I felt a flood of hatred towards him. It wasn't up to him to sort everything. He didn't own her, and one day I'd prove it to him. I'd bide my time, but I'd make him pay.

Chapter Seventeen

It rained in the night and in the morning the cushions were sodden, the silvered wood chairs streaked black. Water lay in pools at the outer edge of the terrace, and dripped on to the table through cracks in the canopy. My blood-stained shirt and trousers, which I had washed and hung over a branch of the big olive, clung saturated and heavy. The sky was overcast, the sea grey, with sullen low clouds blocking out much of Albania.

There was no fresh bread. No one had gone to get it. We were out of milk, too. I found a couple of biscuits in the cupboard and made myself a black coffee, which I drank standing at the counter in the kitchen. Dirty dishes from the day before, from supper, even from breakfast, lay submerged in cold greasy water in the sink. I should have washed up, but I didn't have the energy. It felt like the end of the holiday, the end of the party, impossible for anything to be resurrected. Outside it was quiet, the world literally dampened – even the cicadas muted, only the occasionally gurgled crow from a distant cockerel, and the scraping of Artan's broom as he swept the water and leaves off the terrace. I watched him from the kitchen doorway. He was wearing a black T-shirt and jeans, his cap low over his face. His strokes were abrupt and short as if he resented the job. He saw me watching and stopped. He did something with his mouth that was more sheepish than a smile; perhaps it was a wince.

Tina walked in, pulling her pink dressing gown tighter around her waist.

Artan resumed his sweeping. 'Shall we ask him if he killed the dog?' I said, still looking at him.

She yawned, rubbing sleep from the corners of her eyes. 'No. Let's just drop it.'

I turned away. 'At least the builders have stopped.'

'Probably too wet.'

Alice breezed in then, wearing jeans and a 1950s-style cropped blue top. She had slept well, she said. She had had a lovely shower. 'And it's quiet, thank God. Hopefully, they've hit an outcrop of rock and decided to relocate the new development further south.'

'Maybe.' I kissed her on the top of her head, smelling her shampoo. I found her attempts to raise our spirits, or her own, touching.

'I think we should have a barbecue for lunch, don't you? Artan?' she called to him through the kitchen door. 'Do you have a moment to clean out the barbecue at the pool? The barbecue? Down there? Cooking?' She was pointing and miming.

'I think his English is probably better than we realise,' I said.

'What makes you think that?' Tina asked.

I opened my mouth to hint at what I knew and then changed my mind.

Alice came back in and started writing a list, her lip skewered to one side under her teeth. It was sexy: I remember thinking that.

'Paul – you'll do the shop, won't you?' she said, handing me a flap of notes. 'You'll have to go to the bigger supermarket in Trigaki. It's about five kilometres along the road to Pyros.'

I was surprised to be asked, but pleased. It showed I was back in her good books. I was her go-to man. I nodded, pocketing the cash. 'Do you want me to go in Hermes? I'm a bit worried about parking it.'

She thought for a second. 'No, you might as well take the Hyundai.'

Tina found the keys and I got into the car, pushing the seat back to make room for my legs. When I turned the ignition, the compilation CD burst into life – 'Charmless Callous Ways' had come round again. I switched it off and put the car into gear. I was heading slowly towards the drive, when Tina ran after me. I pushed the button to open the window. 'An addition to the list,' she said. 'Alice forgot lye.'

'Alice forgot to lie?'

'*Lye*. For pickling. There's all those raw olives knocking around. Alice has discovered a clever, quick way of pickling them. She found it online. But you need lye. They'll have it anywhere – this is Greece.'

'OK,' I said. 'Tina?'

She had already turned away. 'Yes?'

'It wasn't me who killed the dog. You do believe me, don't you?'

She nodded. 'It was a mistake. I know.'

I was comforted, as I drove off, though of course her answer was ambiguous.

Trigaki was a dusty little town, up a hill off the main road, the outskirts semi-industrial, with small roundabouts and a web of service roads around warehouses selling bathroom fittings and garden pots in trade quantities. The centre, under its overcast sky, was busy with old men playing backgammon, a spankingly modern chemist, women in headscarves queueing by a squawking van of live chickens.

For a moment, I fantasised about driving on, through the town, out through the other side, driving down to the airport,

or anywhere really. The holiday was not what I'd expected, full
of death and sadness, and violence – though not of a type any
of us could have predicted.

I didn't drive on. Perhaps it would have taken a different
man to do so. But how much better it would have been if I
had.

Instead, I found the supermarket and parked in one of the
allotted spaces outside it. Inside, it was air-conditioned – a
shivery shock of cool. Everything on Alice's list was easy to
find, and I collected the items – chicken legs, lamb chops,
dried pasta, feta, tomatoes, beer, charcoal, firelighters. There
was no sign of lye, though I wasn't quite sure where I would
find it. Not with the olives. Not with the vinegars. I asked at
the checkout but the woman shrugged and pointed through
the window in the direction of the town centre. I put the box
of shopping in the boot of the car and wandered back down
the main street, which was dirty, the gutters full of litter. No
obvious outlets selling lye but I passed an 'internet cafe' and,
on a whim, I went inside. It was empty and, peeling off one of
Alice's notes, I paid for a coffee and fifteen minutes of
computer use.

I checked my emails first. I had 127 – most of them spam,
or notifications from Amazon or Abe Books. One was from a
woman called Katie, apologising for not having been in touch.
She had been travelling in Vietnam and Laos ('awesome'), but
she was back and she'd love to pick my brains about journalism some time. Katie, I remembered eventually, was the young
thing I'd met all those months ago in the Crown and Hart.
How long ago that seemed. And how changed I was now. Why
on earth would a girl like her be interested in my opinion?
Why would I be interested in hers?

My agent had emailed too. He'd read through the last thing
I'd sent him and he was very sorry but 'it wasn't quite for

him'. He'd also 'been thinking' and in the course of trying to 'pare down his list', he wasn't sure I was still 'the right fit'.

I drank my bitter coffee down in two gulps and binned his email along with the spam.

The analogue clock counting down on the screen showed five more minutes. I was about to call it a day. Instead, I had an idea. I opened a new window, and in the header for Google search I wrote: 'Florence Hopkins, suicide' and waited.

The internet searched; a circular disc spun across the screen. Several results.

Florence Hopkins Death Records

Birth, Marriage & Death (BMD) Unwanted Certificate Services

Eighty Suicides Linked to Coalition Cuts

Alan Sugar Slams Katie Hopkins for Controversial Comments

But halfway down: Funeral for Tragic Cambridge Student

I clicked, waited while the disc spun again, and then a window opened on the screen – it was an article from the *Hampshire Chronicle*. Two photographs began slowly to download. One was a family group, of parents clinging to each other, a young man with his arm out to steer them into a car. The other was of a young girl holding a sparkler, the glitter throwing flints of light on to her face. She had spiky hair, and a wide smile, and a familiar large gap between her two front teeth.

The article was short: 'David Hopkins, a local businessman, and his wife Cynthia are supported by their son Andrew at the funeral of their beloved daughter, Florence, who died two weeks ago. Florence, known as Florrie, a student at Cambridge University, had been suffering from depression since the spring. 'She was a wonderful person, a joy to teach,' said her former headmistress. 'She is a great loss to the college community and to her family."

'David Hopkins, who is understood to have stood down as managing director of Akorn Investments, was unavailable for comment.'

I looked at the date at the top of the article. July 1994.

It took a moment to sink in. Her funeral was a month after I left Cambridge.

A motorbike-scooter wailed past the cafe. I felt the legs of the plastic chair bow as I rocked back. My fingers held the table. I felt the scratch of sugar on the Formica table, the stickiness of it under my nails.

I have been in league with cruelty . . . and charmless callous ways.

She had killed herself a matter of weeks after we had dated – or whatever it was we had done. Hell: we *had* dated. I had thought of her death as nothing to do with me. But it was. It was the girl I had known who had killed herself, not the imaginary person she had become. We had got to know each other in April or May that year. She killed herself so soon after, in July – a month I had spent being cosseted by publishers, making the deal, being interviewed for the *Bookseller*, my talent held up and marvelled at like a precious jewel.

I sat in the cafe and I thought about Florrie properly for the first time since any of this had happened. I remembered listening to music in her room, the roughness of the wall above her bed, the thin, cheap texture of her pillow. A sunflower motif. A polka-dot top in a slippery fabric. I remember kissing her. I must have slept with her, too, but the precise memory was just out of reach. I had seduced a couple of girls in her year – freshers' week was particularly busy – but Florrie? Of course I had. All my relationships had been sexual. Why would it have been any different with her? I felt regret, and sadness, and a vague sense of guilt – that letter I'd scrunched up and thrown in the bin. Poor Florrie. And did this new information affect my relationship with Andrew? With Alice? Were there conversations I needed to review? Behaviour of my own I needed to think more about? Surely not. Florrie had been depressed, mentally ill. It was nothing to do with me.

The man behind the counter was staring at me. 'More money?' he said. 'More internet?'

I shook my head and pushed back my chair. Its plastic legs tangled with the plastic legs of the chair behind, and I kicked at them to separate them. And then I was out in the street, walking away from the cafe.

I had already started the engine when I remembered the lye. Under normal circumstances, I would have given up. But I was in a mood, dazed still by the news about Florrie, and grateful for a task both to distract my mind and delay my return.

A man I asked outside the supermarket suggested another shop – a five-minute walk in the opposite direction to the town centre. It was more of a shack really, a hotchpotch of homewares, packet food, and what looked like car parts. Two men in vest tops sat on chairs outside it, drinking tiny glasses of coffee. One of them, overhearing my conversation with the owner, gestured me over and, after establishing I had wheels at my disposal, gave me complicated directions, which I only half followed, to Praktiker, a shop on the other side of town.

I returned to the car and drove aimlessly for a while in circles on the outskirts of Trigaki. I found myself deep in the mini-industrial area when I saw the large red sign reading Praktiker across a low-slung home improvement centre.

Inside, among the ranks of paints, buckets and small-scale agricultural equipment, I was directed to a row of large plastic bottles, which, I was assured by an overalled assistant, was lye – sodium hydroxide. As I paid, it struck me that the container was identical to the container I had picked up in the shed. Perhaps I needn't have gone to so much effort.

The police were back. The same car parked in the yard – white with blue writing and a strip of rust above the front right wheel arch. Bloody hell. Groundhog Day. Were they ever going to leave us alone? I pulled up behind as close as I could.

Tina met me as I was getting out of the car. 'You've got a visitor,' she said.

'*I've* got a visitor? What do you mean?'

'Don't worry. I'm sure it's nothing.'

She took the box of shopping out of the boot and carried it around the side of the house. I followed, hands empty but for the plastic bag containing the bottle of lye.

The terrace looked different without the sun, the view flat. No light and shade, no pools of sunshine, no pockets of shadow, just gloomy. The spikes of lavender in their black-streaked pots looked menacing.

Voices at the far end by the kitchen door. Gavras standing, a cup of coffee in his hand; a burst of laughter, all chummy.

He saw me coming towards him and he handed the cup of coffee to someone standing half in the kitchen, then made a wiping movement with the ball of his hands, knocking them together, removing crumbs.

'Mr Morris,' he said. 'We were beginning to think you were never coming back.'

'Just doing a spot of shopping,' I said. 'We're having a barbecue.'

Alice stepped out of the kitchen doorway. She was wearing the Topshop bikini, with a towel over her shoulders – an odd choice, I had time to think, for an overcast day. She did her thing with her lip, biting it, twisting it to one side. 'Paul. Lieutenant Gavras has some questions ... Could you ...'

She raised both hands, palms out. 'Do you want to do it here?'

'Yes, of course,' I said, before realising she wasn't addressing me. I had already sat down. The cushion was damp; I felt the wetness seep into the seat of my trousers. I rested the plastic bag at my feet.

Gavras looked at Alice, and he looked at his watch, and then, making a decision, he pulled the chair out opposite me and sat down, too. He was carrying a briefcase and he snapped the clasp and took out the notebook from the previous day.

I turned my head to catch Alice's eye. Tina was moving about in the kitchen now, putting away the shopping. The suck of the fridge, the click of cupboards. Otherwise, the house seemed quiet. 'Where are the others?' I said.

'They've gone into Stefanos for a coffee.'

I nodded, as if it were a matter on which my opinion had any bearing, and turned back to the policeman. 'OK. So what's this about? More about the dog? How can I help you?'

'So, Mr Morris. I am sorry to inconvenience you in the middle of your holiday. Nothing . . . nothing . . . too important.'

'Good.'

'I can't believe how busy I've been this week. A rape, a dog with his throat cut. Normally it is so quiet here in Agios Stefanos. How much more interesting life has been since you arrived, Mr Morris.'

I shrugged. 'Neither of those things have anything to do with me.'

Gavras spun his open notebook round and peered down. 'A few minor matters,' he said in a conversational tone. 'A couple of curiosities.'

'Go on.'

'You arrived, you say, on the Thomas Cook flight from Gatwick on Monday?'

I tried to will the blood not to rise to my face. I had a split second to decide. If Alice hadn't been present, I'd have told the truth. But in that split second, I cared more for her opinion than his. I managed to say, 'Yup . . .'

'Do you still have your boarding pass, or ticket?'

I shook my head. 'No.'

He nodded very slightly. 'So you were still at home in London on Sunday night?'

'Yes.'

'In the property you own at . . .' He looked down at his notebook and read out Alex's address in Bloomsbury.

I hardly faltered. 'That would be correct.'

'Odd,' he said musingly. 'The registered owner of that property is a Mr Alex Young.'

Alice took a step closer. She was frowning, her head on one side.

I said: 'Alex Young is the freeholder.'

Gavras studied me, his chin lifted, the corners of his mouth downturned. 'Ah. I see. We can return to that. At any rate, wherever you left home that morning, you took the Thomas Cook flight, leaving London Gatwick at 5.10 a.m., and landing at Ionnasis Vikelas International Airport, Pyros at 7.40 a.m.'

'Yes.'

'Mr Morris,' he said kindly. 'It doesn't take my team long to check these sorts of things. Passenger lists.'

I rotated my shoulders as if they were stiff.

'Where are you going with this?' Alice asked.

'I am just keen to establish that Mr Morris was not in Pyros town on Sunday night at the Pig and Whistle bar?'

'No,' I said.

'And Laura Cratchet is unknown to you?'

'Yes.'

'Despite the fact that Mr Hopkins remembers you saying hello to her in Stefanos earlier during the evening of the rape, greeting her –' he looked down again at his notes '– "like an old friend"?'

'I think she said hello to me first. I had seen her on the bus.'

'And noticed her?'

I closed my eyes briefly. 'Enough to recognise her later, that's all.'

'And when I saw you in the nightclub on your own on Thursday night, you had just wandered in by accident?'

'Not by accident, but as I explained, because I thought I saw Andrew going in there.'

Alice was standing right next to me now. She brought her hand up and rubbed the ball of it across her eye. Then, taking it away, she said, her voice cool: 'Mr Morris has confirmed his address and the arrival of his flight from London, and has reassured you that he was neither in Pyros town on Sunday night, nor a close personal friend of the rape victim. Was that all you needed, Lieutenant Gavras?'

Gavras was writing in his notebook. He put his pen down on the table. 'One other curiosity.' He sighed. 'A conversation we had regarding the guard dog.'

'I didn't do it – you know that. It was almost definitely Alice's caretaker, Artan.'

'My question,' he continued as if I hadn't spoken, 'regards your whereabouts during the hours when the creature had its throat cut. To be precise, the trip you took to the Helladic Settlement at Okarta.'

I said, 'I don't see why this is a police matter.'

'Enjoyable, was it?'

'Yes.'

He leant back, tucking his shirt into his trousers. 'It amazes me, Mr Morris, that you found so much to interest you at the

Helladic Settlement, since the site is temporarily closed for renovation.'

'What are you talking about?' Alice said.

My eyes felt dry and my tongue swollen.

'I did go,' I said. 'I did see the ruins. There was no one in the ticket office to pay; I thought that was a bit odd. But I got in and walked around OK.'

'And you got the bus?'

I nodded.

'How fortunate you were to find "a bus" going into the interior of the island. Unusual.'

'My mother used to say I had the luck of the devil.' I looked at him and he looked at me. His eyes were narrowed. 'So if that's it. I might go and have a shower.'

I stood up, without waiting for an answer, and began to walk casually across the terrace towards the bedroom door. As soon as I had my back to him, I felt a desire to run, a sort of explosive panic in my feet. I was ready for the sound of footsteps, for the winding thud of Gavras's body, for the twist of my arm. But there was nothing. The squeak of my shoes. The cockerel in the distance. Cicadas.

I spent the rest of the afternoon playing the role of model boyfriend. I attended the barbecue, turning and basting the chargrilled meat, my eyes filled with smoke, my hands scalded by tiny splatters of oil, without complaint. I served up, and I cleared away. I charged people's drinks. I found fresh ice. The sun broke through the clouds and reminded us we were on holiday. The builders hadn't yet returned and the peace was like a gift. Pigeons coo'ed and swallows swooped, darts across the pool. There were jokes and laughter. Someone swam – small splashes, sharp intakes of breath, sighs of pleasure. Normally, I'd have slept after lunch, but today I kept myself alert to other people's needs. Tina forgot her paints and I went back up to the house to collect them. Yvonne was hot in the sun and I moved her lounger to the shade. Frank and Archie needed a third to play a card game called 'Cheat' and I was the first to volunteer.

We played at the table under the gazebo, next to a plant with big trumpet-like white flowers and dark pink centres, yellow stamens. The petals were dropping on the ground, where they lay crinkled like tissues. I won the game – the best cheat there, it turned out – and afterwards the boys leapt into the pool. Alice was sitting on a chair next to Yvonne's lounger and she smiled across at me. 'Thanks,' she mouthed, wrinkling her nose. One of the flowers had flopped on to the table. I picked it up and stroked it across my lips. It was soft and velvety, and smelt like almonds. It felt like promise, like sex, like hope.

I wasn't worried about Gavras – not now he'd left. They were small lies I'd told; what mattered now was Alice. I'd tell her the truth later, as soon as we were alone. The sort of mistakes I'd made, the kind that were natural to me in the past, I wouldn't make again. Not now I was with her. Small lies, small errors of judgement – they added up. It was better to be truthful, to be honest, to take care of other people. Take Florrie. Poor dead Florrie. I should have known she was vulnerable; I should have picked up on the danger of it. She had loved me – I could hear her voice whispering it in my ear; feel her lips on my neck, remember pushing my tongue into her mouth, my body against hers. But I had gone to London and left her. That letter, screwed up. Phone calls I didn't return. I should have been kinder.

I gazed across again at Alice, hoping to catch her eye again, to convey how I felt. I was different now, I'd turned a corner, all because of her. But she was leaning back stiffly in her chair, her lids closed. Yvonne basically ignored or snapped at her. Nothing was ever right with Yvonne – the meat was burned, the wine too warm, Karl was telling a story she'd heard too many times before. She was sour and strangely resentful, and someone like me might find that suspicious, but Alice stayed by her side, stuck with her. That was the definition of goodness, of kindness. And I would learn from it. Maybe I'd confess about Florrie, explain my guilt. And what else? Artan and Daisy? Should I divulge what I saw? Or should I keep my promise? What was the right thing, the most honest thing? Oh God, it was a minefield. The selfish response to events was so much more straightforward than the morally correct.

'Dropping off, are we?'

I must have closed my eyes for an instant, and Andrew was leering down at me.

'No. Thinking.'

'Planning your next book?'

'Something like that.'

'Nice work if you can get it.' He slapped me on the shoulder before heading for the steps. 'Got some calls to make,' he said loudly.

'But it's Saturday,' Tina said. 'I thought now you were partner . . .'

'No rest for the wicked.'

Of course I ruined it by drinking too much. I don't know what happened. I think the lamb at lunch was too salty and I downed one too many beers or glasses of wine to compensate. Perhaps that was the problem – I was mixing. Or perhaps it was the stress of the day, the shopping trip, and the efforts to impress. I was aware of dusk falling, and the lights flicking from the house, the steps up to the terrace rickety and uneven, the shrubs closing in on me as I climbed. I was aware of Andrew enjoying every minute. 'Oopsadaisy,' he said as I stumbled. I tried to make a joke. 'Oops your own Daisy,' I tried to say, but I don't think it came out right.

A hand under my am, plates clattering, conversation louder and then quiet. The dark bedroom. The cool of the pillow against my face. My head was full of Florrie, and of Jasmine, of dead girls and missing girls, of certainty and uncertainty. My head began to pound and I felt a dread that was like sediment blocking the flow of my blood.

When Alice came in, I pulled her down. 'Lie with me.'

Her body moved close, swellings and dips.

'I'm sorry, Alice,' I murmured.

'You just called me Florrie.'

'What did I do? What did I do wrong?'

I was half drugged, but I remember her mouth on mine.

Chapter Eighteen

The workers had been creeping closer. The following morning they started in the copse just beyond the swimming pool. The jack-hammer destroying what was left of the wall woke everyone up. 'Ignore it,' Alice said in my ear. Her breath was damp and hot. A wrench of the sheet as she turned away. 'It's the only thing to do. Keep on as usual.'

The sun was out, the sky a clear new blue, the world dried out, soil-cracking hot. Yesterday had been dull and then patchy. But this was the kind of heat that we'd come for – the kind of heat we deserved. Alice got up and went down to the pool, hoping to shame the builders into stopping, and I followed her. Artan was cleaning out the filter. I remember his cap stuffed in the back pocket of his jeans, the back of his head, the scraping noise. Andrew and Tina came down the steps, and Tina asked after my head. 'I've got some aspirin up at the house,' she said. 'You should drink lots of water.'

Andrew sneered. 'Bit late for that.'

Daisy arrived soon after, and peeled off her sundress, her slim body olive-brown. Artan watched her as she arranged herself on a towel. I remember that. And I remember thinking she knew he was watching and feeling mildly turned on by that, and also guilty, as if there was something I still had to do. Was Phoebe already with us? Details at this point matter. Yes. I remember stepping past her to reach an empty sunbed. I remember noticing the bleach of her hair against her dark roots, and the deliberate attempt she made, seeing me, to cover herself with a towel.

I don't remember the exact moment the construction stopped. It had been off and on all morning. I don't remember a shout, the alarm first being raised. If I had heard it, I would have assumed a problem with the machinery. Possibly distant shouting filtered through into my consciousness. I was still fuzzy from the booze. I expect when the noise stopped, I sank with relief into the silence.

On the sunbed, the world was still – that's the impression I have, thinking back. Alice, lying on her front – her head turned to one side, a rigidity in her neck, the hand that held a book trailing on the ground. The laced pattern of the pool reflected on the underside of an umbrella. Gnats in the grass. Olive leaves silver in the sun. A hornet low and dangerous across the pool, a gurgle from the water filter.

But then the voices changed and grew louder – an urgency in them, an alarm. Shouts like bullets. The sound of a car bumping up the field. The roar of a motorbike. Footsteps running. Boots on cracked vegetation, getting closer. I remember sitting up and seeing, through slowly clearing eyes, Gavras. Right there. In the scrub just below the pool, in the dappled shade of the low trees. Muscles bulging below his shirt sleeves. Too dark to see his face, but an arrow in his head – no, a twig caught in his hair, at an angle. Gavras took a few steps forward, out of the shadow, up the slope. There was something ghastly about his expression. Did he mouth something to Alice? I'm still not sure.

Things I remember next: a violent clatter as Andrew's sunbed jack-knifed. Alice running towards Gavras, and then away again back towards me, stumbling, stubbing her toe, her face stretched. Tina, throwing her dress on back to front and

226

saying, 'What is it?' and Phoebe and Daisy wrapping themselves in towels and standing by the barbecue, and Andrew bent double, the tips of his shoulders pink with sunburn, scrabbling on the ground under the collapsed lounger for his phone. I remember seeing Artan talking quickly, in a language I didn't recognise, to one of the labourers, and Gavras shouting into his phone in Greek.

But most of all, I remember Alice's voice, over and over again: 'They've found her. They've found her.'

I was extraordinarily calm. I felt like a bystander, a witness. Gavras put the phone back in his pocket and pushed his palms out at us, gesturing for us to go up to the house. I righted Andrew's sunbed and picked up his phone. I rescued a towel that was dipping into the pool. And I put my arm around Alice's shoulders and forced her up the path after the others. She was limping. Her toe was bleeding. She left smears of blood on each step. I made her sit on a chair while I washed it. I took her foot in my hand and inspected the loose flap of skin on one side of the toe and once I had stemmed the flow, I wrapped it tightly in some toilet paper. The blood soon began to seep through.

Louis, huge and ungainly in a pair of pyjama bottoms, came out of his bedroom. 'What's happening?'

Alice said: 'It's something to do with Jasmine.'

Tina shook her head. 'We don't know that.'

I looked up from Alice's small, bleeding foot. 'We don't know anything,' I said.

No one came for hours. We huddled on the terrace, like actors in an Agatha Christie novel, waiting to be told what to do. Andrew, changed into beige chinos and a pale pink Fred Perry, went down to the pool to find out 'what the hell was going on' and was sent back. Gavras had asked permission to use the house for access and he had given it. 'That's all right, Alice, isn't it?' She nodded. Tina brought out some cold lamb chops, left over from the day before, and some tomatoes. Nobody ate. I cracked open a beer and then, watched by the others, wished I hadn't.

Archie and Frank walked down to the end of the drive and said the lane was blocked with police cars. They had stretched tape across the gate. 'It can't be another dog,' Frank said. 'They didn't bother with tape for Paul's dog.'

'The dog Paul murdered,' Phoebe added.

'It wasn't my dog,' I said. 'It had nothing to do with me.'

'We should ring Yvonne,' Alice kept saying. Her foot was still up on a chair, the blood-stained paper unravelling. She didn't notice. I reaffixed it whenever I could get near her. 'Just in case. She'd want to know.'

'We shouldn't.' Andrew shook his head, and then nodded a few times, watching to check she understood.

'It's the way he nodded at me,' Alice said. 'I can't get it out of my head.'

She buried her face in her arms and rested them, crossed, on the table. Every few seconds her body convulsed in a silent shudder.

'They might not have found anything. It might just be that one of the workers has been injured,' Tina said. 'Broken his leg or something. An industrial accident. They'd send for the police if it was serious. If machinery was involved. If it was the company's fault.'

'It's Jasmine,' Alice said, lifting her head. 'I know it is.'

Shadows shortened and then began to lengthen. The three boys had gone into the house and were playing on the Xbox. Tina was clearing up in the kitchen. Phoebe and Daisy had retired to my fag seat and were watching something on an iPad. Alice and Andrew were sitting, side by side, staring at the sea. I was pretending to read my book.

A middle-aged man in a blue suit came round the side of the house, holding a briefcase, walked straight past, and descended the path down to the pool. Two younger women in white overalls followed a few minutes later, carrying heavy bags full of equipment. One of them nodded, but neither of them spoke. A few minutes later, the older man in the blue suit returned and stood on the edge of the terrace with his back to us, making a phone call. His suit jacket was cheap and too tight – the central seam was beginning to pull away.

Alice lifted her head. 'I wish we could speak Greek,' she said.

'How does he know we don't speak Greek?' Andrew said. 'How does he know we don't understand every word?'

'It's just so *rude*. Treating us like we don't *count*.'

I was looking at her while she spoke so I saw it on her face: the precise moment they came up the path. I saw her eyes darken, the hollows in her cheeks sink, the colour in her lips drain away.

A small procession. The women in the white overalls came first. When they reached the terrace, they stood silently on either side of the path, waiting. Two men were bringing some-thing up, carrying it between them, at the lowest reach of their arms, slowly, carefully, gingerly, keeping their burden level, trying not to jolt it. It was light. The men weren't struggling under the physical weight. But there was something in their posture, in their expression, as if this was the heaviest burden they'd ever carried. The first man, Gavras's handsome side-kick, appeared at the top of the path; following him a few feet behind, the bald policeman from the beach. When they were both on the flat of the terrace, they laid their burden down.

It was a stretcher. On it was a piece of plastic sheeting. And under the plastic sheeting was an angular mass, flat, pale, soft, darkness, a smear of mud. Cloth and bones, and sinew. Not much. A handful of dust and dirt. The bald policeman leant forward with his elbows on his knees to get back his breath. Angelo, Gavras's sidekick, crouched down to readjust the plastic, to tuck it in at one side. He did it delicately, with reverence. His throat moved; he swallowed, closing his eyes.

'I am very sorry.' Gavras had come up behind and was standing at the top of the path, his face grim. 'Mrs Mackenzie – I . . . I am so very sorry.'

Alice had stood up. Her hands were pressed to her cheeks. She was staring at the body on the ground with pity and terror in her eyes. Blotches had appeared on her throat.

Andrew took a couple of steps forward and the chair behind him clattered over. His eyes were hollow. 'Is it a body?' he said. 'Is it Jasmine?'

Tina in the kitchen doorway let out a moan.

'I can't say anything for sure, but we have found some remains. I'm sorry.'

I felt a hard lump at the back of my throat. Even at this point I was still expecting a different explanation. Some ancient horror, some mechanical mishap, some misunderstanding. Now I could feel their shock like ice on the surface of my own skin. I could feel it burning on every nerve ending.

Angelo got back into position, checked he was in sync with his partner, and the two policemen lifted the stretcher up again and carried it, past the teenage girls, around the side of the house and out of sight. The women in the white overalls followed. Gavras stayed where he was.

'It seems extraordinary if she was here on this land, so close to the house for all these years,' I said.

Alice spoke for the first time. Her voice came out gravelly, almost inaudible: 'Have you told Yvonne?' She cleared her throat and repeated the question more loudly. 'Have you told Yvonne?'

Gavras put his head on one side. 'We don't know for sure that it is Jasmine Hurley. Relevant procedures need to take place.'

'You've found a body, haven't you? Who else is it going to be? Of course it's Jasmine.'

'Mrs Mackenzie, I understand you are upset . . .'

'HAVE YOU TOLD YVONNE?'

Gavras stood up. 'I'm on my way to talk to Mrs Hurley now. Some of my men will stay on the property while we arrange for a thorough search.' He looked quickly from left to right, apparently overcome by indecision. 'Um, I'm sorry for the inconvenience. Is it all right if . . . We'll need to search. We'll need to talk to you, if it's . . . Even if it isn't . . .' He seemed to have lost his confidence, his arrogance.

Andrew stood up and took control. He put his hand out – an invitation to Gavras to shake it. 'We'll be here. No one is going anywhere,' he said. 'Is it all right if we use the house? Yes? That OK? We'll just be here.'

Gavras took his hand. 'Thank you. Yes. Yes. I am sure that is . . . yes. I will . . . I will be back in, um, due course.'

He turned and took a step away and then he paused. 'Mr Hopkins? If I could have a word?'

Andrew peeled himself from the table, resting his hand very lightly for a moment on Alice's shoulder, and the two men walked together across the terrace where they stood in conversation.

I tried to follow their lips, to read what they were saying.

'What do you think they're talking about?' I said to Alice.

She didn't answer. I turned. Her phone was on the table but she'd gone.

'Alice?' I called. 'Tina?'

No answer.

Andrew was walking back across the terrace.

'Paul,' he said. 'A word, if I may.'

A word. Same phrase Gavras had used. I didn't answer but nodded. He had to run everything, organise everyone.

'Of course,' I said.

'Do you want to sit down?'

'No.'

'OK, then. I should tell you the lieutenant is particularly keen that you shouldn't leave the house for the time being. I've told him I will ensure that.'

'Me?'

'I know a lot else is going on but he still has a few further questions for you, regarding your relationship with Laura Cratchet. Nothing to worry about unduly.'

'*Laura Cratchet?*' It took me a second to work out who he meant. 'I have no relationship with Laura Cratchet.'

'I'm only repeating what he said.' He was loving it. The little fucker.

I stared at him but I wasn't going to stare him out. Behind him the sea crawled. A motorboat sped, churning a tiny white path like an aeroplane trail.

I went straight to the bedroom to look for Alice. Tina was leaving as I got there. She brushed past me in the doorway. 'Be kind,' she murmured.

Alice was lying on the bed, her dress wrinkled up and twisted around her thighs, damp, her face buried in the pillow.

'I'm so sorry,' I said. 'I'm sorry. I'm so sorry you were wrong.' I sat on the edge of the bed and stroked her hair, noticed the pearls of perspiration on her forehead. 'I'm so sorry. If it's right. It's just awful – for Yvonne, for you, for everyone.'

She let out a deep, long, trembling sigh, and I forgot my own worry as another of those overwhelming tides of tenderness and pity crashed over me. I thought about all the time and money she had spent on this campaign, how much of her own heart she had given over to it, how the loss of Jasmine, a girl she had never met, had driven her half mad, and I wanted to wrap her in a blanket, and to hold her in my arms, close to my chest.

I pulled a strand of hair loose and smoothed it back. I said quite a lot more about how much I knew people depended on her, and how extraordinarily self-sacrificing she had been, how much she had supported Yvonne, how much she had personally shouldered, what a burden the hope had been, and what an amazing mother she was. 'I think you're . . .' I began to say, and then my voice cracked, 'wonderful.'

She didn't say anything.

The afternoon lengthened, the heat sank from the day. After a while, I lay down next to her.

Andrew was standing in the doorway. A dark shape. He couldn't have been there long, watching us. He stretched out his hand. Alice's phone lay on his palm. He said, cupping it with his other hand, 'It's Karl. I answered. I couldn't not.'

She sat up, stared at him. Her hair clung, damp, to her face. Red creases from the pillow.

I thought of Salome bringing the head of John the Baptist to Herodias.

Andrew said: 'He wants to speak to you.'

Alice swept her legs sideways off the bed and stumbled across to him, her dress crinkled. She tucked her hair behind her ears and, taking the phone from him, pushed open the door to the terrace. I heard her voice, distinct, outside. 'My dear Karl. How is she? . . . I'm sure . . . Unimaginable . . . The worst . . .' A noise, half-sigh, half-shudder. 'Can she bear to? If she wants to. If she can. Yes, of course.'

A long silence, and then, her voice clear again, 'Darling. My darling girl. We don't know for sure yet, but yes . . . Words can't express . . .' A long silence and then: 'Yes. I know.'

Andrew had followed her out. I wondered if he had his arm around her.

'We've been asked to stay here,' she said. 'But I'll come to see you the moment I can.' A long pause, and then her voice softer: 'We don't know . . .' Another silence. 'All my thoughts, all my love . . . Yvonne. I'm sorry. I'm so sorry.' Nothing for a moment, and then she said: 'She's gone. She's hung up.'

Alice came back into the room alone. I was lying where I'd been when she left. I hadn't moved. 'How is she taking it?' I said.

'Still in shock. The police are with her.'

'Of course,' I said. 'If nothing else, they'll want to see how she reacts.'

'What do you mean?'

'Haven't you ever wondered?'

'Paul. Don't.'

'Would she have known about the well? Whoever killed Jasmine might have known about the well. How close was the apartment block where they were staying?'

'For goodness sake, Paul, not now.'

She crossed to the bathroom and I heard the sound of water splashing into the sink. She washed her face, I think, and cleaned her teeth. I sensed the dampness of her cheeks when she lay back down, smelt the mint of her breath.

It wasn't me that started it. I wouldn't have dared. She peeled her dress off, followed by the red bikini she was wearing underneath – and, naked, she rolled on top of me, pressing the length of her body against mine, and brought her mouth down hard. I kissed her with some alarm, but equally hard as it seemed to be what she was expecting. She pinned my arms above my head and pulled up my T-shirt. Her hands moved under the waistband of my shorts, her knee thrust between my thighs, her breasts against my chest. She rubbed her body from side to side, pushing much harder than I would have dared.

In one movement I wriggled my arms free and lifted her until she was underneath me. Her breathing was fast, her eyes tightly closed. She tugged again at my zip. I bent to graze her mouth and then kept her waiting for as long as I could before I was inside her. Her mouth opened, her tongue sought mine. When I lowered my face, I felt her teeth pushing hard against my lower lip. I pulled away. Her hands were tangled in my hair. 'Don't stop,' she said. 'Don't you fucking stop.'

So I didn't. But I slowed it down. I slowed it right down until she could bear it no longer. And I watched her face again as she cried out, as, finally, she came.

We didn't eat that evening, or leave the room. I don't know what the others did, whether Andrew forced them to carry on as if nothing had happened. I don't know if the police left the house alone for the night, or whether one of Gavras's men stood guard at the gate. Alice and I stayed where we were. When we were thirsty we drank from the tap. Mainly she slept and I lay next to her, listening to her breathe.

I should have felt wonderful. The big man. Her first orgasm in more than ten years. She didn't any more, she had said. *I don't come.* Why didn't I feel pleased with myself? Six months previously that's all I'd have thought about. But something in me had changed. I felt a deep, heart-ripping tenderness for her, and with it a terror I couldn't explain.

Chapter Nineteen

Gavras was back early the next morning, with a search warrant for the house and grounds. There were men in overalls everywhere, in the yard, and in the garage, in the pool area, in the copse. It was like being invaded by ants. I felt itchy and claustrophobic, desperate to get out.

I was sitting on the terrace with Alice, Andrew and Tina – all four of us in a mood that was both desultory and tense – when Gavras came over to join us. He was cleanly shaved, and wearing a newly ironed white shirt, which looked a little tight around the collar. He kept moving his neck, jutting his chin forward, as if trying to loosen it. He sat next to me, his hand on my chair, apologised for 'ruining our holiday' and, at a prompt from Andrew, cautiously filled us in on what he knew so far.

The remains had been sent to the medical examiner in Pyros town for DNA testing and it now seemed very likely that they belonged to Jasmine. The coroner – the middle-aged man in the blue suit, it turned out – had been unable to pinpoint the date of death with any exactitude, but had agreed that the body had been in the well for 'between five and ten years'. Growth plates, bone composition and sutures in the skull suggested it belonged to a Caucasoid teenager, between the ages of thirteen and sixteen, not fully grown. The skeleton had a female pelvic structure. Most importantly fabric fragments found with the body matched the description of clothes

Jasmine had been wearing, though there was another garment that didn't. There was no doubt this was a murder enquiry. She hadn't fallen. She had been thrown in the well, after death. A blunt force trauma to the head. Subsequent to that, someone had recently tried to destroy evidence.

'I can't believe she has been here all this time,' Tina said. 'I just don't understand.'

Gavras told us he personally would be taking a back seat in the investigation – a superior officer would be arriving soon, and he would be handing over to him. In the meantime, he was keen to tie up a few loose threads regarding other recent crimes. He was getting close, he said, smiling.

He turned to me. 'In fact, Mr Morris, I have a few more questions regarding the inconsistencies we discussed on Saturday.'

I nodded, unperturbed. I had known this moment would come. 'Yes. I understand.'

'Maybe we could meet in private later this morning?'

'That would be fine by me.'

He looked at me for a moment, and then also nodded. Directing his attention to Alice, he told her that Yvonne was in 'an extreme state of emotion'. A doctor had been called and was on his way up from Trigaki. But Yvonne was adamant she wanted to speak to Alice first.

I caught Tina's eye. 'That's interesting.'

'So I give my permission,' Gavras continued, 'for you to join her in the hotel. One of my officers will be there when you get there.'

Alice stood up. 'I'll go now.' She picked up her car keys from the table. 'Tina, could you check the kids are OK when they wake? I haven't had a chance to talk to them properly. Andrew, we should start working on a press release. It's going to leak, isn't it? We need to do that before it does.'

'I'll come with you to the car,' I said. As we walked away from the table, I put my arm around her shoulders and felt her tremble.

In the front yard, I opened the driver's door for her and she got in. I walked in front of the car and then got in on the passenger side. 'I'll come too,' I said. 'Just down to the village. It'll be nice to get out for a bit.'

She looked across at me. 'OK,' she said, switching on the engine. The car filled with 1980s alternative rock. Tracey Thorn sang about how much safer it was to break down and cry. Alice spun the air-conditioning to full – hot air blasting – and turned the car round. Angelo, the young policeman with the good looks, was standing at the entrance to the yard. Alice rolled her window down. 'Lieutenant Gavras has said it's OK for me to go into town.'

'You can go. But him –' he jerked his chin at me. 'He must stay.'

'I'm sure it's fine,' Alice said. 'We're not going to be long.'

The policeman shook his head. I didn't move, but Alice leant across me. A whiff of orange flower and fig; a tang of chlorine. She pulled the handle to open the passenger door, just a crack, as far as she could reach. 'Maybe you'd better do what you're told.'

'Really?'

'Yes.' She kissed my cheek. 'I won't be long.'

Angelo came round to my side of the car and pulled the door wide. I stepped out, put my hands up in an ironic gesture of surrender. The door shut behind me and I heard the bang of the policeman's hand on the roof. The engine turned and Alice drove slowly off. I watched the vehicle bump down the drive and then I turned away and walked quickly around the side of the house, and headed for my fag bench. From inside the house, I could hear Andrew talking on the phone – pompous, lawyerly.

'. . . Grounds for that would need to be verified . . .'

I lit up, hoping I was out of sight. I felt mildly disconcerted at being stuck there, trapped, *bored*. Nothing more.

Andrew came out of his bedroom doors, slipping his phone into his back pocket. He didn't see me at first, but he looked around, chin forward, and then came straight towards me.

'Paul,' he said, sitting down on the bench. 'Hi. I thought you'd gone with Alice.'

'Apparently she's the only one of us who is allowed to leave.'

He moved his head up and down slowly, a careful nod. 'Hm.' Boring, I know. Some things just won't go away.'

'I don't know why he still wants to talk to me about the poor girl's rape.'

'Unfortunate it took place the night you arrived in Stefanos.'

'A coincidence.'

'Notice—' he laughed, 'I didn't say "the night you arrived in *Pyros*".'

'A minor misunderstanding,' I said, looking at Andrew carefully. 'I'm going to clear that up when I speak to Gavras.'

He swept some invisible dirt from his shorts. 'Of course it's a misunderstanding, but you can see how Gavras might make the connection. Policemen being what they are.'

'Luckily, I was up here at the house that evening. I was nowhere near Stefanos. I've got an alibi. Alice was with me.'

He said: 'I think Gavras's issue is that you don't actually have an alibi?' He used the upward intonation of his children, making a statement sound like a question. 'The main problem, annoyingly, is that she wasn't with you? She was with me?'

I tipped another cigarette out of the paper packet, though I didn't light it, just rolled it between my fingers. 'Yes,' I said carefully. 'I know. The two of you were collecting Louis from the harbour, later in the evening than anyone –' I shrugged lightly '– sorry, than *Gavras* is aware of. I'm hoping he's going to drop the matter, because I really don't want to have to go into all that.'

'Yes, he let a beat pass, stroking the carved wood of the bench between us. I don't think he needs to know Louis was in the village, do you?'

'I don't want to tell him, but I'd tell the truth if necessary. I'm sure Alice will too, if she thinks I'm in any trouble. She loves me. She'll back me.'

He pulled his chin in. 'Back you over her son? I don't think so.'

I felt something in me sink. 'I don't think he did it, but I still think he should be made to own up. I'm sure Alice does too. I don't know why you would stop her.'

'No, Paul,' he said. 'No one is going to make Louis do anything. Be realistic. Alice'll do anything to protect her son, and under the circumstances, so will I.'

'But the truth – that matters.'

Andrew said, 'The truth is a strange thing, Paul. All truth is subjective. We all have responsibilities. Didn't we all hear you suggest that what Louis needed was to have sexual inter-course? Do you think the other boys didn't tell him? And didn't you refer to those half-clad girls as slappers, or was it jailbait? I forget your exact term.'

'But if there is the slightest doubt that Louis might be a *rapist*?'

'Again – a subjective term. Take Florrie . . .' His tone was so casual and calm, you wouldn't have known there was any emotion behind his words. 'My sister. You made certain assumptions. And she allowed you because she thought herself in love.'

'What do you mean, "assumptions"?'

'You know – that she was more experienced than she was, that she was "up for it", an easy lay.'

'I don't think I—'

'You did, Paul. She was a virgin and it meant a lot to her. Do me the favour of not even trying to pretend it meant anything to you.'

My chest had tightened. I felt floored, found it hard to breathe.

'I'm sorry,' I said, unable to meet his eye.

I fumbled to light my cigarette.

'It might just as well have been rape for the amount of thought you gave to her. You didn't for a minute think about the damage you might be doing.'

I managed to bring a cigarette to my lips but I was having trouble lighting it. 'I'm sorry,' I said again. 'I didn't realise . . .'

'No, you didn't.' I was aware of him looking at me, sizing me up, and I wished he wouldn't. 'She loved you,' he added after a moment, 'that's the thing.'

'If I had had any idea . . .'

'That she cared so much? Or that she would kill herself?' He let out a laugh that had no humour in it.

I managed to light the cigarette. 'It was a mistake.'

'Yes. We all make mistakes. And sometimes we need to live with the consequences.'

I stood up and left him then, my eyes blurring, the world out of focus. In the bedroom I sat on the bed. My legs were shaking, my heart pounding. The heat of the room, the lazy, pointless droning of the fan. My clothes spilled from the hold-all. My books – the Dickens, the Truman Capote, *Moby-Dick* – were on the floor. A bag of shopping I'd brought in here by mistake. I put my head between my legs and took some deep breaths. The walls were closing in. I couldn't stay here any longer. I needed to get away. I didn't want to look Andrew in the eye again. I didn't want to think any more about Florrie.

And I didn't want to have to talk to Gavras, to wriggle and explain. I needed to get out of the house. If I got down to the village and found Alice before they did, if I explained, got her on side, then everything would be all right. This whole Greece thing – she was right, it had been a terrible mistake. I needed to get back to London, where she and I could be together properly, without Andrew, without Gavras, where everything could be sorted. That's right. I just needed to get away. I went into the bathroom and had a long shower. When I came out, I put on my linen trousers, washed but a little crumpled, and a denim button-down shirt, slipping my passport and wallet into my back pocket, picked up *In Cold Blood*.

A shadow passed at the window, darkened the vertical crack between the two shutters, and stayed there. I heard someone clear their throat.

I opened the door. Angelo, the handsome policeman, was standing outside. He stepped back.

'OK?' I said.

He nodded.

Tina was sitting at the table, reading an old copy of *Vogue*, and I pulled one of the wicker chairs out from under the table and placed it a few feet from her.

'Alice not back?' I said.

'No.'

A fly buzzed. A Coke can lay on its side at the edge of the flower bed; wasps hovered over it, one of them landed and crawled inside, its body quivering. Tina let out a deep sigh. I looked up. Her paints and watercolour book were at her feet. She was picking at her nails, then biting the skin to the side of her thumb, frowning, as if it were a job that had to be done.

I read for a bit, and then I put my book down carefully on the ground. 'Can I get you anything? Cup of coffee? Glass of water?'

She looked at me for a moment, as if she needed time for the words to make sense, and then said, 'Oh. A coffee. OK. If you're making one.'

I stood up. 'What about you?' I said to Angelo. 'Coffee?'

He moved his legs slightly apart, rooting himself in, and shook his head.

'Lieutenant Gavras? Do you know where he is? He might want one.'

The policeman shrugged. I walked round the terrace to the front of the house and stood in the yard looking around. No sign of Gavras there. I walked a very small distance down the drive and then saw him, about 100 yards away. He had his back to me and he was talking into his phone, kicking at the wiry plants on the verge.

I went back the way I had come. 'Can't find him,' I said.

In the kitchen, I filled the kettle to the brim with water and spooned coffee into the cafetiere. Then I stepped outside again. 'Andrew want one, do you think?' I said.

'I don't know.'

'What about your colleagues?' I said to the policeman. 'Can I get them anything to drink? Hot work down there.'

He looked confused. I mimed drinking from a cup and pointed to the area beyond the pool. He shrugged.

'Maybe water?' I said. 'I could go and ask.'

He shrugged again.

'OK. I'll do that.'

'Or you could just take a jug down?' Tina called, but I had already set off down the steps, taking them two at a time, adrenalin squeezing my chest, my eyes filled with explosions of light and colour.

I scrambled down to the bottom, tripping on the last step and stumbling on to my knees. I stood up, pulled myself together, and walked cautiously the few steps to the pool terrace. I glimpsed two of Gavras's men, at the far side of the water, in the trees down the slope to the right – where I had explored earlier in the week. The flash of a white shirt. A bowed head. One of the two men walked a short distance and then stopped and said something. The other man grunted. They both had their backs to me.

On this side, the pool was built up on a platform. From the edge, the land dropped at an abrupt angle: a scarp of red earth tangled with low undergrowth that ended in a tumble of concrete, stones and bricks: rubble left by whoever had built the pool. I'd have to clamber down here, without attracting any attention, if I were to have any chance of getting into the field beyond.

I walked to the edge and shuffled slowly downwards on my bottom, using my arms as leverage. At the base of the slope, I crouched, listening for sounds of alarm. OK so far. Keeping my head down, bending over as far as I could, I didn't so much run as lollop over some thistly rocky ground into an area of scrub where I fell to my knees and waited. In front of me was a haphazard pile of white stones, what was left of the wall, a dip in the land, a ditch, and beyond that the field where I could see the hulk of a rusty yellow digger, its claw resting like an elbow on the churned earth. Sweat had collected on my brow, and across my chest. I could taste blood at the back of my throat. My hands stung where I'd scratched them on a spiky plant. *Shit.* I didn't have long.

I peered over the pile of stones, using it as cover. In the distance, I could see the headland, beyond which lay Agios Stefanos, and a triangle of dark blue sea. I'd have liked to have waited a moment, to have scouted out the field from this vantage point, to check there weren't any more of Gavras's men waiting beyond the brow, but I didn't have time. I hoiked my leg over the pile of stones. They shifted under my weight,

244

clattered off, a mini avalanche. I scraped my back, lowering myself into the ditch. I was at the edge of the construction site, the ground on this section riven with deeply grooved tracks. A hundred metres away what they'd built of the main hotel sat like an alien landing pad. On one side of it a heap of sand, on the other a mountain of gravel: for a moment I considered hiding in one of those, letting the weight slither over me, waiting until the heat passed.

No. Madness. Keep moving, that was the answer. I ran quickly, taking long strides, along the edge of the field, towards the gate, paused there to look up and down the lane. No sign of Gavras. Perhaps he had already gone back up to the house; perhaps he was looking for me.

I clambered over the gate and ran down the lane towards the main road. It was speed that counted now, putting distance between me and him, me and *them*, heels rubbing, chest hurting, getting the hell out of there.

I paused at the junction. Should I abandon my hopes of finding Alice and cut loose on my own? I could turn left, head away from the port, towards the relative anonymity of Trigaki, hitch a lift or hail a bus? Somehow get to the airport? And then I thought of her face, the way she twisted her mouth when she was thinking, how she laughed sometimes at the ordinary things I said. A moment of indecision. Has my whole life since been down to that moment? I don't know. You can drive yourself mad wondering.

I turned right. The road here was wide but it narrowed as it fell downhill, the olive groves on either side pressing in. White heat, black shade: a chequerboard. I was running at a slower pace, in the gutter. A mini-bus came towards me, with Delfinos Beach Club written on the side, and I stood back as far as I could to let it pass.

I had reached the lay-by where the bus had dropped me on

the first day, by the shrine, when I heard a car coming down the hill behind me. I leapt behind the shrine, ducking down. The car passed – a flash of white and blue. I strained my ears – a pitch in acceleration, the car slowing down, the swish and rattle of the wheel on the road, another car coming – and then the engine was killed. Slammed doors. Voices.

I stilled every muscle. I remember the taste of my hand at my mouth: salt, coffee grains, dust. A motorbike approaching from the other direction, pulling in closer to where I crouched. And then the sound of feet, more voices, getting closer.

I spun round wildly, and ran deeper into the grove, to where the black netting was folded at its thickest, threw myself to the ground, rolling round, getting my foot tangled, wrapping what I could grab over my torso, burying my face in the earth.

I lay there, trying not to make a sound, feeling sick. Footsteps on the road, and voices – Gavras's and another man's, and Alice's. The crackle of a walkie-talkie. Gavras: 'Please return to the house, Mrs Mackenzie. Leave this in my hands. We will find him and bring him back. I know where he will be headed.' And Alice, tearful, saying: 'Find him, please.' Their voices dwindling, disappearing. Vehicles returning. Another voice, deeper, speaking in Greek. I heard the word: 'Trigaki.'

It was hard to breathe. My chest felt tight, as if I'd inhaled soil. *We will find him and bring him back.* Tiny stones dug into my chest and arms. I lifted my head a fraction, my eyes focusing on a heap of dead flowers, and what looked like maggots. No, white candle-ends. A damp smell of soil and rotting vegetation. I became aware of tiny movements near my ear, the vibration of a million insects – spiders? Beetles? A tickle across my face. My muscles shrieked. I forced myself not to move.

Time passed. The light changed, shadows shifted. The slight breeze now dropped and the heat intensified. More vehicles passed. Chickens fussed somewhere nearby. An elderly woman walked within a few feet of me. An hour passed, maybe two. *Find him, please.* Had there been love in that plea? I didn't know. It was too late to find out.

It was more of a physical surrender than a mental one. I lost the feeling in my right foot. It became a solid object, dead flesh. I imagined myself in my own grave. The discarded flowers, the redundant candle nibs – they began to make sense: rejects from the shrine at the corner of the road. They'd outlived their purpose, been left to decay. My own rotten shrine.

When I stood up, it took a while for my limbs to move, for the blood to circulate. My foot was a useless club. I had to stamp several times to get the feeling back. I unpeeled olive stones, which had been so tightly pressed into my upper arms they were lodged like bullets, and crept quietly forward to the edge of the grove.

I looked up and down the road. It was deserted. 'Trigaki,' Gavras had said. That's where he thought I'd gone. Who in their right minds would have come this way? Once you were in Stefanos there was no way out. By road, anyway. But by water? I thought about the little jetties, and the fishing boats, and the party boats, the boats for hire. It was risky, but I could be down there in ten minutes. I could possibly be away in five more, watching Agios Stefanos disappear behind me. I would take the back route I'd discovered on the first day; plenty of alleyways to hide in, and I could come out at the harbour not by the supermarkets, but at the far end, opposite the main pontoon.

I set off at a steady jog, conserving my energy. When I reached the white house on the corner, the old lady was sitting on her plastic picnic chair, the white chickens pecking in their ratty little yard. I took the passage to the right, stumbling up and then down the uneven steps, out of breath too quickly for my own good. I almost tripped twice, once on the tendrils of a plant that sprouted in a crack in the stones, and then again on a sleeping cat. I passed several abandoned buildings with broken bars across the windows. I smelt oranges and fresh bread and piss. Must stay calm, must stay calm. I repeated it like a mantra, kept sane by a voice at the back of my brain: *you've done nothing wrong.*

A bolt of water through a crack between buildings – soft velvet, draped around the boats at mooring. The odd strain of music. A few voices. Mid afternoon – not a busy time. I reached the corner, where the passage widened, and leant against a wall. Should I skulk here or head down to the harbour? Or was this pointless? Was I trapped? I felt all confidence drain. Was it too late to go back? *Find him, please* – surely there'd been concern in her voice? My forehead began to throb. I slunk down to the ground with my back to the wall, and then, on the air, I caught the strains of music, distorted, bending upwards. The tavernas played Euro-pop. This was the bouzouki, starting slow, speeding up: 'Zorba the Greek'. It was coming from the water. A horn sounded. This was what I'd failed to respond to ten years before. Saffron had been demanding I make decisions about 'when we got back', talking about how it was 'time I settled down'. I'd missed the boat on purpose.

I ran down the last flight of broken steps, to the service road behind Club 19, and peered down the alley to the harbour. Voices and laughter were louder here. Several fishing vessels were moored on the jetty and at the end a large galleon, with lights strung along its empty rigging. A group of girls in headbands and long neon shirts was walking towards it; several sunburnt lads followed, swinging bags of beer. And then around the corner came four older men, in their late thirties – a stag break or a university reunion – with short sensible hair, socks with trainers. I counted to three and then ambled down the alley, and into the open. A moment of exposure, in which the hairs prickled on the back of my neck, but then three more strides and I was on the pontoon. Water gleamed in the gaps in the boards; the ground swayed slightly. I could feel the vibrations of someone behind me, but I kept walking at the same pace, ignoring the shiver up my spine, the desire to turn and run, to *scream*, until I reached the boat.

The queue had thinned and the last two men ahead of me were climbing on to the gangplank. It was a full-on fake pirate ship, shiny with orange varnish, a huge pronged steering wheel, a packed top deck, and a large lower area with seats in a circle around the rim. 'Captain Jolly', a sign said. Most of the seats were taken now; people hung over the side on the upper level, shouts of laughter, drunken shrieks, the clinking of bottles.

I waited, staring ahead, until it was my turn to board. I felt a firm hand on my elbow. I jumped, nerve ends on fire. It was the captain – 'The Boss' read his T-shirt.

'Ticket?' he said.

'I haven't got one.'

I got ahead of him, on to the boat, body rocking, water smacking against the wood beneath my feet; I could feel the relief of it. The smell of fish and wine. 'Zorba the Greek' clattering and whistling loud in our ears. The engine already shaking. 'But I can pay. I've got money.'

I opened my wallet and drew out Louis's ten-euro note. The man who had held my arm – tiny shorts, black beard, red face – was shaking his head. 'You buy ticket in Elconda,' he said.

'I can pay more money,' I said again. 'When we get there.' It wasn't strictly true, but at least I'd have time before then to think. 'A credit card!'

He shook his head.

'How much do I need?' I looked around. 'Can someone lend me some money?'

The couple making their way to a seat along the side turned. They looked at me and gazed over their shoulders, at the water.

'Please,' I said. 'Someone?' I raised my voice. 'Someone? I'll sort the loan out with interest, as soon as we get down the coast. I just need to get away from Agios Stefanos.'

If my dirty clothes and dishevelled demeanour hadn't alienated me from the crowd, this did. One of the lads, with a bottle of beer in his hand, got to his feet, legs apart to keep his balance. 'Off you go, mate,' he said. 'Do what the nice man said and fuck off.'

The captain had his hand around my elbow, and hauled me up out of the boat. 'This boat is ticket only,' he was saying. 'Ticket only. You buy ticket in Elconda next time. Return trip.'

'Please,' I said. But he had untied the rope now, leapt back into the boat, brought in the plank. The engine rumbled, throttled, the water swirled, a gap grew between the vessel and the pontoon. Shouts from the cabin. The Boss shouted back. A rope slapped, the boat's engine churned the water and it was gone.

The strength drained from my legs and I sat down on the edge of the pontoon. I could still feel the bastard's thumb on my lower arm. My nostrils were filled with the stench of diesel and dead fish. I watched the oil in the roiling water spread. I should get out of sight again, keep listening for another boat. But for the moment I couldn't move. The *Captain Jolly* had reversed out into the harbour and, with several revs of its engine, was turning, the lights on the rigging flapping. I sat and watched as it motored towards the headland, past Serena's fucking rock, and disappeared.

I stood, bent to shake the dirty water from my trousers, and turned.

A figure was standing at the other end of the jetty, one hand tucked in his back pocket. I could see the caverns in his face, the shadows beneath his eyes and, as he smiled, the gap between his teeth.

He took a step forward. Andrew: the person I realised I was most afraid of.

Chapter Twenty

He put me in the back seat of the car – that stung – and drove along the harbour road and through the village. 'I knew you'd be there,' he said conversationally. 'Gavras, everyone else, they were all convinced you'd be heading towards Trigaki, that you'd hitch a lift to the airport. But don't you remember, you told me.'

'What?'

'That you'd find a boat, escape by sea.'

He caught my eye in the rear-view mirror and tapped his forehead with his finger.

When we reached Circe's House, he got out of the car and stretched out his back muscles – showing me how free he was, how powerful – and then he let me out of the car, led me by the arm around the house and pushed me into his bedroom. He left, locking me in.

I banged on the glass door to the terrace.

'Tina!' I shouted. 'Alice.' I tried to lighten my voice, to suppress the panic. 'Help. Save me!' For ages nobody came. I sat on the edge of the bed. The room was meticulously tidy – even Tina's jewellery was hanging neatly over the mirror. Finally there came a tap at the internal door – the one that opened on to the lounge, and Alice opened it. She came in, leaving the door unlocked behind her.

'Paul,' she said. 'What's the hell's going on?'

She was wearing a silky dress that clung to her breasts, her hair in a ponytail. I put my arms out. 'Andrew's keeping me a fucking prisoner,' I said. 'He's behaving as if I'm dangerous, as if I might kill someone or something. Though I'm so angry I might kill him.'

She drew back.

'I'm stupid,' I said, trying to sound calmer. 'I know I am. I shouldn't have run. It was madness.'

Her brow creased. 'Yes. It was. Now everyone's behaving as if you're guilty of . . . I don't know. But what did you think you were doing? Why did you run away?'

What should I have said? That I thought Andrew, or Gavras, or both were setting me up? That I'd been looking for her? Or the real truth – that running away was just what I did? It was what I'd done to Florrie, and to Saffron, and to every woman since. That it was why I lived in someone else's flat, on someone else's time, skipping from job to job, from relationship to relationship, in the belief that if you keep moving nothing is ever your fault?

I sat down again on the edge of the bed, and looked down at my hands. 'I don't know. I'm scared of Andrew. He said some weird things earlier about the rape, as if he thought I might have something to do with it. Now I think I was right – the way he chased me round the village, bringing me back here, locking me up like a criminal . . .'

'Don't be ridiculous. If you've got nothing to hide you've got nothing to be scared of. No one's going to frame you, or make things up.'

'Andrew hates me because of Florrie. He was shouting at me, saying I killed her.' I put my hand on my heart, and looked across at her. 'I didn't know she was so vulnerable; of course I regret my behaviour. I wouldn't have treated her the way I did if I'd known. But she didn't kill herself because of me.'

Alice half smiled. She picked up a necklace that was hanging on the mirror and trailed it between her fingers. She wasn't looking at me. I said, 'You don't think that, do you? It's not true, is it?'

She balled the necklace in her hand and said casually, 'What do you want from me? Do you want me to lie?'

'No, I want the truth.'

'Well then, yes. I do blame you for Florrie's death.'

'Alice . . .'

She threw the necklace on to the chest of drawers and turned back to me. 'You did know she was vulnerable. I told you. At her birthday party. I warned you then, when she was *insane* for you. Do you not remember? In the garden. I found you at the bar and railed at you. I begged you to look after her or to leave her alone. I looked you in the eye. I said I would kill you if you hurt her.'

'What were you wearing?'

'Oh for God's sake, Paul. How can you ask that? I don't know. A black dress. I was fatter then, and spottier. I probably wasn't flashing any cleavage. That's why you don't remember – I didn't register for you sexually. Christ, if only I had: perhaps you'd have got off with me, and abandoned her then, rather than two weeks later when it was too late, when you'd slept with her and left her feeling worthless.'

And now I did begin to remember. A short fat girl at the bar, ranting at me. But Florrie, a sure thing, waiting for her drink, and mates laughing in the corner as I wriggled away. If I'd known it was Alice, if I'd known what I knew now. But I hadn't; that girl was nothing like the woman standing here.

I put my arms out again, desperate for her to come close. 'I'm sorry, Alice. I really am. If I could reverse the time . . . I was young. I was so immature. I did a lot of damage – I know that. But it's no reason to treat me like a criminal.'

Alice hesitated and then sat down next to me. Her voice flattened. 'That night in Giorgio's ten years ago – you said terrible things. I think that's why Andrew is so angry. Being here has probably brought it all back.'

'What kind of things?'

'You asked after Florrie.'

'I wasn't to know she had died. I can't be blamed for not knowing.'

'Paul.' She took my head between her hands so she could look me in the eye. 'You said, "How's your little sister? Still hoping for a man to trap? Still dead from the neck down?"' She let go of my face as if she had seen enough. 'I'll never forget it.'

'I'm sorry. What's wrong with me? I am so sorry. Please.'

'We were sitting there, trying so desperately to pretend everything was all right, when Harry had just died. I was a mess. Andrew was doing all that he could to make the holiday nice for me. And then you, suddenly there, filling the restaurant – so boorish and rude. You never knew what you had done. All that pain you had inflicted. And you had no inkling. You had never *felt* it. It's the main reason I had to get away. I shouldn't have been drinking. I shouldn't have been driving.' She let out a small cry. 'You never *felt* it,' she said again. 'You had just got away scot-free.'

I took her hand, pulled it to my lips and tried to hold it there. My eyes had filled with tears. I was saying, 'I'm sorry, I'm sorry. I'm going to change. I am feeling it. I am feeling it now,' but she pulled her hand away, shaking her head.

'The others have gone down to the port,' she said. 'But Gavras is here. I was told to come and fetch you. He's waiting outside.'

It was dusk. Gavras was sitting alone on the terrace. Mosquitoes floated in the light from the kitchen. 'Ah, Mr Morris,' he said, when he saw us approach. 'You were in a hurry to get away from us today, I hear. One might think you were evading questions. But just bored of our company perhaps? Still, it has been a busy day here, ripe with revelation. I'm thankful to Mr Hopkins for ensuring your return.'

I sat down across the table from him. 'Please. Let's just get this over with. I'll answer any of your questions. I'll tell the truth.' I looked in appeal across at Alice, who was standing by the door to the kitchen. 'I want to make this right.'

'OK,' Gavras said. 'Well, that is what I like to hear.'

A leather satchel lay on the table in front of him and from it he carefully withdrew a foolscap file, which he opened on his lap. He placed a photograph from it on the table in front of me.

'This woman,' he said. 'Have you seen her before?'

It was Laura Cratchet – a photograph taken against a white wall. Her full mouth was bare, her eyes naked without their heavy liner.

'Yes,' I said. 'I have. It's Laura Cratchet.'

'And you first met her when?'

'She was on my bus, but we didn't talk. We caught each other's eye.'

'You caught each other's eye? You mean expressed interest in each other?'

'No. That's not what I meant. We smiled, that's all. I can't remember why.'

'Did you wink, in a sexually suggestive way?'

'No.'

'But you had followed her on to the bus, having met her the night before, at the Pig and Whistle in Pyros where, according to Miss Cratchet, she cheerfully rejected your advances. You were drinking heavily and had to be escorted from the bar at the end of the evening. But you were persistent. You had listened to their conversation and took the same bus you knew she and her companions were taking north the following morning.'

I looked over at Alice and shook my head.

'Or is this a case of mistaken identity?' Gavras continued. 'We are dependent on Miss Cratchet's word – she was with me in Club 19 the other night when you wandered in. But perhaps she picked out the wrong man. Really, the truth of her story hinges on whether you were in Pyros town on the second of August or whether, as you claim, you arrived on the Thomas Cook flight the following morning?'

I spoke carefully. 'Yes. I lied about my arrival,' I said. 'But it's not what it seems.' I turned to address Alice. 'I'm sorry. I didn't want you to know how broke I was. I got the cheapest flight I could find and I *was* on the island that night.'

She took a step towards me, frowning. 'What about the meeting with your publisher?'

'I lied about that.'

'And the book deal?'

I shrugged.

'Another lie,' Gavras said. 'You seem to make a habit of them.'

'But I didn't follow her.' I turned back to him. 'I was already on the bus when she got on. She wasn't even staying in Pyros town. She was staying in Elconda. And I didn't stalk her. I saw her after supper but it was a coincidence, that's all. And I certainly didn't wait for her outside the club. You know that, Alice – I came back to the house with you that night.'

She lifted her chin but didn't answer.

Gavras was drawing another photograph out of the folder. He placed it on top of the picture of Laura Cratchet. 'Does this look familiar to you?'

I bent to look closely. It was a close-up of a small crinkled object, gold, on the ground, next to some gravel. 'Not really. A packet of some kind.'

'Do you have your wallet on you, Mr Morris?'

'Yes.'

'Would it be a huge inconvenience to hand it over to me? You are quite within your rights to refuse.'

'It's fine. I've got nothing to hide.'

I pulled it out of my back pocket and threw it across the table.

He opened it carefully, and with a small smile, produced the three gold condoms. 'Interesting. The photograph is of a condom wrapper, found in the alleyway where Miss Cratchet was sexually attacked. This make of condom is not available in Greece. LifeStyles Skyn.' He made a face. 'An identical condom packet to the ones we find unopened in your wallet.'

'They're not mine. They're Andrew's. Or at least . . . I took them from his washbag. As a joke.'

Alice let out a small noise, a muffled gasp.

'A joke?' Gavras made a movement with his hand, as if waving away an invisible fly.

I stood up. 'Listen. I didn't rape Laura Cratchet. I couldn't have. I was here at the house, already in bed, when it happened. Wasn't I? Alice, tell him. I was with you. Alice –' I turned.

She was standing very still, head up, breath held.

'Alice – I was in bed all evening. Tell him.'

Her body had stiffened. 'But you weren't.'

Gavras got to his feet. I felt a prickle of fear deep in my stomach. 'I was,' I said. 'I got up and . . . oh, I see, this is about Louis. Tell him the truth. You have to.'

The corners of her mouth dipped down. Her fingers were knotting and unknotting. 'Tell him what?'

I studied her for a moment. Andrew had been right. Of course she would choose her son over me. What mother wouldn't? Would she hate me for telling the truth? I had no choice. I turned back to Gavras. 'I got up in the night and saw

258

Alice and Andrew helping her son Louis out of the car. It was well after the girls had got home. It was 1.30 a.m. or later.'

'I don't know what he's talking about,' Alice said. She spoke slowly and clearly, her hands clasped in front of her, as if already preparing for court. 'I woke up in the middle of the night and I saw Mr Morris standing on the terrace. He was fully dressed. I don't know where he had been all evening. As far as I was aware he had not yet come to bed.'

'Alice, why would you say that? Don't do this.'

I stared at her, pleadingly. But in the dusk, with the light behind, her face was in shadow.

Chapter Twenty-one

Gavras took me to a building on the other side of Trigaki. It was dark when we got there. Outside: the edge of an escarpment, a dried-up fountain. Inside: concrete pillars, a web of narrow corridors. The room was bare, save for a stinking bucket and a wooden bench, on which I lay motionless, staring at mosquitoes as they abseiled down dirty grey walls.

The heat was pressing, airless, unbearable. He took my phone and I lost track of time. Muted light glowed weakly from a high window. A plate of food – some sort of sausage, a heap of flabby courgette – congealed by the door. My innards solidified, turned to chalk. I had believed in the power of charm. It had served me well, throughout my gilded life, but it had lost its power. Looks, clever words, lies – all useless.

In the morning, I was taken by a short, thickset official with no English to a different room in the same building. Gavras was waiting for me behind a solid wooden desk. A woman with heavy make-up and glasses on the top of her head was sitting by a smaller desk in the corner. A shorthand pad rested on her knee. The room smelt of pine and sweat. A vase of silk flowers collected dust on a windowsill.

When I sat down, Gavras pushed a piece of paper across the table towards me. 'This is a warrant for your arrest.'

I twisted it round and studied it, then spun it back. 'Can I see a translation?'

'You will be provided with an interpreter in due course.'

'Do I need a lawyer?'

'Mr Morris. You find yourself a fortunate man. You are blessed with very useful friends. Mr Hopkins, he has volunteered to represent you legally.'

'I don't want Andrew. I'm here because of him.'

'You are refusing the help of Mr Hopkins?'

'I don't want Mr Hopkins anywhere near me.'

'Ah – Alethea – please could you record that Mr Morris is refusing the offer of a lawyer.'

I let out a hollow laugh. 'Are you being deliberately belligerent?'

'Please also record that Mr Morris is being abusive.'

I spoke between gritted teeth. 'Perhaps you could outline to me my rights? Or do I not have rights here? You have kept me locked up overnight. I'm innocent. I've been set up. It's Louis, Alice's son, you need to look into. I've done nothing wrong.'

Gavras studied me hard. 'Why did you try and run away, Mr Morris?'

'You wouldn't understand.'

'You have no obligation to answer my questions. Your silence cannot be used against you. That – Mr Morris – is one of your rights.'

He smiled, and then nodded at the middle-aged woman, making sure she had got every word.

I was led to a different room to be photographed and for a DNA swab. I thought about refusing, but what would be the point? They'd take it anyway – rip out my hair or scrape out my nails in my sleep. The police station seemed semi-deserted – a series of empty rooms, echoing doors, the air somnolent and torpid. But the languor of this police force, their sluggishness, it was all an act. I was in the care of wolves.

Back in my cell, flies buzzed above last night's food, and against the small high window. Fresh mosquito bites rose in weals across my neck and ankles. I heard the whine of a motorbike, and the braying of a donkey. The water they had brought tasted chemical and sour. I lay down on the wooden bench, aware of every bone in my own head, and finally slept.

I did eat. Fresh food was brought, if you can call it fresh. A piece of gnarled fatty lamb in a watery sauce. On the side a boiled potato and a raw tomato. I was too hungry to avoid it, though I worried about my stomach. The bucket they had left me in a corner already stank.

Time crawled. I felt filthy with heat and sweat. I banged on the door several times and on the fifth attempt a slot in the door opened and the eyes of my squat jailor appeared. He moved his head. 'Eh?' his mouth said.

'How long will I be here? You can't keep me here forever. Not without charge. It must have been twenty-four hours now. You've got to let me go.'

The slot closed.

Later, when it got dark, I banged again. Over and over until the heel of my hand was raw. No one came.

I had no cause for complaint, Gavras told me calmly when he came to get me the following day. Thirty-six hours: it was nothing. Well within *their* rights. I should conserve my energy.

Something in his manner had changed, the sleepiness in his eyes replaced by an excitement, a hunger.

He escorted me, his hand firmly under my elbow, into the room where I had been shown the warrant. Someone else was sitting behind the desk – a larger man in a black suit, a pale striped shirt and a wide navy tie. Grey hair, black eyebrows: another wolf. He was the superior officer Gavras had been expecting. I could tell by the small obsequious nod Gavras gave as he came into the room. He also had an authority about him, an insolence, his chin resting low on his neck, his eyes narrow. He was big, but his jacket was too wide across the shoulders and the wedding ring he was fiddling with was loose. I wondered whether he had recently lost weight.

He was introduced to me by his title not his name. 'Anakritis,' Gavras said, with a slight nod of his head. 'He is the prosecuting judge. He collects evidence.'

'I see.'

Gavras asked again if I wanted a lawyer. I told him I didn't, that this was an absurd fuss about nothing, that I had done nothing wrong. He sat down next to his colleague and put his leather satchel on the table in front of him. The woman in the corner had switched on a small recording device on the table next to her. She picked up her notepad and pen.

I asked them why they were keeping me.

A long silence.

'Are you an honest man, Mr Morris?' Gavras's gaze was steady.

'I hope so.'

'Do you tend to tell the truth?'

'I'm telling the truth now.'

'Were you telling the truth when you insisted you visited the Helladic Settlement at Okarta, ruins that are closed for renovation on a bus that no longer runs on Fridays?'

I tried to keep my own gaze level. 'OK. I didn't get the bus to the ruins, but there is an innocent explanation. A group holiday, you know. Other people's kids. I just needed a day on my own.'

'Do you live at the address you gave me?'

'Well, not presently. But I did, until . . . Look, why does this matter?'

I had raised my voice. The Anakritis hadn't yet spoken, but

now he said, in an impeccable English accent, 'Do you have a violent temper, Mr Morris?'

'No,' I said firmly. 'I do not have a violent temper.'

I sat back in my chair, glancing over at the woman writing notes. She was looking at me, but she bent her head again and carried on scribbling.

'When things don't go your way? When you are tired. When you have –' He mimed swigging from a bottle. He was still smiling.

'No,' I said again.

'And your appetites, Mr Morris, would you describe them as normal?'

'My appetites? Normal? Well, yes, of course I would say my appetites were normal. My "appetites", as you call them, ARE normal.'

The judge said, 'Did you see Laura Cratchet outside Club 19 at 1.20 a.m. on the morning of the fifth of August and grab her from behind?'

'No.'

'Did you take her into the alley between Club 19 and Athena Jewellery, thrust her against the wall and pull down her underwear?'

'No.'

'Did you put on a condom and rape her, Mr Morris?'

'No. No. I certainly did not. I wasn't there and I wouldn't have . . . No.'

I was aware of the woman's pen tip-tapping in her notebook, of a shaft of sun casting a square on the floor, the thickness of the dust on the fake flowers, a fly banging its head against the glass.

Gavras said: 'Would you like to rethink your decision about a lawyer, Mr Morris?'

'I don't need a lawyer,' I snapped. 'I wasn't there and I am entirely innocent of the crime that you are accusing me of. And, as such, we're done here and I would like you to release me.'

The woman turned a page in her notebook. She raised her pen. The Anakritis readjusted the waistband of his trousers.

Gavras put his hands together, as if he were in a church. He breathed in deeply. 'So, Mr Morris – let us move on to another matter.'

'What other matter?'

He stared at me impassively. 'Mrs Hurley mentioned yesterday, while you were attempting to leave Agios Stefanos, that you were in the village ten years ago. I was under the impression this week was your first visit to the island but here you were on the night her daughter went missing.'

My heart began to pound. 'Yvonne told you that? Yvonne told you I was in the village?'

'She is understandably keen to leave no stone unturned.'

'It's maybe that she's just making trouble – have you thought of that? It's no secret that I was in Stefanos that night. But I'd left long before any of the drama happened. Andrew put me in a taxi.'

As I said it, I remembered Alice saying: *poured you into a taxi*. Fragments: the slam of the door, Andrew's narrow face sideways at the window, the slap on the roof as the vehicle moved off, the world spinning, nausea.

'Two witnesses place you in Stefanos later that evening – one of them, an English woman who now lives in Epitara, remembers seeing you in Club 19.'

'*What* English woman? Niki Stenhouse? I only met her on Wednesday. She didn't mention having met me before then.'

'The second witness, an elderly resident in the village, remembers seeing you walking up the hill towards the entrance to what is now Delfinos Resort but what was then the Barbati Beach Apartments.'

'What? That doesn't make sense.'

'You were with a young girl.'

'That's ridiculous.'

'You were not with a young girl?'

I racked my brain. 'It's true I met a girl at the club – though this was much earlier, in the afternoon. But she was Dutch. I went back to her room, but it wasn't even dark then. And no, don't ask me what her name was – I've forgotten it, if I ever knew it.'

'And this girl. This *Dutch* girl. She was how young?'

'I don't know. Eighteen? Nineteen?'

'Not fourteen?'

A vein at the back of my neck began to throb. 'This is absurd. Are you seriously interviewing me about the death of Jasmine?' I looked from one man to the other, searching for some chink, some break in their heavy expressions, some indication that this was all a joke. 'This is madness.'

Gavras looked down at the notes and without raising his eyes said: 'Why did you buy sodium hydroxide?'

A moment passed, while I tried to make sense of the question.

'For the olives,' I said eventually.

'What olives?'

'Alice wanted to pickle some olives.'

The policeman shook his head. 'Why would she want to pickle olives? She has no olives. She is not an olive grower.'

'Well, she had some. She had bought some raw ones by mistake that needed pickling.'

'When was this?'

'Thursday? Friday? I don't know.'

'So this week. She had visitors staying in the house; Yvonne and Karl had just arrived; it was nearing the anniversary of

Jasmine Hurley's disappearance. You might have thought her mind was on other things, and yet she wanted to pickle olives?'

'She asked me to buy lye. It was on a shopping list she gave me.' I shrugged. 'I was only doing what I was told.'

A moment of consultation in Greek between the two men. Gavras opened his leather bag and produced a piece of paper in protective plastic.

'This shopping list?'

Alice's writing photocopied on to the page, the scrap of paper at an angle, blurred at the edges. 'Chicken legs, lamb chops, dried pasta, feta . . .'

I remembered her writing it, her look of concentration, the twist in her lower lip as she chewed it.

Gavras said: 'No sodium hydroxide.'

Tina's voice clear and loud calling to me, her image reduced in the rearview mirror. 'Tina chased after me. Alice forgot to write it down. Ask her. Ask Tina. One of them will tell you.'

'The bottle of lye was found in your bedroom, Mr Morris. Not in the kitchen with the other groceries.'

'I don't remember where I put it.'

'And another empty bottle of lye was found on the property, bearing your fingerprints.'

A memory fought its way through the muddle and tiredness and panic. I nodded. 'In the shed. Yes.'

'It bears your fingerprints.'

'I picked it up. I used it to prop open the shed door.'

Gavras made a face, shaking his head as if this was a ridiculous excuse.

'I'm telling the truth.'

The Anakritis leant forward then, his face as close to mine as he could get it. 'Whoever killed Jasmine Hurley attempted over the last couple of days to further destroy evidence by pouring sodium hydroxide, otherwise known as lye, into the well.'

'Not me,' I said. 'For Christ's sake. No.' I racked my brain. 'Artan. Alice's caretaker. Have you talked to him? He's in and out of the shed. He was in the village ten years ago. And he's creepy.' I bent forward. 'He's having a relationship with Daisy. Andrew Hopkins's daughter.'

Gavras waved his hand, dismissing gossip that was of no interest to him. 'Moving on. When Jasmine Hurley's body was exhumed various items were discovered with her.' He produced a larger bag from his satchel and poked it, rolling the contents, several items wrapped in their own plastic casing, apart. 'Does this look familiar, Mr Morris?'

The bag he had isolated contained a large rusty spanner.

'Yes,' I said, staring at it. 'I have seen it before.'

'Ten years ago, Mr Morris?'

'No, the other day.'

'The other day? I don't think so. It was discovered in the well, Mr Morris, along with Jasmine's body.'

'Then it's a different one. I saw a spanner like that recently but it was in the shed, inside the bonnet of the Toyota.'

'What would you say if I told you Jasmine Hurley's skull bears fractures in keeping with a blow from an instrument such as this.'

'I'd say I don't know what you're talking about.'

'What would you say if I said the spanner is covered in your fingerprints?'

'It doesn't make sense. Someone must have put the one from the shed in the well. I don't know why.' My hands were beginning to shake.

He sighed heavily. 'Even more upsettingly, Mr Morris, your DNA was also found on this.'

He produced another evidence bag from the floor. Its

contents looked like everything and nothing, familiar and foreign: a scrunch of fabric, an old rag, blackened in places, rusty in others, the faint strain of a floral pattern. I had seen it before, recently, but because now it was produced so reverently, I realised I had also come across it long ago, in a different setting. In another country.

'What is it?' I said.

Gavras let out a laugh, a laugh without a vestige of humour. 'Oh, Mr Morris. Stop the act now.'

'I don't know what it is.'

The Anakritis wasn't laughing. 'It is a headscarf belonging to Jasmine Hurley, covered in your DNA, also found with her body.'

I peered more closely. The poster on the lamp-post and the flyers on Alice's kitchen table: it was the bandana Jasmine had been wearing. The seat of the truck. The key that didn't turn. The piece of old rag I had used as traction.

'Again it was in the truck,' I said. 'I wiped my hand on it. I used it to turn the key. Ask Alice. She asked me to look at the truck. She asked me to buy the lye. I don't know how the spanner and the headscarf ended up in the well. But it's nothing to do with me.'

The two men looked at each other, something passed between them. 'I'm tired,' I said. 'This is crazy. I want to go back to the cell. I want a lawyer. And I want to see Alice.' I laid my head on the table.

'Oh, Mr Morris.' Gavras's voice was like treacle. 'And you were doing so well.'

I raised my head. 'Tell me what you think I've done. Just tell me.'

The Anakritis stood up. He tucked in his shirt and nodded to the woman in the corner. She turned a page of her notebook, a scrunch of paper, a creak of binding, the threads stretching. When the Anakritis was sure she was ready, he sat down. He said: 'On the night of the tenth of August, 2004, after taking a boat up from Elconda you separated from your companions. You were given money by Mr Andrew Hopkins to leave the village in a taxi, but instead you spent it drinking in Club 19. Is that not so?'

I had a moment of confusion. 'I . . . I don't know.'

'You left the club drunk and when you encountered Jasmine Hurley on the road down from the Barbati Beach Apartments, you were unable to restrain yourself.'

'It's not true.'

'You raped her, didn't you?'

'Was Jasmine Hurley raped? Do you have any evidence for that? She was a *child*.'

He ignored me. 'And to keep her quiet you killed her.'

'You're just making this up as you go along.'

'You then carried her body through the olive groves until you found a suitable dumping ground: the well in the woods on the boundary of Circe's House. Here you hid Jasmine Hurley, along with spanner you killed her with.'

'You're lying. I didn't.'

'Your DNA is all over Jasmine's bandana and the murder weapon; both found with the body. How do you explain that?'

'I can't, but it didn't happen as you said. It wasn't me.'

'If only I could believe that. But there is also the matter of the shirt.'

'The shirt?'

Gavras brought out another piece of paper from his bag and spun it round to show me.

It was a photograph of a dirty, torn piece of clothing: a purple T-shirt with black letters that spelt 'Let Zeus blow your mind'.

I felt something ugly pace along my veins, put its fingers tightly around my heart.

Gavras said, 'It is quite distinctive, is it not?'

I swallowed. My mouth was dry. 'I have one like it,' I said. 'But this isn't it. I've worn mine recently.'

His expression was almost pitying. 'DNA, Mr Morris.' He shrugged, one hand outstretched, as if he would change the situation if he could.

'I don't know how it got into the well, but it's a mistake. A joke. If it is mine, it can't have been there for ten years. I wore it in London, a few weeks ago. If you let me go, I'll send it to you. I've mislaid it, but . . .' And then like an explosion at the front of my head, a firework, an eruption of hope. 'You just have to ask Alice. She saw it. I showed it to her. A couple of weeks . . . three, four maybe . . . before we came out here.'

'Ask Alice?'

'Mrs Mackenzie – ask her. Ring her now. She can explain everything. Please.'

Chapter Twenty-two

Back in my cell, after the interrogation, I banged on the door shouting for her: 'Get Alice. Get Alice.' In the sullen quiet of the night, I stood on the bench, my face up to the bars of the small high window, and screamed: 'ALICE!' Did I think my pleas would reach her, that my words would carry over the hilltop, sneak under the door of her bedroom where she lay asleep and creep into her ears?

When the door opened, I was finally sleeping – a snatch of unconsciousness, my throat hoarse, my neck at an angle. In extremis, the body will take its rest anywhere: I've learnt this now.

She was standing in the doorway.

'Alice!' I struggled to my feet. 'Finally. Thank God. You've come!'

I faltered. Gavras was at her side and it was partly the way he moved his body only fractionally to let her through, close against the frame, not allowing a crack; the way he snapped the door shut the moment they were both inside; the way he leant back against it, eyes hooded, nothing conceded. It was partly the fact her outfit was so smart – travelling clothes: three-quarter-length black trousers, a white shirt, a soft cotton jumper tied across her shoulders, navy ballet pumps. Had I lost all track of time? Was it already Sunday? Was she heading to the airport? But mainly it was her expression, the blankness of her eyes. I thought my heart would stop.

'Paul,' she said. She was holding my tweed coat out in her hand. 'I thought you might need this where you're going.'

'Alice,' I said. I took a step forwards. When I didn't take the coat, she laid it on the floor. Gavras made a gesture to indicate I was to sit. I didn't. I just stood there. 'You will help me, won't you?' I said eventually. I put my hand out, trying to reach her. But she didn't move any closer. My hand dropped.

'Help you how, Paul?'

Had Gavras said something to turn her against me? I just needed her to understand. 'Alice,' I said, lowering my voice, trying to speak quickly so he might not follow. 'They've made up all this stuff about me. It's all wrong what they say.' I looked over at Gavras, who shrugged. 'Alice, please, I need you just to explain that I had nothing to do with Jasmine's death. And the rape. It's serious now. I need you to tell them the truth.'

She was standing very still. Did I imagine a softening in her shoulders? 'What do I need to tell them, Paul?'

'Starting with Jasmine, tell them about the truck, the T-shirt. Tell them about the lye.'

'What lie? There have been so many.'

'Tell them you told me to buy the lye to cure the olives.'

She wrinkled her brow. 'What is lye?'

'It is sodium hydroxide,' Gavras said with a small bow.

Alice gave her head a short, baffled shake.

'And that you told me to mend the truck,' I went on. 'That's why I was inside the shed, that's why I touched the spanner, and the bandana. I don't know how they both got into the well – someone must have put them there to frame me.'

Alice's hands gripped each other in front of her stomach. Her eyes were empty. 'If I wanted the truck mended, why would I ask you?'

'Because you knew I once had a job as a car mechanic.'

'Did you?'

She was staring at me, and the air turned to ice.

'I told you I had. Remember . . .?'

'A genuine mechanic?' she said.

I felt a dark uneasiness, a tremor on the surface of my skin.

'The T-shirt,' I said slowly. 'The one from Zeus nightclub, the one you hated. Can you tell Lieutenant Gavras that I had it in London a few weeks ago? You saw me wearing it.'

Her tongue darted across her lower lip. Her fingers still clenched, she rolled her palms together.

'What T-shirt, Paul?'

'The one from the nightclub in Elconda. "Let Zeus blow your mind".'

I saw her chest move as she exhaled slowly. 'The one you were wearing the night Jasmine went missing?'

'Yes. Yes. That one. Tell him you saw me wearing my one in London. *Tell him.*'

She glanced over her shoulder. Gavras moved his weight from one foot to the other, lifted his chin.

'I wore it under my jumper and showed you in your bedroom in Clapham – that night. You remember. It was a joke. "Let *me* blow your mind."' I lowered my voice. 'Don't you remember? You said you hated it. You took it off me. We had sex.'

She shook her head.

'Alice. *The T-shirt.*' I could feel every sinew in my face stretching, the air against my teeth. It was my last chance, *her* last chance. 'Why won't you tell him?'

As she pulled down the corners of her mouth, shaking her head, a chasm opened in my chest.

Only Alice could have taken my T-shirt; only she could have put it in the well.

I thought about the expression on her face, down at the pool, before we knew what Gavras had found. How quickly she had got to her feet. How close to fear her shock had seemed. It was because she already knew Jasmine was there. For days, listening to every crack and churn of the diggers and drills, she'd been expecting it. When she saw Gavras standing in the shadow of the tree she knew what he'd found. She'd been *waiting*.

'Oh, Alice.' I sat down suddenly on the hard bench. 'You know who killed her.'

She turned, made for the door. One of her ballet pumps slipped off her heel and she ducked down to secure it. The leather was bent and soft, concertinaed. Her fingers fumbled. 'I don't know what you're talking about.'

'You're covering for someone, aren't you? Oh, Alice. Just as you're covering for Louis too.'

She faltered, looked towards Gavras, and then back at me. I didn't have much time. I said, 'Was it Yvonne? Or was it Andrew? How can you let them think it's me? What are you doing? You know I had nothing to do with Jasmine's death.'

She hesitated. Gavras opened the door and was halfway out, beckoning for her to follow.

Her shoulders were shaking. I thought she was crying, but she wasn't. 'Can I have a minute alone with Mr Morris?' she said to Gavras.

She and Gavras conferred; the whisper of their voices, then the door clicked shut. She crossed the room to the bench and crouched down, her mouth next to my ear.

'You had *everything* to do with Jasmine's death,' she said.

She shuffled even closer, pressed her chest into me to support herself, our cheeks brushing together. 'In Giorgio's the night Jasmine died.'

'I don't understand.'

'The cruel things you said about Florrie.' She rocked back on her heels. She was speaking calmly now. 'If you say things like that, if you are that horrible a human being, it has an effect; it has consequences. I had been feeling better. Andrew and I – we'd got into conversation with that French couple. For a few seconds, I'd let myself forget my grief. And then you – YOU. I couldn't bear it. I couldn't stay any longer. Andrew begged me not to leave, or to let him drive me, but I had this feeling I had to get out, to get away from people . . . Any people. I . . . I shouldn't have been driving. I was drunk, I was crying. I couldn't see straight. I wasn't fit to drive. ' She was gritting her teeth. 'And it was because of you that I did. So yes, you are to blame, you did have something to do with Jasmine's death.'

A long silence.

'Do you *feel* it?' she said. 'Do you *feel* it now?'

'*You* killed her,' I said. 'You killed Jasmine.'

She studied me, as if she were considering whether to respond. 'It was an accident,' she said almost conversationally.

'All these years – ten years – you've sat at Yvonne's side. You knew her daughter was dead. You let her suffer. I thought you believed in truth and honesty. I thought you were good.'

She didn't answer. Her back stiffened and she stood up, stretching out the back of her legs.

'Guard,' she called.

I stood up to face her. 'And now you're *framing* me. Me. Does our relationship mean nothing?'

She looked straight into my eyes. She wasn't whispering now, but her voice was low and there was a hard, cold tone in it I had never heard from her. 'Of course it means nothing. Do you think I felt anything for you? Ever? I've had to put up with your absurdly inflated sense of your own looks, your snobbery and sponging. Your affected little French phrases, your desperate made-up stories. Why would I be interested in a loser like you? I did it all for Florrie, but I actually hate you. You are a loathsome, self-centred, self-satisfied human being. You deserve everything I've done to you.'

I felt so winded I could hardly get the words out. 'I was in love with you.'

'You can't have been in love with me.' She pushed her mouth so close to mine I thought she was going to kiss me. 'Because you have no idea who I am. You never bothered to find out.'

I looked into her face, at her pinched narrow cheeks, her pale green eyes, the scar that defaced her upper lip. I thought about her orgasm the day they'd found Jasmine: it hadn't been sexual release, it had been *relief*. I thought about my tenderness towards her, how I had stroked her damp hair, how much I had longed not just to be with her, but to *be* her, and my stomach turned.

And then she was re-tying the jersey around her neck and straightening the lapels of her shirt over it and turning for the door in order to knock and be released.

I said: 'This doesn't end here. When I explain what you've done . . .'

She didn't bother to lower her voice. 'Who do you think people will believe, Paul? Who do you think people have *ever* believed? You? Or me?'

And then the door opened and she was gone.

AFTER

Chapter Twenty-three

They moved me to the mainland that evening. The journey was tortuous and hot, the police van airless with small tinted windows, the road nauseatingly twisted. I remembered it from the bus: all the braking and accelerating, the rattling, the serpentine doubling back. This time I didn't sleep. My thoughts churned as did my stomach. On the six-hour ferry crossing to Patras I vomited several times, first in the toilet, then later, when I was too sick to move, where I sat, attached to my police minder, over myself, on my coat, in my hands.

Gavras had stayed behind in Pyros. He told me before I left that I was to be held in pre-trial detention, which could be as long as six months to a year. I was formally accused of the rape of Laura Cratchet and the murder of Jasmine Hurley, and at the last minute, of a third crime – the physical assault of another female, one Greta Muller, the hippy from Epitara. As a proven danger to society and as a flight risk, I was refused bail. The investigating judge had prepared the cases against me. No translation was available at this stage, though in Athens, this would be rectified. Gavras portrayed Athens as the Promised Land. I would have a larger cell, with the company of other felons. I would be visited by the British consul. An English-speaking lawyer would be appointed. He shook his head, a small smile on his thick lips. 'He will listen to the ridiculous claims you persist in making against Mrs Mackenzie and will advise you accordingly.'

I had been allowed one phone call. Michael answered his mobile in the garden. I could pick out the pattering sound of a hose; the rattling snarl of a distant lawnmower, the scrambled cries of children. I filled him in as quickly as I could. He listened without interrupting, made no comment except to ask exactly where I was being taken and to assure me he would be on a flight to Athens the following day. I wept when I hung up. It was just hearing his voice, the realisation that I was a long way from Beckenham. An English summer afternoon: I think I already knew it would be a long time before I saw another one of those.

The ferry docked in Patras at dawn. I felt the cool of the early-morning air through a crack in the van door. I was given a bottle of water that tasted of hot plastic, a small packet of dry biscuits, but no clean clothes. We drove for about half an hour and then the van stopped. The back door opened and two other men were thrown in – one blond with muscles bulging from a vest T-shirt; the other dark-skinned and wiry. They sat, staring at me with open antagonism, probably because I smelt of vomit. It was my first experience of other felons, of the constant suspicion, the threat, the incipient violence. I'm used to it now. I've learnt wiles of my own, to keep my distance. At that point I was still naive. The wiry prisoner had cigarettes. I could see the packet lumped in his T-shirt pocket. I was desperate enough, using sign language, to barter my Vans.

He folded up the flip-flops he'd been wearing and stuffed them into his back pocket. He put on the Vans – they were far too big. He handed me a single fag, not the whole packet, and made an aggressive gesture, neck extended, face in mine, when I tried to protest. I sunk back, barefoot, into my seat and they ignored me after that. I didn't care. I was numb, devoid of emotion, and any sense of self. All I could do was try to make sense of the events that had taken place ten years ago, and of the previous six months; all I could do was sift and sort things that had happened, searching for reasons and explanations.

Alice filled my head. Her lopsided smile, the habit she had of fiddling with her hair. Alice cooking supper, on the phone to colleagues, in bed with me. This Alice had killed Jasmine. This Alice, the Alice I had fallen in love with, who was she? All this time, she'd known where Jasmine's body lay, and lied and concealed, and plotted. It was unimaginable, and yet her face in mine in the police cell – the way she'd almost spat her words. I didn't know her. I had no idea who she really was. She'd been right about that – I'd projected on to her the attributes I desired. And everything fitted. She had killed Jasmine, run her over in the truck. Drunk. Upset. And then she'd panicked, hidden the body in the well at the edge of her own property. (With Andrew, or without him?) And then how clever she had been, to involve herself in the search, to stick close to the investigation, to Yvonne. Was it supposed to be just the night at first, and then become a week, and then a month? Did it snowball? Become an addiction? *For ten whole years?* The campaign, the ball, the benefits, the fund-raising – why? How had Tina put it? *Alice has to be in control. Without her in the driving seat everything goes wrong.* It must have been a way of masterminding the operation, diverting police attention, keeping Yvonne in her thrall. It kept the case alive too – and why would she have done that unless deep down she wanted Jasmine found? Closure: how many times did she use that word? But for the poor grieving mother, or for herself?

Was it a coincidence meeting me at Andrew's dinner? Already hating me for Florrie, blaming me in her twisted way for Jasmine's death, did she see her chance to use me, to set me up for the killing? How clever she had been, if so. The redevelopment of the land would have unearthed the body.

She needed a suspect. I thought back to how courted I felt that night, how flattered. She came into the garden to find me. She cadged a cigarette; her first and last, choking it back. The tactic worked, though. She got my attention.

All the time I thought I had been playing her, she'd been playing me. She'd dangled the promise of a next stage, but never clinched it. She'd offered a holiday at Circe's House and then withdrawn it. It was all hints and delay, and hard to get. I'd been manipulated. It was the chase that made me keen. It was *not* being invited to Pyros that had made me determined to come. And then, once I got here, squeezing me into the boot of the people carrier, making me feel like a spare part, when all along I'd been the *main* part. All the acting and the smokescreens, the cooked-up hysteria about 'sightings'; I thought I was a witness to someone else's drama, when all along I was the star of her show.

How beautifully I had played the role she had written for me. Every one of my failings worked in her favour. My arrogance, my greed, my need to prove my own virility, my tendency to show off. My cheesy stab at seduction with the T-shirt – she must have been thrilled with that; it was the clinching piece of evidence she needed. And getting me into the truck, where she'd left the spanner and the headscarf: how easily I'd taken the bait, wanting to please her, convinced by my illusory sense of superiority that I might be able to fix it. Wonderfully underestimating my own incompetence, I had fiddled, left my DNA where she needed it, on the spanner, on Jasmine's cotton bandana – all she had to do was move them into the well.

Every step of the way, I had played into her hands – my laziness, my moral cowardice. If only I hadn't lied about the flight; if I hadn't stolen the condoms. I shouldn't have fled from Circe's House, but there you have it. It's what I do: I run

284

away. She had watched me, groomed me from the start, exploited my weaknesses every step of the way. She had reeled me in. But how easy I had made it.

The van lurched to a halt. The back doors were thrown open and a man stood there in the narrow gap, with a gun at his hip. Behind him, a flat, faceless building with yellowing water-stained walls, and row upon row of small barred windows.

'Welcome to Korydallos, your new home.'

I got out, leaving my tweed coat on the seat.

Chapter Twenty-four

I've been writing this at night in my cell – wanted to get it down before the trial in case it doesn't go my way. The act of writing has been its own form of therapy. It's clarified matters in my head. I've been here fifteen months. You know sometimes when you look back on things that have happened, you pity yourself, your own naivety, your own foolishness? Well, I don't. I'm not that man any more.

Ironic, really, that I've finally found a place to call my own.

I've had more comfortable gaffes, no getting away from it. Six men to a cell, often more – particularly after the austerity riots. There was a period when a particularly nasty drug-dealer from Macedonia forced me on to the floor, but he's moved on now and I have my own mattress again. The physical discomfort – the sores, the blackness on your fingers, in your pores (there is no hot water), the bone-cold in winter, the lice, the psoriasis, the scars from scuffles and beatings – you get used to that. It's the psychological pressure that's the hardest thing. The fear of violence, the dread of boredom, the guilt.

My trial could be any day. Andrea Karalla, the lawyer assigned to my case, is hopeful we'll go to court in the next few weeks, although we have reached this stage before. Always some delay or another, some lost paperwork, some witness inexplicably indisposed. Sometimes, I'm not sure she is worth the money. Or whether she isn't simultaneously being paid by someone else. Other times, I'm simply grateful. She is a plain woman, heavy browed, fond of severe black suits, and of scraping her hair from her face. She is way out of my league, far too good for me. She wears no make-up and, I noticed last week when she reached across the table to take my hand, that she bites her nails. But she is kind and clever and careful with me, and her eyes are a beautiful chestnut brown. If I weren't shackled to my chair, I would want to lay my head in her lap. God, just the thought of it makes me want to weep.

My spirit isn't broken (the phrase you are supposed to use in memoirs of this kind). I still have hopes of freedom. There have been useful developments in two of the cases. Karella is confident, for one thing, that the charge of physical assault against the woman we now know as Greta Muller will never reach court. Ironically, although we are convinced Alice persuaded her to press charges, it is the one crime of which I am, sort of, guilty. I did push the caravan door into her face and though I didn't mean to hurt her, there was an aggression and force behind that push, a desire to impress, that I am not proud of. Karella says it doesn't matter. Muller has proved evasive. She is no longer in Greece; in fact she is currently in Amsterdam partaking in a music festival called 'the Cannabis Cup'. The owner of the supermarket in Stefanos has identified her as a petty thief. Even if she returns to speak against me, Karella feels her plausibility has been weakened by her 'lifestyle choices'. So there you go – just as my personality traits count against me where I am innocent, hers count against her where I am not.

It was me who engineered that encounter in the first place. Alice, I'm sure, kept 'seeing' Jasmine in an attempt to reinforce her own innocence, and how taken aback she must have been at my insistence that we pursued that particular sighting. She adapted quickly enough, though – introducing me to Niki

Stenhouse, one of the witnesses to testify against me. That's one thing you can say about Alice, how resourceful and inventive she has been. She couldn't have predicted my attack on Muller, though she has clearly used it since, just as using the rape could never have been part of her initial plot against me. All she had to do after it happened was remove my alibi and leave the rest to me – my lies, my thieving, my casual sexism did the rest. Whether Louis was guilty, I still don't know. During my first meeting with Karella, in a windowless room in the bowels of the prison, I explained about seeing him being brought home paralytic and about finding the condoms in Andrew's bag. Karella was cautious at first. I think she assumed I'd raped Laura Cratchet, that it wouldn't have been out of character. Lots of people carry condoms they don't use, she said – the ones I found could have been in Andrew's bag for years. But since then we have had two small breakthroughs. A private investigator employed by Michael has found a witness, the owner of a jewellery shop near Club 19, who remembers seeing Alice and Andrew hoisting Louis into a car at 1.15 a.m. – which at least proves she was lying when she said I was the one who hadn't been in bed. Michael has done some research too. It's a small thing, but the gold condoms, LifeStyles Skyn, not available in Greece, are sold in Johnson and Co, a small chemist around the corner from Louis's school. They are also widely available in most branches of Boots and Superdrug, but we will keep quiet about that.

Neither Alice nor Andrew has so far returned Karella's requests to discuss either of these issues. She says she finds that unusual enough to be considered suspicious, 'particularly from fellow lawyers'.

Andrew's role is an interesting one. I've thought about it a lot. Artan's papers are not in order, it turns out, so with very little duress, he admitted to the private detective that Andrew had paid him to 'get rid' of the dog. It wasn't a misunderstanding. It was a commission. Is that better or worse than having blood on your hands? Worse, surely. I mean, what kind of person takes out a hit on an animal? That Andrew also helped Alice cover for Louis is now obvious. But what else has he colluded in? Their closeness, their body language. I don't think they were having an affair. It was deeper and darker than that. They watched each other – out of fear of what the other might give away. He was in on Jasmine. I'm convinced of it. He helped Alice hide the body, encouraged her to do it. I've pictured the terrible impact, and her running down the road to find Andrew, on his way up to check she was all right. It would have been Andrew who persuaded her not to tell the police, who reminded her of the well, who said her children needed her, that it wasn't her fault. I have decided it was Andrew who forced her to turn a tragic accident into a serious crime, to live with a lie.

Karella says she wishes there was proof of an affair – that it would be leverage of some kind. She's asked if I would write to Tina about it, but I'm not sure. I've been keeping the information about Artan and Daisy to myself, too. Tina was the only person who was genuinely nice to me. Despite everything, I don't want to upset her.

We have made some progress. The bandana, the one on which I wiped my hands, has my DNA on it, but none of Jasmine's. The prosecution claims the lye destroyed that, but Michael has discovered the scarf was part of Cath Kidston's 'classic' range. It's our contention the original scarf was never found; this was a replacement. The spanner is also clear of Jasmine's DNA. The prosecution claims I wiped it clean. But Karella has found a medical examiner who will testify that the injuries to Jasmine's skull could also be explained by impact with a car, and a forensic expert who will argue that the damage to the front panel on the Toyota is commensurate with such an injury. As for the witnesses, Karella is working hard to discredit their credibility. Niki Stenhouse, who placed me in Agios Stefanos later on that night, is a friend of Alice's and therefore biased, and the other, the elderly resident who saw me with a young girl, has recently taken possession of a 40-inch flat-screen TV. Our PI is confident it is only a matter of us finding the right price for her memory to begin to fail. Meanwhile, he is still trying to track down the Dutch tourist I had sex with that evening. My alibi. If only I had got her number. If only I had got her *name*.

The case against me rests on the supposition that I raped Jasmine and killed her to keep her quiet. Her body, however, is too disintegrated to provide evidence and it's my character Gavras has put forward to back the case. I am the main witness for the prosecution. I am literally my own worst enemy. And here it's the dossier the Anakritis has compiled of my moral failings that has done me the most damage.

To be honest, it's shocked me. I didn't see it coming. The character references sting. Nothing has gone unnoticed. They've closed ranks, the Mackenzies and the Hopkinses. Their central accusation that, when I discovered the property was to be redeveloped, I 'groomed' Alice in order to have a reason to return to the house and destroy evidence is patently absurd. But even Tina, who will now know all about my treatment of Florrie, has been turned against me. They've listed all my lies – that I don't own my own flat, that I haven't worked properly in years, that I am never where I say I am. They claim I am shadily unscrupulous: an affidavit from Hertz proving I drove the people carrier without insurance, that I 'ride roughshod' over laws and rules, believing myself above them. I am 'devious': nobody remembers Alice or Tina asking for lye. Alice has also provided examples of my 'arrogance', my 'obsession' with class and status. A section in the dossier reads: 'He claimed to have been awarded an academic scholarship to his public school, whereas this was in fact a bursary, awarded to poorer students whose parents worked for the church.' Big deal. More painful: 'He lied about a publishing auction for his latest "novel", and greatly exaggerates his earlier literary success. A work he describes as his "great oeuvre" [unfair, that – it was Andrew's phrase], *Annotations on a Life*, sold only 1,500 copies and is out of print. It is important to him to be seen as a significant literary figure. It is the deceit that raises alarm, in conjunction with the raised sense of his own intellect – what psychologists call Delusional Disorder.'

Andrew, in turn, provided examples of my dishonesty – not just the petty cash I stole at Circe's, but the Diptyque candle lighter I fingered from his house, the Martin Amis first edition (actually it was a present) which I later 'sold on the open market' and the hostess gift he and Tina brought Alice which I took home to give my mother. They've pooled their information. Only Alice knew about the Amis; only Tina could possibly have caught me out on the soap.

More painful still are the details of my 'sexual appetites'. Phoebe has detailed times in which I made her 'uncomfortable'. She includes the incident with the can of cold Diet Coke, in which, as we fell into the pool, I apparently 'fondled' her breasts, along with numerous occasions when I spied on her, or 'undressed' her with my eyes, including that moment, early on, when I watched her through the crack in her bedroom door. Andrew's mobile phone has been taken in as evidence. I was confused by this when Karalla first told me. But then I remembered that photograph, the one of me watching Daisy on the beach. I wondered if there were more.

One detail stings: an addendum from Tina, contending I

made a sexually explicit pass at her the afternoon we were alone at the house. And the following day, I behaved in a manner that was 'creepily intense'. I thought that was unfair. I was only being kind.

At first, I thought a lot about the little things that change your life. If it hadn't been raining, if I hadn't walked into the bookshop, if I hadn't been rejected by the girl behind the desk . . . But more recently I've realised it isn't just fate – though that plays a part, like a backdrop. It's the small things inside you, the slants and notches, the defects, that trap you. In the night, I feel afresh the force of Andrew's hatred. It wasn't a coincidence, that meeting in Charing Cross Road. He knew where to find me; he'd planned it. If he hadn't bumped into me there, he'd have bumped into me somewhere else. And that wasn't because of him, but *me*, and my unkindness to Florrie. It was only a matter of time before my behaviour caught me out. Poor Florrie, a sweet girl who should never have met me, whose life I ruined. One thing I've learnt – long-lasting damage can be caused by casual cruelty.

I do deserve the blame for her death, if not for the one I'm here for.

Alice was right.

Saintly Alice. I saw her once more before I left Pyros. It was that last afternoon, as I stumbled out of the police station, Gavras's hand on my elbow. We crossed a small square to reach the van on the other side, and I looked around desperately, absorbing every last detail, of the square, the buildings, and a wall, a fountain carved in stone, and behind it a dip, as the land fell into the valley. And then there they were, standing in the shadow by a small stone fountain, Alice and Yvonne Hurley, waiting for me. Yvonne's face was riven, grey, desperate with grief. Alice was supporting her, but I caught an expression in her eyes – panic, dread. She was the one who looked trapped.

I've wondered since which of us is actually in the worst kind of hell. It's a pact with the devil Alice has made – not casual but considered cruelty. All these years she has watched Yvonne live with not knowing; the worst kind of agony as she herself so often said. And now, with the accusations against me, she has led a mother to believe that it wasn't an accident that took her child, but the worst kind of death.

If it wasn't for that, I might even drop my defence and take what's coming. Because the thing is, I'm writing properly for the first time in years. It's amazing the things I've heard, the people I've met – the stories they tell you if you bother to ask. So no, I don't feel sorry for myself. I am a different person now. This whole experience – it could be the making of me.

Acknowledgements

For invaluable help with research, thanks to Ben Thorne, Andrew Watson and Ruth Bouratinos. Thank you to my editor Ruth Tross and to everyone at Hodder; to Grainne Fox at Fletcher and Co, and to the team at Greene & Heaton, especially Judith Murray and Kate Rizzo. Thank you to Barney, Joe and Mabel and special gratitude, as ever, to Giles Smith.

You've turned the last page.

But it doesn't have to end there . . .

If you're looking for more first-class, action-packed, nail-biting suspense, join us at **Facebook.com/ MulhollandUncovered** for news, competitions, and behind-the-scenes access to Mulholland Books.

For regular updates about our books and authors as well as what's going on in the world of crime and thrillers, follow us on **Twitter@MulhollandUK**.

There are many more twists to come.

MULHOLLAND:
You never know what's coming around the curve.

www.mulhollandbooks.co.uk

HODDER